MW01116154

Exceptionals

Bowen Gillings

Published by Bowen Gillings, 2023.

EXCEPTIONALS

First edition. April 18, 2023.

Copyright © 2023 Bowen Gillings.

ISBN: 979-8987772812

Written by Bowen Gillings.

Dedication

Dedicated to Aeryn, my Julia, the wonderful,
exceptional girl who keeps me off balance.

Praise for Bowen Gillings

"READERS OF CARL HIAASEN and Christopher Moore will be hooked by Larry and his crew of misfits in *Exceptionals*. You don't want to miss this book!"
   – Fleur Bradley, award-winning mystery author

• • • •

"WHAT FUN. *Exceptionals* is an entertaining fast adventure that boggles the genre mind. This thriller meet comedy meet mystery meet fantasy meet marital disfunction self-help book relives the 80s better than I remember them, and I remember them fondly."
   – Johnny Worthen, bestselling author of the Tony Flaner comedy mystery series.

• • • •

"HOLY SHIT, BOWEN! WHERE have you been hiding?"
   – John Gilstrap, NYT and USA Today bestselling author

• • • •

"*A Night to Remember* was an all-nighter for me. After reading it, this author is on my auto-buy."
   – Donnell Ann Bell, award-winning author of *Black Pearl*

• • • •

"IN *Dawn Trouble*, Bowen Gillings' characters made me laugh in between holding my breath."
   – Rachel Howzell Hall, NYT bestselling author

· · · ·

"*Dawn Trouble* is a tale in the classic vein of fantasy action adventure. Witty with a twist, it's a fun addition to the genre." – David R. Slayton, award-winning author of the Adam Binder series

· · · ·

"NO DOUBT ABOUT IT, you are the real deal as a writer and storyteller." – Anne Hawkins, literary agent, John Hawkins & Associates

· · · ·

Acknowledgements

THE AUTHOR WISHES TO acknowledge those who contributed to bringing *Exceptionals* to life. John Gilstrap, whose patience with my questions, freely given wisdom, and rallying support were a constant godsend in ensuring this book was ready for the world when the world was ready for it. I owe him many martinis. Angie Hodapp, for being a shining light of positive and constructive input. I owe her many a Kapu Kai. Deb Courtney, without whose inspiring and motivational Write Drunk, Edit Sober sessions the seeds of Larry, Julia, and Exceptionals among us would never have taken root. All the agents and editors who told me, "Love it. Don't know how to sell it." My critique partners, beta readers, and fellow creatives at Pikes Peak Writers and Rocky Mountain Fiction Writers who keep me honest.

• • • •

THANK YOU TO SUSAN C. Kelly for her great cover design.

• • • •

THANK YOU TO LOU J. Berger for his editing and enthusiasm.

Chapter One

A clown walks into a bar.

Clown jokes aren't funny. Not to me. Not after sprinting the past five blocks in these huge goddamn squeaky shoes, polka-dot poofy suit, and Raggedy Andy hair. Not now, sweating through face paint, stumbling down chipped concrete steps into the chatty hum and incandescent buzz of the Rubyfruit Jungle. Not one thing funny about a clown walking in here.

The cramped basement bar is packed with women. Women in leather and flannel sipping from glasses and slugging from bottles. Women in business suits and dresses. Women on their feet, perched on stools, or poured into padded booth benches.

None of them wears a spangly peach leotard.

Damn.

Clasped drinks stop before reaching lips. Stories halt in mid-sentence. Unsettling quiet strangles the room as every eye turns to me.

I gulp. Jimmy's boys are close behind, so I can't worry on being a circus rooster in an unfriendly henhouse. Pop always said to focus on the task at hand. Once again, Julia's my task. She's in here somewhere and she won't be safe until I find her.

Down the steps —*thump, squeak, thump, squeak, thump, squeak*—through a choking haze of cigarette smoke and estrogen, careful not to prod any shins with my big red water skis. No way a six-foot four man-clown is gonna casually slip through here.

The lady-crowd gives way with a smatter of grumbles, glowers never leaving me as I head to the bar.

Sweat drips from my nose.

A buzzcut in a popped-collar sleeveless IZOD tends the bar. Neon Schlitz and Old Style signs bracket a slinky advert for Black Velvet behind her. She leans over the polished wood and looks me over the way, well, the way anybody would look over a circus act tromping into a lesbian bar at happy hour. With a cocked eyebrow she says, "I have to say…first time for everything."

"I'm looking for a girl." Regretted it the moment I said it.

She laughs. Most of them laugh. Some get back to their business. Those around me keep staring.

"Funny," she says. "Don't know how many times I get that line. But, never from a guy dressed like you."

"She just came in here. Short. Lean. Black hair in a braid. Acrobat costume."

The bartender eyes me carefully. Her hands don't leave the bar. That's good. Hidden hands send my highly trained, deeply suspicious, and profoundly defensive instincts into overdrive, which always makes me want a gun at my hip.

"Please."

We have two minutes until the bad guys show, maybe less.

She considers, then leans back and crosses her arms. "Is the young lady in trouble? Or did she *give* you trouble?"

EXCEPTIONALS

The patrons are watching us like we're the best show in town. Guess if I were in their shoes—definitely more practical than what I'm wearing—I might pause sharing the tale of my day to pay attention, too. A few press closer. None look amused. A big redhead, neck as broad as her skull, grinds away on a mouthful of gum like she wants to chew me up and spit me out.

My right hand twitches. No badge to reach for. No sidearm. Not anymore. I clear my throat. "She's in trouble. Real, life-or-death trouble. And it's on its way here, now."

For all this barkeep knows, a desperate, sweaty clown is chasing his circus honey through her beloved establishment. A great story for weeks to come. Then again, the scars on her knuckles and the Marine Corps tattoo on her bicep tell me she's seen some shit in her day. She has to be asking herself if she wants any more.

Her fingers drum on the bar top. Her eyes tighten to angry slits.

Please, lady.

"Bathroom. That way." She jerks her head to signal around the bar.

"Thank you." Courtesy never hurts.

Thump. Squeak. Thump. Squeak. The ladies of the Rubyfruit Jungle grudgingly part to let me pass, each one giving me her personal stink-eye along the way. Conversations hum back to life and someone sets Pat Benatar to blasting away on the jukebox.

Two rough brown doors flank a sticker-covered payphone and a glossy poster of Bill Cosby mugging for New

Coke. Both doors bear the circle and dangling cross. Guess a men's room here is a moot point.

I push open the closest door to an assault of bleach and lavender, purple and beige. Stalls are all open. No legs below. No window to get out. She's not here.

A tall clone of naughty Sandy from the last scene in *Grease* steps from bathroom number two.

"What?" She sneers at me, like a clown at happy hour is nothing new.

"Excuse me." I shoulder past and through the swinging door.

Julia's here, hiding in the last stall, trying to keep quiet, but her whimpers echo off the tile.

"Julia. We need to go." Maybe a minute before the goon squad arrives to make things hairy. Then me and these shoes are her only chance at avoiding a life of needles and tubes while wearing a hospital frock in a cold white room.

"Aw fuck Larry, really?" she shouts through frightened sobs. "Here? You followed me here?"

I shuffle slowly forward, shoes scraping and wheezing. She's been through so much. Hate scaring her any more. "They're coming. We have to leave. Now."

"I'm not going anywhere. If those clowns want to come drag me away, they can damn well try." There's a sniff, then the honk of blowing her nose.

Goddamn clowns. "I'm trying to keep you safe."

"Oh, stow it. That's what you said when you brought me *to* the circus. 'No place safer,' you said. 'Won't have to hide here,' you said."

4

I did say that. Taking her there made sense. She could be who she is right out in the open. Just an acrobat—an acrobat with perfect balance who I've seen juggle flaming torches perched on one foot, atop a broomstick, atop a basketball, in a swimming pool. An Exceptional like her can do things the other ninety-nine point nine percent of humanity can't, no matter how hard they work or what drugs they take. Of course, that's the goal of the Opposition pricks hot on my heels: distill Exceptional abilities into illicit compounds for sale to the highest bidder. A black market of metahuman power pills. Yay.

I grip the stall door. "All I can say is, I'm sorry. Please, come out so we can get you someplace safe."

"Just leave me alone."

She knows I can't. Keeping Exceptionals safe is my job. Keeping *her* safe is also…personal. "Julia, either open this door or I'll break it down."

Another sniff. Slippered feet shuffle into view. The locking bolt slides free and the stall door opens. She's like a fairy—barely tall as my chest, pale tights, golden spangles on her leotard shimmering in the fluorescent light. Black trails of mascara stain her cheeks.

"I hate this," she whispers.

"I know."

Bar noise outside gets quiet.

Sweat trickles from under my wig. Heart does a drum roll against my ribs. And my old scar starts itching.

"Shit."

The bathroom door creaks and I push Julia behind me. My hand goes for the grip of my Smith, a Smith I haven't carried in years, and finds only some gauzy pink frill stitched around my middle.

The bull-necked gum-chewer steps in, closing the door behind her.

"You bring the whole damn circus or what?" she drawls between wet chomps.

Christ, they're here. So much for slipping away.

Chapter Two

"How many?" I ask.

"Four."

"All clowns?"

"Yep."

Tomorrow's headline will read, *Clowns Crash Lesbian Bash*.

"One of 'em a little person?" Jimmy hates the word "dwarf." Consideration of physical features is another thing Pop taught me. He'd say, "Why judge someone for something they can't change?" If Pop knew this malicious little shit like I do, he might make an exception.

"Uh-huh. With a red ball of a nose and a goofy big hand."

And a TASER, a blackjack, and likely some brass knuckles. *The* Jimmy. Jimmy the Fist. I knew it.

"Huge fucker with 'em, too. Bigger even than you."

That would be Bart. Wherever Jimmy goes, Bart follows. Real name: Bartholomew Rockentanski. *Special Agent* Rockentanski. And he can military press three hundred pounds with a bad case of the flu. Why wasn't a guy like him snatched and probed by The Opposition? Maybe he had been. Maybe hunting down his own were the terms of Bart's parole from their "program." Whatever the case, I can't let him or Jimmy recognize me and I can't let them get ahold of Julia.

"We're in trouble, aren't we?" Julia asks behind my back.

Yes, we damn well are.

"We'll be fine." I look at Bull-neck. "Can you stall them? Give us time to get out the back?"

She stuffs her hands in her jean pockets and shrugs, looking past me to Julia. "He the good guy?"

A pregnant pause.

Really? After the past six years?

Then, "Yeah, he's a good guy."

The throttle eases on my thudding heart. Jangling nerves quiet.

"Why not?" Bull-neck says with a shrug. "Might be fu—oof!"

She reels forward as the bathroom door slams into her back, banging her off the counter. Bart's bulk looms in the open doorway, terrifying despite the bald cap, fake green beard, and clown getup a few sizes too small.

"Stay behind me." I say in my best it-will-be-all-right tone.

She does as I ask, thank God.

Bull-neck is on her ass, rubbing the back of her head and groaning.

"In here," Bart bellows over his shoulder then squints at me, "Well I'll be... That you, Lawson? I thought something looked familiar. You always did run funny."

So much for not getting recognized. "It must be the shoes."

How in the hell were we getting past him?

"Goddamn, Larry Lawson, alive and kicking. So what, you adios the Bureau and join the circus?" He looks past me to Julia. His gears grind slow, but they do grind. "You some sort of bodyguard or something?"

8

"Or something." I widen my stance on instinct.

"I'm not going with you, Bart," Julia shouts.

"You don't got much choice girl. Took us this long to find you. You're not getting away again." He steps forward. "You gonna make me do this the hard way, Lawson?"

"I don't got much choice Bart." He's not after her on orders from the FBI, but from his *real* masters, the ones running a covert cartel built on abductions, abuse, and murder. I got orders, too. Mine come from those trying to keep Exceptionals safely out of the public eye, a skeleton agency so ragtag it hasn't got a name. Hell, it's barely got a budget. And until today it's gone undetected by The Opposition. But protecting Julia? I'd do that for free. I owe her that much at least.

"You don't." Bart shrugs, a broad smile breaking out on his shovel of a face. "You know, things'd be a lot different if I'd been there that day."

"Maybe, maybe not." I whisper to Julia, "Run when I tell you."

Time to live up to my protection agent title. *Thump. Squeak. Thump. Squeak.* Gonna be a bitch throwing down in these shoes.

Bart strides forward with that special disregard of a big man coming into a fight. He smirks down at me, raising his fists. One punch from those frozen turkeys and it's lights out. He pays Bull-neck no mind.

She stands behind him, big vein bulging on her temple, lip curled in an angry sneer.

"Excuse me," she growls.

Bart doesn't even look at her. "Stay out of this, dyke. It doesn't concern you."

"That's no way to treat a lady," Bull-neck says in her grizzly bear voice. She punts him from behind, square in the crotch.

Bart's eyes bulge. His jaw drops open and he doubles over, squealing like air from a pinched balloon.

She plants her foot against his ass and shoves, sending him past me into the wall, a sprawling tumble of striped socks and flopping beard.

"Christ," Bart hisses through gritted teeth as he balls up, both hands jammed between his legs.

"Situational awareness, Bartholomew." Not Pop's wisdom, Army's. A solid right to his temple and big bad Bart slumps to the floor. My knuckles throb. Like punching a block of marble. If we were alone I'd strangle Bart with one of his denim suspenders. Keeping secrets requires extremes. Though I'm not about to make Julia witness to more death.

"Let's go." I grab Julia's hand, giving Bull-neck a cursory nod as we pass. The lady can handle herself. She heard my name, but she looks the type to conveniently forget such things.

Another clown steps into the doorway as we're about to leave. Bright yellow cotton-candy-explosion hair.

"Hey, Bart? What the—gah!"

A quick jab to the throat and he goes down coughing. I shove past him.

The other two clowns are struggling through the crowd. One I don't recognize, a tall broomstick with rainbow suspenders and a foot-wide necktie. The little person I know all too well—Jimmy the Fist. His clown outfit is complete with a single giant, telltale glove all stitched and stuffed to look like a massive cartoon hand. But that's not how he got the nickname.

My groin gives a shadow ache at the flash memory of hand-to-hand training sessions with that prick. He hasn't seen us, yet.

"Come on." I drag Julia down the hall to the back. *Thump-squeak-thump-squeak-thump-squeak.* My thanks to whichever government entity mandated marked emergency exits.

"Where are we going?" she puffs from behind me.

"Outta here." She won't like that answer but specifics have to wait.

The hall ends in a dark paneled wall with a sticker-ridden steel door on the right.

I slam against the candy-stripe bar marked "Emergency Exit Alarm Will Sound." And whaddya know, a weak bell clangs like an old brass clock. The door, however, doesn't budge.

"What is it?" Julia shouts.

I try it again. Nothing.

"Damn thing won't open." I take a step back and hit it again. The door moves a rusty, grating half-inch. The alarm bell gains vigor and rings piercingly clear.

In the main room women react to the alarm, jostling for the front door and adding to the clamor. They balk at Jimmy and Broomstick shoving against the tide. Cotton Candy struggles up from the checkered tile floor. No sign of Bart.

I hit the door one more time, so hard my teeth ache. Maybe another quarter inch.

"Let me help." Julia sets her back against the cold steel then walks her feet up the opposite wall until she's suspended, horizontal, five feet off the floor.

Incredible.

She grunts. The ropey muscles of her acrobat legs bulge and strain. She screws up her face and heaves.

I shove with her. Jaw clenched. Shoes wheezing. Breath hissing with the effort. The door creeps open a hand's breadth.

She eases off a bit, sucking in air for another go, then yells, "Behind you!"

I spin in time to see Broomstick's charge—arms pumping, oversized tie flapping out to the side. He dips low for a tackle. I shift with his momentum, pivot, and launch him like a goofy cannonball beneath Julia, tumbling over my own shoes in the process. He smacks against the panels with a wood-splintering crunch.

"Keep pushing!" I grab Broomstick by those silly suspenders and drag him away from the door. He struggles, kicking, groaning, blood dribbling into his chalk-white face from a cut on his scalp. A hard clip to the base of the skull and he goes limp.

I turn around and *BAM!* Every muscle fiber locks up. My back arches. My mouth goes rigid. Teeth grind in a vibrating rictus. Hands jiggle like a fish just pulled from a lake. I taste ozone and the salty copper of my own blood.

Pain. Searing pain.

"Gaaaw!" I gurgle, then go all jelly and drop into a heap on the floor beside Broomstick.

Jimmy *did* have a TASER. Little bastard.

Chapter Three

"Oh, crap!" Julia gasps and gives one last, desperate shove. Metal shrieks, but the door only cracks open another inch. There's daylight in the gap. Not enough for her to get away, but enough for the bar's A/C cooled air to rush by blessedly, invigoratingly across my damp face.

For a brief instant she hangs there, muscles quivering, face twisted with fear and strain, stretched out like a magician's assistant waiting for the silver rings to be drawn over her. Then she tucks her legs into a backward summersault and touches down, more graceful than a leaping house cat.

Just a glimpse of why I'm here, and why they really want her.

She stands poised on the balls of her feet. Her wide eyes slip from me to the two clowns coming down the hall, to the motionless one in suspenders, and back. A cornered deer hoping for rescue from one already dropped by the hunter's bullet.

I'm no help. Pins and needles stab up my spine. I can feel my limbs, just gotta get them to work. A couple minutes and I'll be right as rain. If only we had a couple minutes. I focus on what I can see and hear, working fast on a way to get Julia out.

"Now hold on," Jimmy bellows in his deep baritone. Always creepy, that voice coming from a body no bigger than a first-grade boy.

EXCEPTIONALS

Jimmy edges closer—smarmy smile on his tricolor face, hands up like he's approaching a squirrel in the park, TASER wires dangling from the fat middle finger of that enormous glove. Cotton Candy Hair is right behind, coughing and rubbing his throat with his own, normal-sized, white-gloved hand.

"Impressive." Jimmy calls over the alarm. "You always were impressive, Julia." He glances at me, but his eyes don't register recognition. "But this all ends right now. You and your yarn-haired boyfriend have given us a good chase."

"He's not my boyfriend." Julia stays poised, fingers flexing.

"Whatever. There's nowhere to run. So come quietly. Some folks want to ask you a few questions, that's all."

Oh, Jimmy. After finding her family murdered, being forced into a new life in the circus, and two attempts at kidnapping, you really think a little soft talk's gonna ease her down?

Julia doesn't disappoint. She gives him the look. That look of someone who's reached the edge and won't be pushed a step further. The look I saw in the mirror the day I left the Bureau and decided to do something good with my life. The day I took this job. Julia's whole body has that look. Hips cocked, arms at her sides, eyes narrowing in her tilted head. It is a look that says she's done with this shit. Or perhaps she's embraced the ridiculousness of running across town to hide from angry clowns in a lesbian bar.

She shouts, "Fuck off, Jimmy."

God, I love her spunk. Fatherly pride, were I her father. I can wiggle my toes.

Jimmy stops. Cotton Candy sidles up, no longer rubbing his throat, but shielding something vaguely pistol-like from Julia's view behind his pint-sized boss.

Jimmy shakes his head. "Such language." He twists that big mitt of a hand, a fishing reel whine squeals and the wires zip back into his glove.

I fight to roll over, to get up, to stop them from taking her. But I might as well be a baby trying to walk on day one. All I manage is to sit up a few inches then flop back down, spent. C'mon kid, stall for thirty seconds more.

The alarm stops. Eerie quiet after the incessant clanging.

Tromping, clacking footsteps come up the hall from the bar. Many footsteps. Angry footsteps.

Jimmy stays put. Cotton Candy doesn't, he turns to face what's coming. His pistol has no slide, no cylinder. That's no gun. Not the firearm variety anyway.

Women are what's coming. Women in leather. Women in flannel. Half-a-dozen very determined looking women, the Marine-tattoo bartender and Bull-neck in the lead. The former brandishes a twelve-gauge pump that could turn this corridor into a charnel house with a single blast.

Oh, thank Christ. I miss carrying a piece.

"There has got to be a clown joke in this somewhere," the bartender says, no hint of amusement on her face.

"A fuckin' funny one," Bull-neck chimes in, still going to town on that gum. "Something like, what do you do when you're attacked by a gang of clowns?"

The bartender shrugs.

"Go for the juggler."

The ladies snort. One laughs.

Jimmy grinds his jaw, shoulders hunched as he turns around.

Cotton Candy lets him past, clenching and unclenching the grip of that weird weapon. The smooth body of it ends in a narrow point.

"Ladies, there's no need for all this," says Jimmy.

He keeps talking. My feeling is coming back. It's like moving through clay and razors, but I'm moving. What Cotton Candy's carrying has a small aluminum sphere where the hammer should be.

Recognition dawns.

"Are you alright?" Julia whispers, hunching over me. She adjusts my yarn wig.

"I've been better," I say, ears buzzing, straightening one leg. "Now, listen. Things look to get messy. I need you to do exactly as I say."

She nods and I keep the instructions brief. My other leg slowly uncurls from beneath me.

"Funny," Bartender smirks, "You don't look like Feds to me. What do you think, Irene?" She keeps the shotgun dead sct on Jimmy.

Irene is Bull-neck. She shakes her head. "Sounds like horse shit."

Jimmy clenches his little fist. "Look, you're about to be in some serious—"

"Got any ID?" Bartender's chewing on the story.

Jimmy practically vibrates with aggravation. "No."

"What, you leave it in your tiny car?" Bull-neck Irene snorts.

"We are undercover." He spits out the words, big hand pointed right at Bartender.

Irene sniggers. Her knuckles are bloody. Guess she went an extra round with Bart. Good for her. "So what, you guys are—"

"Yeeegh!" Cotton Candy screams high and tight.

Bartender twitches.

Jimmy jumps, spinning to check his man.

Cotton Candy's head wobbles. His knees slowly give way, held up only by Julia's grip on his arm behind his back. Held where she'd grabbed his gun hand, pressed the slim barrel into his spine, and squeezed the trigger. The clown's pneumatic injection pistol shot some anesthetic cocktail I'm sure ends in "caine" deep between his vertebrae. He slumps to the floor.

"Fuck," Jimmy shouts, little foot stamping in impotent rage. "I wanted this to be simple!" He spins back, bringing that hand around to take aim at the gathered ladies. Something tells me there's more than a TASER in there.

Bartender must have thought the same. She kicks at the circus prop.

Jimmy's hand goes up and a gunshot booms.

Julia drops to the floor and covers her head.

I cringe, managing to go fetal. Hey, my body works.

A tiny shower of plaster rains down, along with a few tufts of drifting polyester padding.

Jimmy has a smoking hole in the tip of his cartoonish pointer finger. He levels the weapon again and roars. But Bartender is faster. A cannon blast and Jimmy's legs are swept from under him. He belly flops onto the floor with a sickening smack. Groaning, he draws his knee to his chest.

A whiff of brimstone. The click-clack of the shotgun. The hollow rattle of an expended shell clattering on the tiles.

Julia looks up at me.

"We should go," I grunt as I fight to my feet.

Chapter Four

JULIA'S faster and helps me stand. I wipe my bloody mouth on my sleeve. Bit my damn cheek. We hobble up to the ladies.

"Thanks," I say, voice cracking like the morning after an all-night bender.

Bartender raises an incredulous eyebrow. "You got maybe four minutes before the cops show."

I nod and shoulder past, Julia in tow. *Thump. Squeak.*

A strong hand catches my arm. Irene. "You ain't getting very far looking like that. Neither of you."

Guess not. A clown and a high-wire acrobat strolling through town? Pretty sure folks would be happy to tell that one to a curious officer. I look at Julia.

She tilts her head, smile cracking the dribbled mascara. "I didn't pack for an extended stay. What you see is what I got."

Me, too. Everything is back at the fairgrounds.

"Help 'em out, Cherry," comes a voice from the back.

The bartender shoulders her gun and looks us over. "Might have some stuff that'll fit you in lost and found." She heads behind the bar.

"What about this one?" Irene gestures at Jimmy.

The Opposition team leader sent to seize a twenty-year-old girl to make her a lab rat slowly rocks and curses under his breath. Much as I'd love to knock him into next week, we're in a hurry.

"Have fun," I say.

Irene smiles.

The rest of the ladies wave off and leave, not wanting to be here when the boys in blue show up. All of them except Irene, who renders Jimmy unconscious with a crack to the nose, and Cherry—the proprietor, manager, and bartender of the Rubyfruit Jungle Lounge and Bar.

Three minutes and a combined heaving shove from all of us later, Julia and I stride out the emergency exit as sirens approach the front. She's thrown on black jeans a size too big, let her hair out, and sports a tie-dye shirt emblazoned with the image of a crab. Big red letters read, *I Got Crabs at Duke's!*

I'm not much better off, wiping my face with a dishrag as we leave, dressed in a men's XXL button-up and slacks Cherry claimed were left by one of her ex's. The pants are women's, but they fit. Roomy in the hips.

Shoes were the problem. Luckily Irene and I weren't too far off. She offered up her engineer boots as a sort of thank you present for the evening's entertainment. Hopefully the cops will be too distracted by the semi-conscious cluster of clowns to care why a witness wore nothing on her feet but woolen socks with a hole in one toe.

My new boots crunch on the gravel. The modest skyline is silhouetted against a lowering sun. I focus on checking for surprises between parked cars. We make it through the back lot with no cops shouting, no clowns flouncing after us. Place smells of piss, fryer grease, and stale beer.

"There wasn't any blood," Julia says as we hoof it toward the bus stop two blocks down.

"What?"

"She shot Jimmy. But there was no blood."

"Bean bag round," I say with breathy disappointment. "Not lethal, but at that range...he won't be dancing any time soon."

We reach the plexiglass shelter of the bus stop, one side plastered with a movie poster for some time-travel teen comedy with the kid from *Family Ties* and an over-accessorized DeLorean.

Streetlights start to flicker on. No one else is waiting. No one walking by. Passing cars rumble and hum, the faint roar of a jet far above. I scan the bus schedule then check the bank clock across the street.

"Five minutes."

Julia flops onto the faded plastic bench, swinging her legs in obvious frustration, leather slippers scuffing the concrete.

It's a lot to deal with at twenty, knowing you're different. Knowing that your difference got people killed, cost you friends, cost you any type of life you'd ever dreamed of. Knowing that difference means you're hunted.

She's a tough kid.

I try not to worry on my own burden—a classified operative not officially on anyone's books, tasked with protecting persons of measurable biologic exception. I keep them secret and safe from Opposition goons like Jimmy and Bart, who will use their FBI credentials to explain away the mess back there and likely be back to "protecting and defending" within the week. Protect and defend my ass. They'll be right back to tracking down Exceptionals for their Opposition overlords. Shit keeps me up at night.

EXCEPTIONALS

"I could've been in the Olympics," Julia mutters, staring at her shoes. "Balance beam. Uneven bars. Gold medals and Wheaties boxes. Nope. Not me. I get the circus. Come see the girl who can't fall! Be amazed!"

I put my hand on her head.

She looks at me with those tired eyes. No tears. She shed them six years ago when she came home to bodies on the floor, to men with handcuffs and a black panel van. Then Yours Truly spirited her away and set her up with a new life in Barney's Big Top and Traveling Show.

She whispers past a false smile, "Be fucking amazed."

A police siren blares behind me. Red and blue dance across the grimy shadows of the bus stop.

I freeze.

Julia's eyes go wide. Her upper lip trembles.

"Stay calm," I mouth, then turn, as any normal joe would at a sudden wailing siren.

A white cruiser rolls up, light bar flashing. The patrolman is talking on his radio. He glances at us then down the street.

Julia stands, pressing against my back with a nervous hand.

The officer gets off the mic, races the engine, then speeds past, evening light shining off the Milwaukee police badge on his door. Lights and siren fade in the sunset distance.

Julia collapses back onto the bench. "They'll never stop, will they Larry?"

No. Not ever. "You'll be fine."

"It's not like I'm bulletproof or can fly or read minds or anything. Why me?"

That's all comic book stuff. What she can do is far more real, and useful, and valuable. "Some folks are afraid of those that are different. And some assholes see that difference as a way to make money. And you...you've got one hell of a gift, kid."

She nods, jaw set hard. "Perfect balance."

"The things you can do... You said it yourself, you can't fall."

"Unless I'm knocked down. Or some big clown tackles me." She playfully bumps my shoulder, then smiles. It's weak, but it's real.

Two minutes until the bus.

"I still think it's funny," she says shaking her head. "Two super-secret groups. One wants me as a lab rat. The other wants me hidden away and paying my taxes. I live in a fucked-up world, Larry."

I pat her leg. "We all do, kid."

"I've figured out one thing, though."

"What's that?"

"I hate clowns."

Thanks for the smile, Julia. How you keep it up after all this is beyond me.

Throaty diesel rumbles around the corner one block down. Headlights sweep the pavement. It's our ride.

We stand.

She takes my hand.

Folks dribble off the bus. We step on, moving to a seat close to the middle doors. The engine revs and we're off, still holding hands in the bumpy quiet.

"Where are we going?" she asks.

Where indeed. "I don't know, yet. But I'll think of something."

"How about L.A.?"

"Oh, hell no."

She stares out the window as the world passes by, squeezing my hand tighter. "Are you coming with me?"

"Yeah." I squeeze back. "I'll get you there."

And I will.

A clown and an acrobat get on a bus. Clown jokes aren't funny.

Chapter Five

IF Chicago is the Windy City, D.C. is the Windbag City. Everybody here talks all the time, everywhere, to anybody in earshot. Dulles baggage claim. Taxi stand. Waiting for the walk signal on the corner of Fifth and G.

"Gonna be a game changer, don't yah think?" The guy's voice is high and excited, keening above the grumbling downtown traffic and my grumbling stomach. He bounces on his leather-loafered toes like a terrier needing attention.

"This new premier. The talks. I mean Reagan has to see it. The commies are done." He jerks a thumb at me, Rolex flashing in the sweltering midday sun. "But what's with that mark on the Ruski's head? Damn thing looks like a map of Albania. Christ."

I caught Tom Brokaw saying something about the new head of the Soviet Union on the Nightly News. Didn't really pay attention. Too many problems of my own to fret over international affairs and bald leaders with odd birthmarks.

Took me a month to get Julia settled. A month get her new identification, new backstory, new residence, source of income, bank accounts, transportation, the works. No circuses. This time something with a better future, somewhere she can blend in and still have a taste of normal. And it isn't a place The Opposition will be keen to look. Small town, but not too small. Nearest FBI division office is Denver, four hundred miles away. She's safe as I can make her without bunkers and blast doors.

She waved goodbye when I left.

EXCEPTIONALS

Hard to leave her—always hard with her—but I was overdue. Checking my caseload by phone doesn't give me the same warm-and-fuzzy as visiting them where they live. Three days each in St. Paul, South Bend, Lansing, and Dayton proved my other Exceptionals were all frustrated and paranoid, but otherwise fine. Tough living false lives. Lives I've set up for them.

The light changes and WALK shines in white. My yappy companion trots off the curb.

"I tell ya, buddy, same time next year there'll be a McDonalds in Moscow." He waves like we're parting friends.

I stay put, leaning against the light post and waiting as traffic flow switches again. A shiny blue Datsun zips by, then a Honda amidst a cluster of Mercedes-Benzes. Guess nobody buys American anymore.

How things change.

I move my draped trenchcoat from right arm to left then wipe my brow. Leaves are turning out west and D.C. feels like Florida on the Fourth of July. From the coat I tug last Sunday's *Tribune.* I've read it three times already, but it gives cover while I surveil lunchtime crowds schlepping up the sidewalks, hailing cabs, and collecting on the Pension Building lawn to brown bag it beneath the trees.

The light changes a half-dozen more times. I flip through the sports section, skimming an article on Dwight Gooden favored for the Cy Young Award, and wait. I hate waiting. Worst part of the job. Pop always said, "Waiting's a test." Of course, he was talking about Christmas morning not about connecting with my handler on a street corner one block from the headquarters of our nation's top law enforcement agency. A place riddled with Opposition infiltrators. A place where my handler currently works, and I used to. Nope, he wasn't talking about that.

"Bit hot for the overcoat, isn't it?" A hard-faced black man in a JCPenney suit steps around me to the curb.

"Raining when I left," I say, putting away the paper. "Haven't gotten to the hotel, yet."

He stays stoic and shakes his head. "Nice to see you, Lawson."

"Nice to see you, too, Jack."

The light changes. I sling the duffel at my feet over one shoulder and we cross to head west on G Street.

Jack Underwood looks the same as always. Same iron gray landing pad hair. Same square jaw that a sledgehammer couldn't crack. Same narrowed eyes that don't miss a thing, including my new look.

"You went blond," he says as we walk slow enough to let the crowds pass us by, but not so slow as to attract attention. "The mustache is a bit much."

"I was going for Burt Reynolds meets Robert Redford."

"What you got is ex-trucker meets male prostitute."

I'm no master of disguise, just a guy with a varied shaving routine who goes through lots of Just for Men. Keeps The Opposition guessing (I hope).

We cross another block passing a group of rowdy school kids and an exhausted tour guide.

"By the way, this is the last time we'll meet," says Jack, as casual as if he'd brought up the weather.

I stutter step but recover quick, switching my bag to the other shoulder. "I assume there's an explanation coming."

EXCEPTIONALS

Jack stops at an empty bench to feign tying his shoe. "Eight-four was an election year. My guy lost. The new chair felt it best to"—Jack yanks on the strings—"separate organizational efforts from those of the Bureau. Entirely. Something about conflict of interest, etcetera, etcetera. Anyway, badge carrying veterans like me are out. Not out too far, mind you. I know too much to simply get cut loose."

He straightens. "Advisory capacity they call it." Jack turns and trudges on.

He's three steps ahead before I trot after, befuddled. Jack's always been my go-to. He recruited me into this protection gig, showed me the ropes, screened me from the FBI's radar after, well, after that first time with Julia. The federal effort to protect Exceptionals is bigger than just him and me but for the longest time it's felt like the two of us against the world.

As I catch up, nostalgia pricks me. I should wish him well or buy him a drink. Then he shades his steely eyes against the sun, and it dawns that I don't know squat about the man. He's a lifer at the Bureau. Other than that.... Our relationship never went further than reports, assignments, and respectful handshakes. Hell, he wears a gold band and I don't know his wife's name, whether he's a widower, or if he wears it despite having been divorced for fifteen years. I sympathize with the woman, whoever she is. I've always liked Jack, though he has, from what I can tell, the emotional depth of a dented spoon.

Foot traffic thins out enough for me to ask, "What does this mean?"

"It means these past months have been all about guaranteeing my pension and guaranteeing my silence." He snorts. "It also means that after our lunchtime soirée with your new boss I have five other protection agents to coordinate with. Look, this third-rate witness protection schtick we've been playing couldn't last. You knew it and I knew it. We've been scrounging, doing our best with scraps from other agency budgets. Meanwhile The Opposition gets more sophisticated every day."

"You don't have to tell me."

We round a corner. Jack stops in the shade of a bookstore awning. The change in light shows his age. Jack looks tired, smaller, shoulders hunched under unseen burdens. "Yeah. I know I don't. You've been in the thick of it for years. Taking shit as it comes. You're good, Lawson. Probably my best. Which is why, over all the others, she wants to meet you in person."

"She?"

"I told you things are changing. We've talked. She's read your file. You're the one agent she wants to handle personally."

"Should I be honored?"

"You might be in trouble. Anyway, that's the place." He steers me toward a fancy brownstone a few doors down boasting an ivy-clad facade and a valet station out front. Once more Jack's age shows through the granite exterior. "You're young. You'll do fine."

Jack hands the attendant a twenty. "Hold on to my friend's bag."

EXCEPTIONALS

The valet doesn't balk, just smiles and sets my duffle behind his stand. "Welcome to Cavanaugh's, gentlemen."

Chapter Six

CAVANAUGH'S is all dark wood and brass and forest green accents obscured by clouds of Marlboro and cigar smoke. Nicer than a parked car or locked office. Still, if the meet must be over lunch, give me a place with sticky vinyl chairs, stickier countertops, and a menu consisting of burgers and fries. Someplace not stuffed with congressional staffers, lawyers, and other capitol leeches. Doubt there's a top-secret clearance or humane soul among them.

The hostess intercepts us at the door, nods, and guides us upstairs to a hushed room of walled off little alcoves, all isolated from one another. No smoke, thank God, only stomach-rumbling scents of good food well-made.

She gestures to one of the snug nooks, says, "Your table, Mr. Underwood," then leaves.

Only it is not just Jack's table. It is Jack and intense-lady-I-do-not-know's table. Pale skin. Tight bun of black hair. Perfect posture. She glides a chewed-up Bic across a legal pad with long fingers that display ruby-red nails. One of those new-fangled portable phones—a beige brick with a rubber antenna—rests on the table beside a picked over plate of salad. Two other places are set, empty save for glasses of ice water.

Jack said FBI ties are severed, so my guess is she's some executive assistant political something-or-other. She's no functionary that's for sure. My apparent new boss exudes a force of authority to match Jack's and then some. She can't be more than thirty-five, yet she makes my neck hairs tingle like wiry old Ms. Harkness, the Doggette Elementary School librarian who terrorized third grade me for talking too loud behind the encyclopedias and slouching in my chair.

She doesn't greet either of us, only glances up at our entry then turns to her writing. I catch apple cheeks, lips to match the nails, and eyes that command and tease at the same time. I don't know what to think, only that my scar itches and that's never a good sign.

Jack hangs his coat on a hook in the corner. He says, "Great steaks at this place. You like steak, right Lawson?" before trundling into a chair. His walnut brown complexion is dappled with sweat he didn't have outside.

I prefer facing the door, but young Harkness has that chair. Exposing my back runs counter to both training and experience. Still, I don't want to be rude.

Young Harkness pauses her writing and shoves a forkful of purple and green lettuce between those red lips. The brick by her makes a startling electronic jangle and she lifts it to her ear. "Tabor here," she says, leaning back, placing the pen between her teeth and giving me a quick wink.

Itchy scar and now my throat's gone dry. This Tabor lady's got a vibe I can't place. I sip from my water glass then tip my head at the portable phone. "First one of those I've seen."

Jack smirks, "Wonderful modern world we live in. They tried giving me one of those boat anchors. What for? Damn things only work here, New York, maybe Chicago. Besides, I already have a phone in my car, and I've only ever used it to call ahead for pizza. Pointless. Show me a hundred-yard stretch of any city and I'll show you a dozen pay phones."

Cumbersome as that brick looks, there is something to be said about having communication at one's fingertips. Hell, if my Exceptionals could reach me anytime anywhere I might not have to bop between states week after week getting jet lag and back pain.

Quick footsteps precede a bright-faced young man in an immaculate white shirt and black bowtie arriving to take our order. "Welcome to Cavanaugh's. My name is Terence, and I will be serving you today. For our luncheon special, the chef has prepared a—"

Jack lifts an interjectory hand. "Two twelve-ounce strips, Terence. Inch thick. Medium-rare. No chives on the potato. Chives for you?"

I'm still contemplating the utility of that portable phone.

"No chives for him either." Jack slips his napkin onto his lap. "And tell Arnie at the bar to make us a couple California Old Fashioneds." Jack grabs the glass of water and takes a big swallow.

Our waiter leaves, drawing a thick green curtain across the entrance to our intimate dining experience. Tabor scoots her plate aside, wedges that massive phone between shoulder and cheek, and returns to attacking the legal pad with her pen. "Yes," she says to her writing. "I understand."

I smooth my mustache, glancing at the curtain.

Jack says, "Don't worry about it. With that drawn, this booth is soundproof. Perks of the profession. Wonderful modern world and all that."

Tabor gives a brusque, "Three-thirty," thumps the phone back on the table, and finishes off her salad in three bites.

After a prim napkin dab at the corner of her mouth she fixes me with a disarming smile, but the evil librarian is still there around the edges. She extends a hand, "Geraldine Tabor."

I reach across the salad plate. "Larry Lawson."

Her grip is firm, easy, and business-like, not frigid, but cool. It's a politician's handshake.

"Underwood tells me good things about you, Lawson. Says you're the best protector of superhe—"

Jack and I lift synchronous fingers to stop her. Jack grunts out, "Exceptionals, please. I've told you. That *other* word has too much baggage."

She recovers without so much as a speed bump. "Jack says you're the best we have." She lifts a sleek leather portfolio from beside her then tugs out a manilla folder. "He also tells me you spent most of the summer dressed as a clown."

I clear my throat, "That was a one-time thing."

"Really? I assumed operating in disguise was standard practice." She gives me the once over. "You're not really a blond, are you?"

Not hard to see from two feet away. "I change up my appearance with each Exceptional. Recognition could lead undesirable elements to those under my watch."

"Makes sense." She lays open the folder and slowly leafs through its pages. "Especially for you, what with your history."

This woman is doing little to put me at ease. Jack's silence isn't helping, either.

"Still." She runs her finger down a page. "Six years on the job and only one asset lost. That's good."

"Thanks, I guess." Niles Fergusson wasn't lost. I found him where he was supposed to be, in his apartment. They shot him at 2:45 a.m. on Friday, November 13, 1981. Unlucky day. For him and for me. Added another corpse to my nightmares.

"Before Jack brought you over, you served with the FBI for..." She taps the page. "Eighteen months. What happened?"

New leadership always needs to learn their people but usually there's a bit more... decorum.

"Personality conflicts," I say, folding my hands in my lap and sitting up straight. "What about you Miss Tabor, what's your story? Harvard Law? Campaign staffer? Shook a few hands, greased a few more."

Her smile doesn't shift. "You got one out of three. And it's *Missus* Tabor. Now, what I'm asking is why you left. Five years in the Army including two tours in Vietnam before a discharge for...psychiatric reasons. Post-traumatic stress?"

She's good at keeping me on my back foot, I'll give her that. "I did the therapy. My file's clean."

"So you did. Earned your degree, too. Worked odd jobs and took the FBI entrance exam four times"—she lifts four fingers for emphasis—"before making it into Quantico. You graduated in the middle of your class, but with high marks in unarmed combat and decisiveness under pressure. Your first-year proficiency report states that you were, well, let's call it above average. You could have had a good career. Made your mark. Why would a man that worked so hard to get in, suddenly ditch the Bureau?"

Jack interrupts, "Geraldine, now is not the best time for—"

She dismisses him with a pert look. "Your food's not even here, yet." She turns back to me. "Why, Mr. Lawson?"

I take a moment, grasping my napkin beneath the table, battling back memories of gunshots and screams, hunting for Julia through her house while stepping over the dead bodies of her family, and the joyous agony of my knuckles crunching against the skulls of her assailants. An overpowering drive to suggest an alternate use for *Missus* Tabor's stupid phone swells through my chest. I take a deep breath and let it out. "There was an incident. I'd decided to turn in my badge and walk away when Jack offered me an alternate course. So I took it."

Tabor's smile tightens. "In truth, you were facing suspension and possible criminal charges pending an internal investigation over the shooting of three fellow federal agents, members of your same task force."

Jack's eyebrows raise and he whispers, "Jesus, Geraldine."

Chapter Seven

MY new boss's statement hangs over the table like D.C. smog. I press my tongue to my teeth to stop from blurting an expletive phrase I'd promised Pop to never use.

"Mrs. Tabor," I say, strangling the guiltless napkin. "Those agents were Opposition moles intent on kidnapping a fourteen-year-old girl. They killed her family to make it look like a burglary gone wrong."

Tabor doesn't flinch. "What happened?"

I clench my jaw and smooth my poor napkin across my lap. "You have the file. Everything's in there."

Tabor doesn't back down. "Not everything."

"I got the girl away." I empty my water glass in three gulps.

"And he'd didn't shoot anyone," Jack says, eyeing me with the disarmed pride of a father whose son just whupped the class bully. "Larry here beat the crap out of them. Those three were in traction for months." He ticks off on his fingers. "Cracked ribs, broken jaw, shattered patella, broken wrists, ruptured spleens, ruptured liver, torn abdominals...I forget anything?"

Yeah, Julia curled up in the back seat as we raced from the scene, her face blank and stony. My panic when she went into shock, and I thought I'd lose her. Her screaming and convulsing in the emergency room. Jack stopping me from tossing my bloody badge in the hospital trash.

"Dislocated shoulder," I mutter, "and concussions."

"Right," Jack says, snapping his fingers.

"I see," says Tabor. She puts a hand on my arm. My skin crawls like she has leprosy, but I stay firm.

"I'm not condemning you for what you did," she says. "You made a hard choice: stick to your sworn duty, obey orders...or protect an innocent and suffer the consequences. In my book, you chose right."

I glare hard at her hand and she pulls it back.

"You are selfless, Lawson. You're a natural protector. The exact type of agent we need in this underfunded, overextended little cabal—a couple of descriptors I intend to change. So, thank you, for what you do."

Jack lets out a long breath.

I relax my jaw but am not ready to meet their eyes yet. Tabor is one tough cookie, and slick. She's a chess master and I don't like being a pawn. Knight, maybe. "Any more questions?"

Tabor taps her pen. "Tons."

A soft knock on the panel wall outside.

I twist in my chair, right hand jerking to my hip. Another ingrained habit. One that makes little sense since I don't carry a sidearm. Protection agents have no license to carry. We're not sanctioned like the Feds, Marshalls, or Secret Service. Hell, even Forest Service cops pack heat. Not us. Too bad we're not in Vermont. Up there an ice cream man can shop for groceries packing a forty-four.

Jack taps the curtain to signal the waiter.

"Your steaks, gentlemen," young Terrence announces, stepping inside.

Wide plates are set before us. A sizzling beef chop, smothered baked potato, and five skinny asparagus spears lay arranged with unnecessary artistry. It's food. Last come rocks glasses filled to the brim, a single ice cube bobs in fizzing, deep amber liquid. A cherry and orange slice lay skewered across the top.

Jack waves the boy away, "Thank you." No one speaks until the curtain is closed once more.

"Great," Jack says, "If you're done with the twenty questions Geraldine, how about Lawson's report before the meat gets cold?"

Tabor taps her thumb with the Bic. "His report can wait. So can your steak. He should know the news first."

Jack picks up his utensils. "He knows about you taking over."

"No," she says, "I mean the rest of the news."

"There's more?" I ask. The day's level of interesting shit was about to keep rising.

Tabor smiles her smile—still warm, still chilly at the edges. She's a conundrum, in her armor of power suit and tight hair, all ambition and political expediency. Yet the complimentary concern over my history reads genuine. And the chewed pen? Anxiety lives beneath that iron facade. When we sat down, I saw a woman who knows exactly what she wants, how she can get it, and is totally comfortable with the means. People like that are best abandoned in the Minnesota backcountry mid-winter. Her strength and surprising gentility remind me of someone I once knew. But that someone had flowing auburn waves and eyes that swallowed me whole. And the story of that someone I'm keeping to myself.

Jack's knife is poised to cut into the beef. He sighs and sets it down. "Fine. I missed breakfast so let's make this quick." He holds up a finger. "For now you need to know one, despite the usual musical chairs following the election, our sub-committee remains committed to ensuring the rights, liberties, and anonymity of all Exceptional citizens. I know, sounds like something printed in an official statement. It is. Still, Americans are Americans no matter what they can do. Our mission hasn't changed."

Jack pops up a second finger. "Two, as I mentioned, our organization—well, *your* organization—is in for a shake-up that includes funding, staffing, research, analysis, you name it. This time next year there may be an office building, maybe even a name."

"That's the plan." Tabor fiddles with her pen. She and Jack share an awkward glance and a pause too long for comfort.

"And three?" I ask.

Jack reclaims his fork and knife. "Three is that the committee has hit a speed bump, more of a pothole actually. There's been a development. You tell him the rest. I'm hungry."

Tabor opens and closes her mouth, searching for words while Jack tucks into his meal with gusto, serrated knife grinding against his fork as he saws away.

Stick, scrape, scrape, scrape.

Jack takes a bite. His shoulders sag and a deep, delighted moan rumbles forth.

Ahmm.

He proceeds to chew with the oblivious relish of a cow in fresh hay.

I remain in quiet, tolerant observation as the scene plays out.

Tabor sets down her pen, folds her arms, and finds her words. "Files have been stolen. The committee and its objective are compromised."

Ah, yes. As predicted: interesting shit up past the elbows.

Stick, scrape, scrape, scrape. Ahmm.

"We found several documents of a sensitive nature had been duplicated." She glances again at Jack. He's working on his spud. "The whereabouts of those duplicates are, at this time, unknown."

Jack grunts mid-chew, whether as a comment on the potential fecal hurricane I've just been informed of or out of beef-induced ecstasy I can't say. My steak no longer sizzles.

"Details," I demand, then remember my manners. "If you don't mind."

"Sketchy. But what has been copied could mean disaster, especially if taken public."

"What, exactly, has been copied?"

She looks to Jack, who wipes his mouth and nods. "Personnel records," she says.

"Of operatives or subjects?"

"Yes."

Shit past the elbows over the shoulders and right up the nose. I need to get past the poop metaphors. It's putting me off my lunch.

And still....

Shit.

I've been compromised before. In the Bureau, in Nam, in...other places. More than once I'd found myself caught by miscommunication, bad intelligence, or poor choices, a few of which I made myself. I can handle bad things happening to me. But now we're talking about people I'm sworn to protect.

"You wouldn't be telling me if this breach didn't involve me. So, who did they get?"

She flips through the legal pad and shows me a list. It reads: Marcus K. Beane, Tiffany J. Johnson, Dr. Archibald R. Grambling, Juanita Carlotta Bienvenidez, and Julia B. Rourke.

My entire goddamn case load—a shell-shocked ex-infantryman with bones dense enough to stop a thirty-eight-caliber slug, a librarian who can accurately recall anything she's ever read, a geriatric former professor of African Studies fluent in one hundred and twenty-seven languages, an insurance rep whose voice could calm a charging rhino, and Julia, the ex-high wire act with perfect balance. Only Rourke is not her name anymore. Nor is she Julia B. Richards, her identity at Barney's Big Top.

"There are more," she says.

Those are not my responsibility. These five are.

Stalling for time to think I take a big pull off the rocks glass, nearly choking when it hits me that the cocktail is nothing more than Diet Pepsi. Dammit, Jack. This day gets better and better.

Chapter Eight

"How long since the breach?" I ask after swallowing what must be the worst concoction ever conceived of by man.

"Sorry. We don't know." Jack joins us, knife and fork dropped unceremoniously on the placemat, his plate clean, wadded napkin tossed atop it. "Whoever did this could have been working piecemeal, over time. Or they could have caught a break and done it all at once. We don't know. No cameras in a records room that's not supposed to exist. You'd think Capitol Hill might have learned a thing or two after Watergate and those blasted Pentagon Papers."

"It was done all at once." I say, rolling my steak knife into my fist.

"And you know this, how?" Mrs. Tabor asks.

"Clowns."

She raises a thin eyebrow. Jack repeats his stentorian nod. "That's how they found your acrobat."

"She's safe and happy for five years without a whiff of The Opposition and then those goons show up? Damn straight." I hate that I'm right.

She lowers the eyebrow. "That fits."

I continue down the rabbit hole. "And nothing's hit the papers. So, whoever did it wants Exceptionals kept secret as much as we do." That's something, I guess.

"True." Jack grumbles.

"Have we lost any?" I ask, looking at Tabor.

She sets down her pad. "No, all the original files are still in place."

"Screw the files. Have any Exceptionals been taken? Any agents?"

"Two agents are overdue on their checks," Jack says in his old stiff-necked G-man demeanor, the demeanor I've grown used to.

"By how long?"

He rolls his tongue beneath his pressed lips. "Ten days."

They're dead. I know it. Tabor knows it. And, by the lowering of Jack's eyes, he knows it, too. Neither handler speaks.

I'm almost afraid to follow-up, but I have to. Need to. "And those I protect? Marcus? Tiffany? What about them?" What about Julia? Bothers me sometimes that she's always first in my thoughts. But she was my first rescue, the first to put her life in my hands. Firsts are always special and, damnit, I like the kid. I've dug a groove in the tabletop with the butt of my knife. Sorry, Cavanaugh's.

Tabor opens her mouth, but Jack coughs and shakes his head.

One of them better talk or I'm stabbing something. "Well?"

Jack tries his tough news smile but thinks better of it. He drags in a deep, nostril flaring breath and lets it out. "The *St. Paul Sentinel* reported a Matthew Carter Benson discovered dead Wednesday in a highway motel bathroom. Stabbed in the solar plexus."

Matthew Carter Benson. The alias I'd given Marcus Beane. Someone just kicked me in the balls.

I'd checked-in with Marcus last week. Engaged after a string of failed relationships, he wanted to know how things would work going forward. He was happy, his persistent anxiety covered in a blanket of eagerness for the future.

I let go the knife and sag into my chair.

"That's not the whole story," Tabor says with a tight voice, muscles flexing in her jaw. "An autopsy revealed that twenty-four hours prior to death, Mr. Benson had a piece of one rib removed by radial bone saw and a marrow biopsy conducted on his left hip. Based on his split knuckles and mass of contusions, he didn't go down without a fight." She's upset and it's not politician theatrics. This really affects her. I did misjudge Young Harkness.

"He fought back," I whisper.

Good for him. Not that it means much now, seeing as how he's dead. Dead because some clandestine pricks want to turn his exception into a revenue stream. That's what The Opposition does—hunts down Exceptionals to see if their abilities can be replicated, turned into a drug or some such. If so, they sell it to the highest bidder. If not, well, people go missing all the time don't they. To The Opposition, Exceptionals aren't human, they're specimens.

Sorry, Marcus. You were killed and dumped in a bathtub because you were special. And because I wasn't there to protect you.

"And me?" I ask. "Was my file... compromised?"

Tabor and Jack share another glance.

"We don't think so," she says.

But they found Marcus. Despite a false identity, they found him. The guy was a tough S.O.B.: a tour in Nam, grew up punching cattle, father beat him until he got too big to beat. The Opposition found him. Did they use me to do it? Follow me? Wait until I'd left?

I rub my stupid mustache. "What changes?"

Tabor's brows knit. "Excuse me?"

"I'm busting my ass to protect people scattered across five states. Me. Alone. There's only so much I can do to keep ahead of The Opposition. What are you going to change, Mrs. Tabor? What do you bring to the table that helps insure no other Exceptional ends up dead in a motel bathtub?"

Tabor taps her pen on her pad. "We have a lot of things in the works."

"What things?" I insist.

She folds her hands atop her notepad. "First, sanctioning. That gets us a dedicated budget. A budget means more protection agents, better trained agents, and better equipped agents. It means field stations and offices, so you won't have to cover so much territory alone. It means operational authority, cooperation with other federal agencies. It means—"

"And when will all this magic happen?" I ask.

"That depends. We—"

"*When*." I don't raise my voice. Tabor's on my side. Still, I make no effort to hide six years of exhausting frustration doubled by Marcus' murder.

Jack sniffs and crosses his arms as if this argument is old hat. Tabor lifts her chin, not put off by my intensity. My guess is this is how she likes it. A simple, "Yes, ma'am," would have diminished me in her eyes.

"Eight months. Six, if everything goes smooth. But we're talking Congress. Smooth is not what they're about."

Eight months. I've held on this long, what's eight months more? A lifetime. Or a death sentence.

I nod to Tabor and glance at Jack. My belly rumbles, but my palate's gone cold as my food. The steak's greasy rather than sizzling and delicious. The asparagus is limp. The potato squats there under an oozing flop of sour cream.

"Fine," I mutter, "but The Opposition might not wait that long."

"What do you mean?" asks Jack. Both he and Tabor lean forward.

"I was with Marcus days before they got to him. Plus I was recognized in Milwaukee. Rockentanski was on the crew going after Julia. We tussled."

"Who's Rockentanski?" asks Tabor.

"FBI Special Agent Bartholomew Rockentanski," says Jack. "Picture a slab of beef in a sport coat. He's been on our watchlist for a while now. Internal Affairs has a file, but not enough to go after him."

"Jimmy was there, too," I add.

"Christ," grumbles Jack.

"Don't think he ever saw my face, though."

"Wait," says Tabor, flipping through her folder of data on me. "Is this the same Jimmy from your recruitment? The Julia Rourke incident?"

I nod. "Same little prick. Good news is Bart thought I was sweet on Julia or just an overprotective carney trying to bring her home."

"You honestly think Jimmy will buy that, with your history?" asks Jack.

"No. Hopefully he'll think I've taken on protecting Julia as a personal thing. Last he saw six years ago was me driving away with her. I gave no reason for him to think there's anything bigger afoot."

"Nothing," says Tabor, "except for your redacted FBI file. You were gone even before this Jimmy and his guys were out of the hospital. Plus, your records are sealed, and no warrant was ever served for your arrest. Now you show up guarding an Exceptional they've been hunting for half a decade? If he doesn't smell something's off, one of his higher ups will."

"And who are those higher ups?" I ask.

"Still working on that," says Jack.

"Whatever the case," says Tabor, closing my file, "it may be best if we pull you from protection duty for a while. At least until I can get you reassigned. Or some backup."

"What?" Jack and I react in stereo once more.

"You can't pull me," I bark.

"You're compromised," says Tabor. "What would you do in my place?"

"I'd wait to be sure," I say.

Jack leans forward. "Geraldine, you need Lawson out there."

"It's not your call anymore, Jack." Tabor taps my closed file. "But you are right. We're stretched so damn thin. Maybe I can swap your cases with another agent."

"No. Please." I won't hand over Julia's safety to someone else. "I know my people and I know The Opposition. You get us sanctioned, get us what we need to do this right. Until then, I have job to do. Four people are betting their lives on me. I won't let them down, no matter what you say."

Tabor flips open my file, again. She turns page after page as she considers her options.

Jack folds his hands across his full belly.

I kill the napkin.

"Fine," she says. "I won't pull you. We'll have some new identities made up."

"My guys can handle that," says Jack. "We have the gear."

Tabor gives him a hard, reasoning look. "Fine." Then to me, "It's an impossible task. I wish we could guard each Exceptional twenty-four seven. But we can't. Not yet."

Tell me something I don't know.

"You save the ones you can," says Jack. "That's all you can do."

Pop would've liked Jack. Too bad.

"Your IDs, travel vouchers, cash, everything we can offer will be at your hotel in two days," says Tabor, loading everything back into her portfolio.

"That's my cue." Jack pushes back from the table.

I reach across to shake his hand. "Thank you, Jack. You take care of yourself."

He grips my hand like a vice. "For what it's worth, I think we did some good. I'll miss that. You keep fighting the good fight."

And he's gone. Heavy curtains swish once at his passing, then hang still as if waiting for what comes next. Six years together and he leaves with all the fanfare of exiting a voting booth.

"Your food's gone cold," say Tabor.

It has, but my appetite's back. I tuck in. *Stick, saw, saw, saw. Chomp.* Never pass up free beef.

"Can you get me a sidearm?" I ask, forcing down an under-chewed mass of potato.

"We'll work something out," says Tabor. "No promises." She packs up her portfolio.

"What about your mole?" I ask.

"Give me a few weeks," Tabor says, standing.

"This can't wait weeks."

She looks me straight in the eye, holding my gaze. "I believe in what we do, Larry, more than you know. I will do everything in my not inconsiderable authority to get you what you need and keep those people safe."

A slice of steak follows the asparagus. I give it a rough chew then wash everything down with what's left in my water glass. I'm not touching the bullshit Old Fashioned. "More agents. More resources," I say scooting back from the table. "And a gun."

She extends her hand and I take it. "I'm working on it."

Tabor steps around my chair and doesn't look back as the curtain swishes closed behind her.

Chapter Nine

"They're not really black, you know." My flannel-wearing cabbie halts at the first stoplight we've hit in a fifteen-minute drive from quaint Rapid City Regional Airport. A smatter of cars crosses the intersection, mostly dented pickups and a lone Jeep Wagoneer. In the distance a modest skyline sits before a backdrop of low, dark mountains.

Rapid's a good place for Julia. A population around fifty thousand means big enough to have things to do while small enough that most don't care it's on the map. Like my driver, the air here is thin and clean. Too clean. I've grown use to rude, smelly people in rude smelly cities. This place and this guy are, well, uncomfortably pleasant.

"Nah, the name comes from the Lakota Sioux, *paha sapa*. See how the mountains look black from here? So..." He shrugs, looking at me through aviator sunglasses. "Black Hills."

The light turns green and our Crown Vic wagon motors gently onward.

He prattles away, but I'm not listening. The past few months have been chock-full of worry over Tabor sealing the leak in our secrets and frustration over my Exceptionals who fought me on how best to save their lives. In the end they saw it my way, as they always do. Juanita and Dr. Grambling, for all their whining and feet-dragging, were pieces of cake compared to Tiffany, who insisted on a move to New York with a job at the public library in Manhattan. She even went so far as to present me with apartment listings in Tribeca that would suit her. Her insistence faltered when I showed her forensic photos of Marcus. Then she agreed that a position with the Akron, Ohio Bookmobile would be acceptable.

My Julia is old hat. She knows the drill. She made her call last night like clockwork. Good kid. Relocating her should be a cinch. Still, I can't rest until each of my Exceptionals are set up fresh and The Opposition mole is found. Even then, sleep won't come easy. It never does. Would be a tad more at ease with a sidearm. Tabor's IOU still stands.

"And here we are, the Hotel Alex Johnson, as requested." My cabbie eases over to the curb. "Best stay you're gonna find."

Don't I know it. AJ's is the only big hotel in town without a six or eight in its name or a waterslide and kids screaming around the pool until all hours of the night. No thank you. Besides, I stayed here last fall when I brought Julia out to enroll her at the university.

The hotel is an impressive building with brown brickwork, creamy stucco, and exposed beam construction. Green awnings over the first-floor windows flap slowly in the midday breeze. The place is like a Tyrolean inn stretched eleven stories high. Nice folks. Comfy beds. Great diner across the street.

I step from the car eager to check in and check on Julia.

My driver closes the trunk and thumps my two bags beside me. "You seen *North by Northwest*?" he asks, adjusting those ridiculous glasses.

I shake my head.

"Hitchcock? Cary Grant chased across Mount Rushmore? Great flick. Anyway, this place was in the movie." He extends his hand to grasp mine.

"Guess I'll give it a look." I say, letting go the gruff handshake to dig out payment for my erstwhile rep of the local visitor's bureau. Big tip. He's been nice, never pushy, and he got me here without once slamming on the brakes. Pop taught me to reward good service.

"Thanks, man. Enjoy your stay."

I hoist my mismatched Samsonites into the broad, wood paneled lobby. After a quick reception that's so courteous I'm worried the attendant is recruiting me as a Jehovah's Witness, I'm rattling a key in the door of room 511. I really need to unwind. My body wants the high, firm, king-sized bed, but I can't risk a nap. Work to do.

Outside phone calls are free so I dial up Julia's dorm while tugging off my shoes. Ring number one, number two, three, four...I let it get to eight before I hang up.

The desk clock says 3:17.

We set her class schedule back in September. She should be free right now.

At the gym?

Visions of rough hands dragging Julia toward a van set my scar to itching. I shove those thoughts back under lock and key. This is a safe location. She has no history in Rapid and neither do I, really. There was a camping trip with Pop when I was ten. Beauty of the area stuck with me. So too the triceratops skull at the university museum. Boys love dinosaurs.

EXCEPTIONALS

Nobody knows this location. Nobody knows her new identity. Julia's smart, tough, and seasoned enough to know what to do when the bad starts happening. Still, my scar itches and there's only one way to scratch it.

A quick shower takes the red out of my hair—leftover look from my time in Ohio checking on Tiffany of the eidetic memory. A clean shave and change of clothes later I step from a different cab where the surly driver got himself no tip, and walk across the broad green fronting Black Hills University. The campus sprawls and rolls, crisscrossed with clean sidewalks, waving pines, and plum trees in blossom. The kids strolling by, deep in discussion or laughing pleasantly, are a generation removed from my college experience—a blur of beer fueled nights, sprints to classes I hardly remember taking, and flipping through girlfriends like the pages of a comic book, all while hoping Vietnam would wrap-up before graduation. Not Lawrence Lawson's proudest years.

Place looked different covered in fall foliage back when I first brought her here, but I find Bennett Hall easy enough. Outside doors are locked. I scan the listed names on a brass wall panel and press a cracked buzzer beside Reardon.

"May I help you?" The voice is high, but distinctly masculine. This isn't a coed dorm, so my itch gets stronger.

I'm worked up just enough to fumble her latest identity. "Hello. I'm looking for Jul-er, Jennifer?" Stupid.

The speaker goes dead for a second. Scenarios race through my brain, none of them good.

"Who is it?" There's the voice I know.

"It's your father," I say. Anyone seeing a mid-30's guy in a sport coat ringing a dorm room bell is going to make that assumption anyway. So, I run with it. Besides, Julia and I've played this ruse before. Jennifer. Damnit, I mean Jennifer.

There's a pause. Then, "I'll be right down." Was it the wind, or did I hear a muttered, "shit" just before she clicked off?

Chapter Ten

WHEN the door opens, a girl I hardly recognize bulls past me with a nonchalant, "Let's go." The long black hair is gone. Short blond spikes tipped with blue stand up off her head like cartoonish gas flames. Each ear holds multiple piercings and she's dressed in an old Army field jacket, jackboots, and baggy purple pants with pocket flaps mid-thigh.

I trot to catch up, my shock at her appearance threatening to derail my train of thought. "Who's the guy?"

"None of your business." She pulls out a crumpled pack of Camels and lights up as we walk.

Julia would never smoke. The look fits rebel Jennifer Reardon. I can't say anything. I'm the one who coached her on giving truth to any new identity. My girl's growing up. Not sure I like it.

"Actually, it *is* my business," I say, using my stern, listen-here-young-lady voice.

"Guess." She drags on the cigarette, blowing a thick cloud for me to walk through.

I blink and push on. "Fine. A boyfriend. I'm happy for you."

She halts mid-stride, eyes filled with tired accusation. "Are you?"

"I'm just worried about you, kid. You know that."

My admission draws a crooked smile.

"I mean, purple pants? I gotta wonder if you're okay." I tap the side of my head.

She snorts and shakes her head.

I smile back. "Just, please, tell me you didn't get a tattoo."

Her shoulders twitch as she chuckles. She takes a quick drag, smoke leaking out around her words. "And what if I did?"

We turn and stroll on. I change tactics. "Well, I hope you'd tell me the where and what of it so I can ID your corpse."

She thumps me in the chest. Camel ash flutters away on the afternoon breeze. "Not funny. Not one, fucking bit."

We stop at a lone bench under a maple atop a high green hill. The tree is just coming into leaf and throws dancing, dappled shadows across my favorite Exceptional's hard-to-get-used-to new look. I turn to the view—treetops, campus buildings, roads that even in this small part of the world seem busy. A slow-rolling train chugs east towards the plains. We sit quietly gazing at it, sharing the moment until she drops her smoke and grinds it out beneath the toe of her boot.

"I like it here, Larry," she says without looking at me. "I don't want to move again. Not until I graduate. It's time I start calling the shots in my life."

I watch the train, not knowing what to say.

"I've got a boyfriend and a job. I'm holding a B+ average. Would be an A but my psychology professor screwed me on the mid-term. Last week I was invited to rush a sorority."

"You?" It comes out all wrong.

"Yes, me. Cocksucker." She thumps me again, this time on the arm. "And it's not that kind of sorority. It's academic. For women engineers and scientists and the like."

Looking at her getup, a layman would think she was some punk kid, likely with rich, disinterested parents. I know better. She's an athlete with abilities far beyond extraordinary. I shouldn't be surprised that she has interests outside acrobatics. That she might want something more out of life than the hand she's been dealt. A hand I had a part in dealing. I owe her.

"Look, Jennifer, I'm not here to—"

"Call me by my real name, can't you? Before, at least I was still Julia even if I had to use Richards and not Rourke. Now? Who the hell is Jennifer Reardon?"

We've had this discussion before, time and again after I set her up in Barney's. I told her when I brought her here. She's just venting.

"I'm not just venting, Larry."

And she's tired.

"I'm just so tired."

"The new name sucks. I know and I'm sorry," I give her a good, long look, the way a father might when sending his daughter off to prom. "It's all to keep you safe."

"Yeah," she sighs, "I know."

A robin lands on the big branch above us and begins to sing its cheery spring song.

I clear my throat. "If it's any consolation, in that getup, I don't think you'll be recognized by anybody anytime soon. I like your hair, by the way."

She looks about to tell me where to go or what to do with myself when the compliment brings her up short. "Really?"

"Really."

Really.

She blushes and turns back to the view.

"Thanks. My roommate did the hair. Takes a handful of mousse to get the spikes working, though."

"What's it like when you wake up in the morning?"

"Like I'm wearing a dead hedgehog." She gives a quick chuckle and the smile I've missed these past months. "You could do with a haircut."

"Probably." This trip Julia's seeing me the way she did our first meeting. No false front. It's another thing the kid deserves.

I halt our conversation until a pair of young men in Army ROTC fatigues pass out of earshot. Their boots grind against the cement path, not yet achieving the matched step that will soon come by instinct. As it did with me. As it does with all who've served. Funny how I can't think of a fond memory of my time in uniform, yet I'm proud just the same.

"Jesus, Larry. You don't have to be so paranoid." Julia whispers.

I take her hand gently in mine. "Part of the job, kid. It's not safe to use your name, even if we think we're alone. There's too much at stake. And too much has happened already."

Jennifer looks up in that sad, curious, tearless way, like she did at the Milwaukee bus stop. Is this parenting? Stopping for time together only when it's bad news?

"What happened?" she asks.

"We found out one of the good guys is one of the bad guys. Some of those we protect...well. We didn't."

She's gone pale. "Any of yours?"

I nod.

"I'm sorry."

"So am I."

"I knew you watched over more than just me. Still, whenever you checked in, I felt, well...special."

I squeeze her hand. "You are special." To me.

She pulls me close and leans her head on my chest. "Yeah, so special a secret society wants me dead."

I put my arm around her. "No, most likely they want to hook you up to a bunch of needles and tubes to find out how perfect balance works. Once they can make a marketable product out of your exception, then the killing."

"Larry..."

"I know. Not funny." We sit there in the afternoon quiet for a moment.

Time to bring the topic back to something normal, something unexceptional. "So, what's the boyfriend's name?" I ask.

She hesitates. "Trevor."

"Oh, dear God," I mutter and she elbows me in the gut.

"Shut up, he's nice."

Of course he is. We enjoy another quiet moment and I pull my mind off what will happen to wee Trevor if he hurts her. The thought of anyone hurting her...

An hour ago I was set to give the speech of all speeches. Pack up her things and disappear yet again. Billings. Maybe Missoula. Now, though, the idea of letting her down, mucking up her life yet again? My heart's not in it.

I never did file a report on moving Julia here—Tabor okayed me compiling reports until the mole is found. I have a stack of thick manilla envelopes in my travel bag just waiting to be mailed. Julia's envelope isn't sealed yet. For a reason.

"You can stay here, kid. Safe a place as any, I guess." Truer and more naive words were never said.

She hugs me tight. I return the squeeze, leaning my head atop hers.

"Ouch!" I jerk back, blinking. "Right in the eyeball."

"Omigosh. Sorry, Larry. Shit, sorry."

I rub my sore eye with the palm of my hand. "Not a hedgehog. A goddamn porcupine."

Chapter Eleven

JULIA drives us to dinner in a dusty blue Reliant K with fake wood siding. As a consolation from our talk, I told her that, in my mind at least, I'd use her real name.

Across from my hotel sits a little diner that makes one heck of a half-pound cheeseburger. I don't let this meal go cold, but get right to business, wiping my mouth only after consuming every juicy bite of firm chewy bun, tender, seasoned beef, gooey melted cheddar, smokey-sweet bacon, lettuce that I swear spoke the word *crisp* with each mouthful, and a beefsteak tomato slice as meaty as the ground beef patty. Some ketchup, a dab of mustard, and three tangy pickle slices put me over the top. If only some genie had granted the place a liquor license so I could wash down this joy-on-a-bun with malted hops instead of iced tea. Still, I cherish the little moments. They get my mind off the harsh reality of someone out there pretending to do my same job while enabling kidnapping and murder.

Come on, Tabor.

Julia stirs the ice in her glass then takes a hard pull at her straw, sucking the last drops of Coke from the bottom. She sets it down, stifling a burp with her free hand.

"Excuse me."

I incline my head as I work the last remnants of tonight's glorious feast from between my teeth with a toothpick.

"Good stuff," I say, finally managing to free a bothersome piece of meat from between my molars.

"Yeah, Sally's does it right, so long as what you want comes off a griddle. Thanks for the food." She leans forward, lowering her voice. "And for not moving me, again."

I follow suit. "You're welcome. On both accounts. None of my higher-ups know you're here. Nor will they, until the 'problem' is dealt with."

"Won't that get you in trouble?"

"It might. Nothing I can't handle. You abstain from any stunning acrobatics, and you'll stay about as safe as I can make you."

We both lean back as our pink-dressed waitress saunters up.

"More tea, sweetie?" She's only a mouthful of gum away from being Flo on *Alice*.

"No, thank you. Just the check, please."

She tears the top sheet from her pale green pad and slides the paper toward me.

"I'll be your cashier whenever you're ready. You two have a good night now."

She winks and walks away, with more saunter than when she arrived.

"She's looking to be more than your cashier, Larry," Julia says with a smirk before giving another try at her empty glass.

"What?" I've missed something.

"Oh, c'mon. She couldn't have laid it on thicker if she'd said, 'I'll be your cashier...and you're welcome in my money box anytime.' Then gave you a squeeze under the table."

Missing a woman's signals can be forgiven. I've been out of that game for years. But, hearing it laid out by Julia makes me squirm.

"She was just being nice." My tea glass suddenly requires my complete attention.

"Sure she was." Julia folds her arms over her chest. "You need to get laid, Larry."

Ice cubes fly across the table as I fumble my glass and cough on tea sucked down the wrong pipe. Some clack and bounce off Julia's plate into her lap. Others clatter to the floor. Dozens of dining heads turn our way.

Julia bites her knuckles, face firetruck red.

I sweep an apologetic smile around the room and immediately try to scoop errant cubes back into their tea-fee receptacle.

"Oh, sugar, don't fret. I'll take care of this." Flo's back, idling beside me like a V8 at a stoplight. Her name tag reads *Marlene* in thick black letters. Then in smaller script, *What Can I Do For You?*

"Nothing. I mean, no—er, sorry. Sorry for the mess."

Marlene gives a crooked smile and winks. Again. "It's my pleasure."

She takes an uncomfortably long time gathering our dishes. And when she bends over to get the ice off the floor, the wiggle of her ass kicks my gaze right up to the brass ceiling fan.

Julia rocks in her seat, battling back laughter.

Once Marlene the Gyration Machine returns to the kitchen, I pull together enough dignity to look at Julia. She, forcing herself calm, returns my look with feigned innocence, as if she has no idea what all that fuss was about. Then something behind me catches her attention and all fun drains from her face.

"Oh, crap."

She's not scared, only shamefaced and trying to be inconspicuous, which is impossible with her hair.

"What is it?" I ask.

"Remember the psychology prof that fucked my mid-term?"

I attempt to see whom she's referring to.

"Don't look!" She clutches my arm before I can turn. "Bitch hates me, always calling me out in class. She gave my paper a D minus. Claims most of it was plagiarized."

She's piqued my curiosity and I'm glad to talk about anything but my non-existent sex life. "Was it?"

"Well, yeah. There was conflicting research."

I don't believe her. She can see it on my face.

"Okay. I didn't do the research. I got busy with other stuff and—crap."

Julia ducks her head.

A citrus sweetness precedes the arrival of a green skirt and matching jacket beside our table. Shapely, nylon-clad calves tapering to a pair of practical heels deserve a moment's pause.

"Miss Reardon, funny bumping into you here. I was just on my way out." Her voice is strong and smooth. And there is something...familiar.

"Well, don't let me stop you," Julia snaps.

I catch her in the shin under the table. "Jennifer," I say. "Manners."

Julia looks at me then up at our guest. "Sorry."

"Oh, that's all right," the professor says in a voice that tells me she's heard worse.

The voice. Those legs. My throat tightens. Please, please, let me be wrong.

"And is this your father?"

I'm not wrong. Shit.

Chapter Twelve

SHE extends a hand. "Professor Holly Chisholm, pleased to meet you—" Her voice catches. Her manicured fingers quaver. Her eyes go wide. The hand retreats, nervously brushing along her coat as if looking for a place to hide.

She's more striking than the day I left her. A short, professional hairstyle has replaced her waterfall of auburn waves. The make-up is still subtle, precisely accentuating the right features. Her green eyes could still swallow me whole. Yet the whimsical sense of adventure is gone, replaced with a steely strength. Pangs of regret, shame, and longing I thought long dead flood right back, crashing over me with power bolstered by years. Were I to stand, she'd be a head shorter than me, yet I feel small as a crumb of burger bun resting on the tabletop.

"Hello, Holly." Her name comes out tight and an octave higher than intended.

She opens her mouth. For a moment, the strong professorial facade cracks. She tries a smile, then tightens her mouth the way I remember her doing when she got angry. With a breath it all disappears. Professor Chisholm reclaims control.

"Larry." She clasps her hands in front of her. "It's been years."

"It has."

We're both at a loss to say more. After all this time apart, where do we begin?

"You two know each other?" Julia says, eyes wide, mouth hanging open.

Holly and I respond simultaneously. My "It's a long story" collides with her "Yes, we do" mushing into something I'm sure came across to Julia and everyone else within earshot as, "This is awkward. Someone please set fire to the kitchen."

Holly, too composed to let herself be wrong-footed in front of a pain-in-the-ass student, recovers first.

"Mr. Lawson and I are old acquaintances."

Is that what we were? A sharp pain hits me dead center, a forlorn echo of the hurt when I left this amazing woman for what I thought would be forever.

Holly senses my weakness and seizes the tactical advantage. "So, how do you two know each other?"

She knows I'm not Julia's dad. We look nothing alike and Holly can do the math. I, on the other hand, can't seem to string three words together to form a coherent sentence.

Damn she smells good.

Julia gives me a raised eyebrow. I can't tell if she's confused over what's going on, quietly delighted at seeing me squirm yet again, or just happy Holly's not drilling her about her studies. Probably a bit of all three. She's not bailing me out of this, that's for sure.

"I'm a friend of the family." Unable to come up with anything better, I default to the textbook response of protective agents under scrutiny. It's hard to improvise with my pulse banging away like a forty-piece drum line. "I happened to be passing through on business and thought I'd check in on Jenn." Way to go. More than three words and not really a lie.

Holly considers then gives a smile I'm sure is reserved for students trying to pull the wool over her eyes. "Ah. Well. You two continue to catch up, then. Miss Reardon, I'll see you tomorrow, with your assigned corrections?"

Julia nods, returning Holly's smile with a false one of her own.

"Nice seeing you, Larry." Holly adjusts the burgundy purse strap on her left shoulder.

"Nice seeing you..." My stupid heart stampedes ahead of my brain. "We should catch up, sometime."

Holly clenches her jaw but never breaks her professional calm. "You said you were just passing through?"

"Uh, yeah, but I've got a few days." Shut up, stupid. Somebody throw a straightjacket on me before I get into real trouble. "Maybe we could grab coffee?"

Coffee? What the hell am I doing? A trip down memory lane with love long lost will not help me keep Julia safe from The Opposition. But a professor would have knowledge of the campus that might be useful to me and—oh, shut up!

Holly smiles once more and this time I get a hint of the playful joy that used to be her constant. Her steel and stoicism soften. "Sorry, but my schedule is full."

Not even a wave goodbye. The brass bell over the diner door jingles as she strides out, determined strides carrying her past Sally's wide windows. I watch her the intense way a puppy might watch its master leave for work, begging with all my being that she'll turn around and play with me. My heart's in my throat as she passes out of sight. Yet, just before she's gone, was that a glance my way?

"Larry?" Julia prods my arm.

"Huh? What?" I refocus, faking nonchalance and failing. Stupid to try. Holly's lingering citrusy sweetness keeps teasing me into what-if daydreams.

"What the hell was that? You and Professor Bitchness?"

"Whoa, easy on the language." How do I explain this? "She's not a...and you know what? She might be nicer to if you didn't cheat on your homework." Pathetic. I suck as a parent.

She leans back, crossing her arms, not buying what I'm selling.

"Like I said, it's a long story." I stand to go. "And it's none of your business."

"Yeah, sure," Julia says with a smirk. She holds her ground a few seconds more then shrugs. "I owe her three pages by tomorrow and the library closes at nine."

I walk Julia to her car and watch her drive east, away from the dimming sunset, before trudging to my hotel. Try as I might to focus on how I can best ensure Julia's safety, my thoughts keep lingering on auburn hair and playful eyes, on that lazy day in when we made love beside a mountain stream, on getting down on one knee and the tears as she whispered, "Yes."

Holly Chisholm. Here. What are the odds?

I stumble into my room, chuck the key on the table, and catch my reflection in the mirror. Holly had changed, flowered and matured and made a life. Me? I flop on the bed.

Several bits of Pop's wisdom race through my mind. None of them help.

Julia is the task at hand. Holly is not why I'm here. I'm here for Julia. Julia has a class with the only woman I ever loved. I jilted Holly so that I could protect Exceptionals... like Julia.

Balls.

Chapter Thirteen

I get no sleep. Even with a double Nytol and the ceiling fan droning away, my mind won't get off the problem of Professor Holly Chisholm.

Problem and possibility.

That was the rub.

What I did. What might have been. What might be. No matter how many times I chewed my own ass for pondering the pointless venture of *her*, my mind just drifted right back. It kept drifting until the night sky out my window turned soft blue and Huey Lewis rocked the alarm on my bedside radio.

Then I started in on the really worrisome notions of how and why she wound up here, now, and what that meant for Julia. Still, it's nice to have a new set of worries instead of the same old, same old.

Those thoughts linger as I complete my morning constitutional then check in with my caseload. Tiffany complains about kids swiping the *Choose Your Own Adventure* books from her bookmobile. Doctor Grambling greets me in Swahili, teaches me how to say, "I don't understand" in that language then says goodbye in Finnish—*hyvästi*. Juanita is my last call, and rightly so. Her ability to clear all tension, all anxiety, any and all negative vibes with a word, is just what I need to start the day. That woman could talk a Pamplona bull into giving her a lift home.

Exceptional.

Mind calm, I brainstorm what to do about the situation here in Rapid. Most ideas mean going back on my agreement with Julia to stay, which would break her heart, which I won't do.

Unless I have to.

What it comes down to is a need for more time and a better grip on the lay of the land. That means a call to the office of Mrs. Geraldine Tabor.

She's oddly chipper, trying to wriggle my location out of me. She doesn't get it. "Just testing you. Each new envelope from you is like a hidden present found two weeks past Christmas."

Sarcasm?

"What's the news?" I ask.

"Capitals won last night. Hell of a game." A slurp and a ruffle of paper on her end intimate Geraldine is handling me, paperwork, and hot coffee at the same time. Maybe tea, but I doubt it. She screams coffee woman.

"Good to hear. Sorry I missed it. How's our mutual problem?" No use beating around the bush. If the powers that be have any new intel on our leak, I need to know. And I have a request.

"Repairs are under way." She cups the mouthpiece and I hear muffled grunting likely directed at someone else in the room. "Sorry. Work goes on. Anyway, to your question. Nothing I can share other than we confirmed your suspicions as to their timeline. Definitely a one-shot job."

Being right is little comfort. "Any news about our boomers and fliers?" I ask.

EXCEPTIONALS

Turns out Geraldine saw *Crocodile Dundee* and fell in love with all things Australia. Says she finds Paul Hogan charming, in a rough, male-chauvinist sort of way. So, when she discovered Aussie nicknames for kangaroos—boomers for guys and fliers for girls—they became code for Exceptionals and agents.

The CIA we are not.

"Funny you should ask. Had two pair go walkabout."

So, they're dead. A pigeon lands at my room's windowsill and promptly squirts on the brickwork. The mellowing vocal powers of Juanita Carlotta Bienvenidez have worn off.

"That's too bad," I say.

"It's no-one you know. Look, I've got five minutes to get some talking points in front my guy." Ah, her employer, the Honorable Representative. "Everything okay? Why the call?"

"I'll be quick." I ask for an extension.

"How much time do you need?"

I can sweep the campus in a couple days. However, there's Holly. "At least a week."

"What about the other boomers? Need someone to cover your rounds?"

"Could you spare someone if I did?"

"No."

"Don't worry. I've got mine corralled. They'll be fine."

"They won't miss their guardian angel?"

"I'll make it up to them later. Put some cash in their Christmas cards."

Quiet on the line. Then, "Fine. I'll scrounge up some more for your expense account. And add me to your Christmas list."

"Will do. Lucky there are still eight months left in the Christmas shopping season."

A chuckle on her end. "I've got to go. Keep me in the loop. I don't care if it's a postcard. Got it?"

"Got it."

"One week. After that it comes out of your pay." She hangs up.

I've got my week. Now, what to do with it?

Chapter Fourteen

O'MARA Hall stands as a testament to practicality. No sweeping lines. No soaring arches. No fancy-pants architecture of any kind to get in the way of Lego-block efficiency—a temple designed by engineers, for engineers.

If the brick exterior promised boredom, the inside hallways deliver blandness at a whole new level. Speckled beige floor tiles stretch away in the distance, reflecting the buzzing glow of fluorescent lights. Beige walls run on, interrupted only by dark beige classroom doors and the occasional corkboard that, despite having notices and fliers of various colors, all carry a certain beige-ness to them. The dusty dry air reeks of a world verging on tan.

I stride through, rubber-soled oxfords squeaking, looking for Opposition clues while imagining what Nazi scientist developed this color scheme. Passersby either ignore me or merely glance up as they scurry along. I peek through a few precisely rectangular windows set in precisely rectangular doors only to see the same repetitive scene of tired profs with bad ties lecturing semi-attentive students.

A corkboard displays various thumbtacked postings including two identical notices of a scholarship application deadline, a four-by-six picture of a battered alto sax with the words *For Sale* written in black magic marker, and a poster-sized advert for a martial-arts tournament happening on campus this weekend.

Nothing smells fishy.

Then again, what do I expect to sniff out by walking through the halls while classes are in session? I've regressed to reconnaissance 101. Learn the ground.

Do I expect to find a hive of Opposition activity at the end of this echoey ecru corridor?

No.

What I do find is a closed door—brown, not beige—marked with an orange plastic sign reading *Social Sciences* in thin white letters. Strange to find that department here. O'Mara Hall is the Engineering building.

Perhaps I should check into this oddity? After all, Julia's safety is at stake and duty demands I be thorough. My actions are in no way self-serving.

Beyond the door it's night and day from what I've just strolled through. Tile gives way to brown Berber. Pale green walls are hung with tasteful artwork and punctuated by small potted plants on small accent tables. The hall ends comfortably, cozily at a large window with soft blue curtains. And the air no longer reminds me of an Egyptian tomb.

Eight doors line the hallway, each bearing a faculty name. Only eight. Shows what BHU must think of the social sciences.

A strong, smooth, lovely, familiar voice drifts from the only open office. The welcoming atmosphere suddenly squeezes the air out of me. I'm on my first high school date. My collar chokes me. My shirt cuffs are too tight. My palms are clammy. I shouldn't be here. But I am.

This is for Julia.

Is it really?

Five feet from Holly's door, laughter. Her laugh, casual and effortless. It helps put some steel in my Jell-O spine, convincing me nothing's wrong here. Nothing at all.

Then, a man laughs with her.

I stop, all steel gone and feet trapped in cement. Is she with a co-worker? A friend? A *boy*friend? Of course she has a boyfriend. No ring on her finger doesn't mean she's single. I've completely failed to assess the evidence.

The slap of Pop's palm against his forehead echoes through my mind.

I shouldn't be here. Holly doesn't want to see me. I abandoned her in the worst way—waited until she left for work then packed up and drove off. She got nothing from me but a one-page note saying we were better apart, that she should not look for me, and some other crap Jack Underwood and his top-secret committee had told me to write.

"Quick and clean," he had said. "Like a band-aid. I'm not saying it won't hurt, but it has to be done."

It had to be done to keep Holly safe. Protection agents sever ties to safeguard loved ones, to eliminate possible leverage, and to keep the truth of Exceptionals a secret.

I turn around, feet suddenly eager to move, and reach for the door back to beige Hades when their laughter precedes Holly and companion into the hall behind me.

"...that's good. I'll have to remember that," he says between chortles. Then all laughter ceases. "Hello, may I help you?"

What now? Stomp out like I'm a nobody who found himself in the wrong department? The door's cool aluminum knob is slippery in my grip.

"Are you looking for someone in particular?" His voice is kind, fun even. Holly deserves kind and fun.

I manage the door.

Just ignore them and leave. Julia might need me and—

"Larry? Is that you?" Holly, voice warm from recent laughter.

Shit. The corridor to freedom lies before me. Instead of taking it, I let go the handle and turn around.

"Yeah, it's me."

She's sheathed in a wine-colored pant suit that, despite its all-work-and-no-play tailoring, does nothing to hide the shape I once caressed during lazy mornings in bed. Holly's stony mask assures me she is not having the same winsome recollection.

Her companion is a much happier looking person—small, cheery, in his early forties. He's all in brown tweed with thinning hair, an infectious smile, and cradling a heavy stack of file folders. There's a tarnished wedding band on his left hand.

That's something. The Holly Chisholm I knew would never dabble with a married man.

"Hello. Dr. Bill Severs. Larry, is it? Are you a friend of Professor Chisholm's?" He shakes my hand clumsily from beneath the paperwork. Firm. Friendly. Not challenging. He's not threatened by me. That's something, too. Hopefully something.

I return the shake, smiling in my best imitation of his broad grin. "More or less. Sorry, to interrupt. I was in the area and thought I'd stop by."

"How nice." Dr. Bill lets go and moves past to open the door. "I'll let you two catch up. I have a class in ten. Holly, see you tonight."

The last is not a question.

Maybe *not* so hopeful.

Chapter Fifteen

HOLLY gives a casual wave and Bill closes the door on his way out, his departing footsteps are the loudest thing in the room for the next couple of moments. She crosses her arms and looks at me as if figuring whether to call the cops now or after she's ripped my head from my shoulders.

My tongue is a dry lump, somehow paralyzed despite my panicky urge to cringe at her feet and beg forgiveness. Right now, groveling seems a perfectly viable course of action.

Anything to break the tension.

"Let's go to my office. We can talk there."

No summary execution? Perhaps she has a trap door in front of her desk leading to a pit filled with malnourished crocodiles. I'm relieved to find her trim office simple, academic, and absent torture devices—a tidy desk topped with a typewriter and empty bud vase, neat bookshelves, a Georgia O'Keefe print, framed diplomas and awards.

"There's coffee if you want." She takes a seat at her desk, the room's only chair, and gestures to a plugged-in percolator flanked by two novelty mugs. One reads *Professors do it with class* and the other sports four nude asses with the caption *Behind Mount Rushmore*.

"No, thank you." I'm not thirsty.

"Really? I thought that's what you wanted?"

"Huh?"

"Last night you wanted to get coffee. Well, there it is."

Not exactly what I meant. She's messing with me and it's working. I feel like a bigger ass than any guy on that mug. What am I doing here?

"What are you doing here, Larry?"

I have no clue. At some point in the ancient history of this morning I had convinced myself this was a good idea, and I had a plan, or at least a vague outline. I think.

"I honestly don't know." To delay making eye contact I peruse her collection of framed certificates. "So you finished your doctorate at Northwestern. That's great. Took me five years to get a BS from Oshkosh Community."

"And that was an extension campus. I remember. So...?" The drum of her fingers on the desktop echo my heartbeat. She doesn't want to play dodge and evade.

Why is it so hot in this place?

"I guess I came to say, I'm sorry." Well that was pathetic.

She chuckles. "Sorry? A disappearing act. Six years without a word and you show up with *sorry*?"

Pathetic.

"If it makes you feel better, I had a really good reason." Moron. Where's that damn crocodile door?

"It doesn't. But seeing you squirm does. In truth, I no longer care about the why. You left. I've moved on. Simple as that."

"Simple?" I haven't moved on.

"Yep." She hits the *p* with a hard pop.

Based on what's in this office, she *has* moved on. Certificate of Appreciation for a thousand hours of volunteer service at the La Croix Veteran's Health Center. A photo titled Platte River Flood 1981 with her and five others in hard hats and muddy grins. A gilded frame housing an oversized document written in Japanese.

"You earned your *shodan*?" I ask, revealing a bit too much surprise.

"My second degree certificate is at home," she says matter-of-factly. "Third degree is at the club."

"Club?"

"Something else I do."

"Ah. Been years since I trained." In a dojo. "I never figured you for one to take karate."

"Kenpo, actually. For a few years there I was in a pretty bad way. You can probably guess as to why."

No guess needed. When I left, she not only had to reset her own life, she had to inform everyone that the wedding was off. Probably still a few uncles and cousins like some time alone with me and a baseball bat.

"I tried therapy groups and journaling and all the things I had used to help vets back when we first...back then. They worked for a bit. Then I found a dojo and turned my rage against the heavy bag and focus mitts. Hard work earned me a black belt and peace of mind."

Stunning. Absolutely stunning.

And her story's amazing, too.

"So, h-how did you end up at a place so far off the beaten path?"

"Fresh start somewhere new and all that. Rapid's a nice town. And there was an opening." Her chair creaks as she rocks, impatience writ large across her face.

"Congratulations. You've really done well for yourself."

She laughs, full and hard and joyfully menacing. I should step out the door and run like hell. But, despite the well-deserved kick to the nuts it is to stand here, I am here, with her, with beautiful, powerful, terrifying Holly and the Larry that loved her six years ago has a knife to the throat of Larry today.

The tide of her laughter slowly subsides. "Oh, part of me really wants to tell you to go fuck yourself."

Can my heart be in the floor and my balls be in my throat at the same time? "Go ahead. I deserve it."

"You do. But what's the point? Sure, seeing you stirs a little mud into my java."

"Uh..."

She raises a cautionary hand. "I don't want the mud. I don't want apologies or explanations. What was us, is no more. It's behind me."

I don't want to believe it, but I'm surrounded by evidence that supports her case. Hell, right now I'd buy her telling me she became a Hare Krishna last year and ran for president.

"When do you leave town?" she asks in a tone bordering on ordinary, friendly conversation.

"End of the week. I still have some business to wrap up." Stick with last night's story.

"And what kind of business is that?"

"Hm?"

"What is your business? What is it that brings you out to Rapid City, South Dakota for a chance visit with one of my more irksome undergraduates?"

"Irksome? Why irksome?" Not my Julia. Though...

"Your little friend filed a complaint with the dean over her mid-term grade. Claims I'm biased against her. That means paperwork and meetings. She also barked at me in front of the entire class, staged a sit-in on the quad, and went on campus radio calling me names I haven't heard used since Nixon."

"All that, over one grade?"

Holly nods, lips pursed. "A mid-term. In a one hundred level class. Your Miss Reardon is a major pain in the ass. Anyway, your business?"

Julia can be troublesome. But I never thought she'd—wait what? "Uh, consulting. I'm a consultant."

Holly raises a questioning eyebrow. "For...?"

"Security."

"For...?" She's not letting me go.

"A government contract. I really can't go into details. Jennifer's father works for the parent company, yada-yada-yada." Please, don't ask me for details. I'm still chewing how best to handle my Exceptional student radical.

"Ah. I see."

"Yeah, I told him I'd check in on her, you know." Dr. Bill mentioned a class in ten minutes. Shouldn't a bell be saving my ass right about now? "Look, this isn't going how I hoped."

"Really? I'm enjoying it."

Nice.

The blessed, aforementioned bell clangs away in the hall. Thank Christ.

"Say your piece, Larry. I have somewhere to be." She gets up, looping the strap of a gym bag over her shoulder.

"I was thinking maybe we could meet for dinner or something. Catch up."

"Wow. Ballsy."

"I'll buy. It's the least I can do."

"It is." She considers a moment. I feel like a bull on the auction block. "Tell you what. You want to catch up? Come by Mountain High Kenpo Club tonight. Adult class starts at seven."

"Um, sure. I'd love to watch you train."

She stands right in front of me, the citrus sweetness of her weakening my knees. "You're not going to watch."

Now I'm even more befuddled.

"C'mon, Larry. You can't stay here." She shoos me out of the office, locking the door behind her.

I follow her into the hallway, not knowing what else to do. As we leave the building, the afternoon sun blinds me back to my senses. Did I just agree to meet Holly at her karate gym? A place where likely every black belt has heard her tale of a tall, ex-Army asshole that left her at the altar?

"Oh, and Larry," she says with a wicked smile. "I'd wear a cup if I were you."

Chapter Sixteen

PAIN is a funny thing. It has so many different forms. There's the sharp, wincing sting of a scrape, cut, or needle prick. There's the hard, throbbing ache of a rough bump or a knock on the head. But there is no pain quite like a shot to the crotch. Attempts to describe it fall short of the true, vomit-inducing, leg-jellying, near blackout agony that comes from a crushing slam to the sisters. Why, just a graze in the general vicinity births trembling trepidation of what misery is about to well up from deep beneath my bowels. Lucky for me, Dr. Bill Severs' lightning front snap kick had been somewhat checked by the well-advised cup I purchased at Shopko.

"Watch the low kicks." Holly calls to the all-smiles little professor.

When Dr. Bill had mentioned he'd see Holly later tonight, I assumed he meant a department cocktail party with trays of those little sausages, not a karate dojo lined with a series of canvas heavy bags speckled by brown dots of dried human blood.

My mistake.

Bill twitches his sparring-helmeted head in acknowledgement of Holly's warning and lunges right back at me.

I have just enough time to swallow the groin nausea before he swarms me with a blur of hands. I bob and weave and shift my stance to avoid the blows.

He circles, stalking me like the world's friendliest barracuda.

Sweat drips into my eyes. The cup drags at my leg hair. My nipples burn from rubbing against the heavy sweatshirt. For an unfortunate moment I wonder what Julia is doing right now.

Dr. Bill seizes my hesitation and sets up a foot sweep that I barely avoid. The happy-faced prof is good. I've touched gloves with seven of Holly's students over the last hour and all of them have been good. A couple were outstanding and one, a lanky nineteen-year-old named Chad, was downright amazing. I got in a single solid shot compared to the dozen or so he landed on me.

I block Dr. Bill's snappy roundhouse kick and creakily counter. My assortment of body aches after an hour's fighting make each move drag. Holly may be over our past. It is painfully clear her students are not. And they're loving getting in some licks on the guy who broke their sensei's heart six years ago. Dr. Bill ducks my punch combo and pops in a straight right hand, adding to my ribs' list of complaints.

Holly shouts a halt. My rubbery arms flop to my sides. The professor and I bow first to each other and then to her. The entire class lines up for dismissal, two rows arrayed in smart white *gi* save for me in a navy and silver sweat suit bought on clearance, along with the cup.

"Good workout tonight," Holly says in a powerful voice any football coach would envy. She's make-up free and glowing, hair streaked with sweat. She'd only sparred twice, but she'd coached the entire night. "A reminder that the Black Hills Invitational is this weekend. If you're competing, we'll meet outside BHU's main gym at eight. If competing's not your thing, you're welcome to come watch our own Chad Ellis go for his third year as all-around champ."

Claps and tired but well-meant praise ripple through the students. Young Chad flicks a blushing smile in return.

Holly bows us out and I shuffle to a folding chair set against the wall. Adult class ran two hours, the last half of which was solid sparring. I, as a guest black-belt, had been awarded the *honor* of fighting Holly's senior students. I don't feel particularly honored. It hurts to sit down. In fact, right now I miss the softer days of hacking through Southeast Asian jungle under machine gun fire.

"You've gotten slow," Holly says, walking over after saying goodnight to Dr. Bill.

"Well, it's been a few hundred cheeseburgers since I last put on sparring gloves." Impossible to keep a regular training routine when I only stay put for days at a time.

"That Chad's going for the hat trick, huh?" I tug off damp helmet, gloves, and footgear. My lips still taste of sweat-spattered vinyl dojo mat, which two-time all-around champ Chad and compadres introduced me to over and over again.

Holly unties her frayed black belt and carefully folds it, setting it on her lap as she sits beside me. "After he won his first tournament without a point scored against him, I sent the story to *Karate Illustrated*. They ran it. When he swept the brackets a second time, they wanted an interview. Plus, we got calls from TV and radio as far away as Denver. Chad's become somewhat of a local celebrity. He goes untouched a third and it's *Black Belt's* Competitor of the Year."

"You sound proud."

"I am," Holly says, eyes distant with memory. "The kid means a lot to me, and not just as a student. He's practically family. He came here poor and skinny. Bullied, not a lot of friends. You know the type."

I smile. "And you changed that."

She dismisses me with genuine modesty. "I helped him find himself. Realize his potential, that's all."

Holly was always modest. One of the things I love about her. "Well, he's damn quick, that's for sure."

"You've no idea. He went easy. When he lets loose, it's like fighting a hurricane."

"Then I'm happy the champ was gentle."

Holly hands me a can of Lysol so I can spray down the borrowed gear from tonight's punishment session. Bending over to shove everything into the community box sends a spastic twinge up my side.

"Are you okay?" She asks with an amused grin. "You got dumped pretty hard."

Okay? Holly's beside me after all these years. So much still unsaid. Julia wants her space. No clue how this is going to work. And damn, even my ass hurts right now.

"I'm fine. And yes, I did get dumped hard. Also punched hard and kicked hard. Your swell bunch don't hold much back." My sweat-soaked shirt clings to me and the smell is noticeable in the way only one's own B.O. can be. "I'm glad *you* didn't step on the mat. I'd probably be wheeled out of here on a gurney."

"No. No gurney. My guys know how to hide a body." She gives me a wink and a sharp elbow.

"Ow," I groan.

We sit in amused quiet for a moment, but that amusement quickly evaporates. I'm at a loss for what to say next. Holly slaps the folded belt gently in her open palm. "So, why did you come here, Larry?"

Because I want to see you, to be around you, to maybe find the balls to tell you I've never stopped loving you.

Because I'm stupid.

My job has rules. Even if it didn't, leaving Holly destroyed me. Whether or not it destroyed her, she's moved on and made something of herself. Telling her how I feel may mess up all she's built since I abandoned her to protect Exceptionals.

"Just a masochist, I guess. Thought I'd give you the chance to knock me around."

"The idea had occurred to me." She smooths the folded belt and takes a controlled breath. "I don't need to knock you around, Larry. I don't *need* anything from you. What happened between us was six years ago. Six years. You get it? I've done the grief and the anger and all the why, why, why crap. That's behind me. And I need it to stay that way, got it?"

Levity may not have been my best choice.

"And now here you are, in my dojo, taking hits you didn't need to, trying to connect with me on some weird, sweat-and-suffering level when we both know you're leaving this weekend."

I didn't need *all* the hits. Sure, I could have avoided a lot more than I did. But I was off my game. There definitely was no dodging her verbal shotgun blast. Had I really been thinking when I came here? No, I'd just let my aching heart lead the way and hoped it would all work out. Pop would not approve.

I clear my throat. "I...just wanted to say, I'm sorry. Again. For whatever you went through after I left. I am so very, very—"

"Stop." She puts up a crossing guard hand. "Save it. I told you I don't want your sorry."

God, but I need to say it.

"You want forgiveness from me for what you've done? Fine, you're forgiven. You obviously had something going on back then that forced you to step away. Doesn't explain why all I got was a goddamn note, but that's neither here nor there." She takes a deep, settling breath. "The point is I would not be where I am if you hadn't left. And I like where I am. So there. Forgiven. Now, stop moping around stinking up my school. Go back to your hotel and take a shower." She gets up and strides to the women's locker room, the door swinging shut behind her with a heavy *clack*.

Dumbfounded is an accurate, but wholly inadequate word. I sit staring at the wood panels of the opposite wall for what feels like a full nine innings. Whatever just happened, happened too fast for my mind to chew on and spit out a response. There was supposed to be shouting and wailing and gnashing of teeth. Holly's words don't make sense and I'm far too tired, too sore, and too sober to process them. I blink and get off my ass. I collect my stuff from the locker room—just wallet and room key—and wait for Holly.

She comes out, changed into jeans, white t-shirt and club jacket, running a comb through her damp hair. "You're still here?"

I give her a sheepish smile. "Sorry. I don't have a car. Can I use your phone to call a cab?"

"Stop being sorry. The phone's on the desk in the back. After your call, wait out front. I need to lock up."

"Okay, but can we do this again?"

She stops mid-combstroke. "What?"

"I mean training. Can I come back and train while I'm in town? You run a great school and you have to agree I need the refresher." I give her my most earnest look. It helps that I'm actually earnest.

Holly considers, eyeing me the way she might a ragged hitchhiker along I-90. "Sure. It's twenty dollars for a week's lessons and you must sign the insurance waiver, got it?"

"Okay." Again, am I thinking or letting my fool heart lead? Does this help keep Julia safe? If I work at it, I'm sure I can convince myself.

Holly nods and stuffs the comb into her tote bag. "Okay. But I expect your best in here. You had three black belts when I knew you. No more playing the lame horse on the mat, got it?"

"Yes, sensei." I bow.

"Shut up and go make your call."

94

Chapter Seventeen

COULD be the five hours sleep talking or maybe the knowledge that Holly doesn't want to roast me on a spit. Whatever the cause, I feel good today. Even with the bruises and aches and stiff joints, even with an iron gray sky and soggy drizzle, my spirits are...peppy. In fact, I forego a taxi ride, throw on my overcoat and walk the three miles from hotel to BHU.

A breeze joins me as I stroll along damp sidewalks under pruned shade trees, cross thoroughfares at designated crosswalks, and pass storefronts still closed in the early morning hours. After two blocks my thighs, tight from last night's punishment, loosen up and I achieve a somewhat normal gait. I search for breakfast on the go but, to my disappointment, the only food option between downtown and campus is a garish MiniMart with questionable frozen burritos and a scalding hot, bitter brown liquid mislabeled as coffee.

The breeze blows off the drizzle and a weak sun peeks through gaps in the cloud cover as I turn into the quad, ready to walk the ground some more, check-in with Julia, and maybe pop by Holly's office.

A sheet of paper stapled to a telephone pole flaps in broken rhythm. The paper is a homemade flier for a missing dog. The photo shows a sad, lovable pup with eyes so full of longing that my breath catches in my chest and my flippant mind slams hard into focus.

Two more Exceptionals dead as of yesterday. Two. Here I am chowing on a burrito while The Opposition is sneaking around snatching and killing. I'm taking a stroll while there are human lab rats as forlorn and hopeless as this pup hidden away in who-knows-where, wondering who will come save them.

I'm worried about the *possibility* of a future with Holly? How dare I. How dare me? I'm not sure of the grammar, all I know is that my appetite is gone, and I need to get serious about ensuring that there is never a flier on a pole about a missing girl named Jennifer Reardon. That reminds me, she and I need to talk about the campus activist thing. Too much attention.

As I tramp across the grounds, I pore over my options. Shadowing Julia is out for sheer practical reasons. First of all, she'd hate having a tagalong and let me know of it, constantly. Second, it would draw more attention to her, the opposite of what I want. And third, if I ever caught this Trevor or some other "dude" putting the moves on her, I'd likely strangle him with his own damn Walkman.

Normal procedure with Exceptionals is establish false identity then regular follow-ups, like life-or-death welfare checks. However, the breach in D.C. means improvisation is required. I need a way to keep eyes on Julia, and on the rest of my caseload.

My one advantage is I know The Opposition, how they work. Eighteen months in the FBI on a task force made up of the assholes made me a quick study. Too bad I learned who they really were after the fact. The Opposition sticks to a limited playbook not due to lack of resources, but because those plays have worked for them time and again. Working within federal law enforcement gives them almost unrestricted access to anywhere they want to be. Plus, the ease of making an arrest covers for snatching up an Exceptional.

Like they tried with Julia.

Twice.

As I cross onto campus, I pass a three-wheel Cushman Truckster painted school colors with a collection of bound trash bags on the deck. I dump my burrito amongst the garbage and carry on, running down options in my mind.

"Aw jeez, whatcha doing there?" a mild-mannered voice calls from behind a waist-high row of boxwoods.

I stop, the gears of my thoughts grinding to a halt as well. When I turn toward the sound, no-one is there.

"Oh ja? You think it's okay to discard your loose refuse like that do ya?" the disembodied voice accuses.

I make no move to recover the burrito. "Um, sorry. I thought all that was trash."

From behind the shrubbery pops a broad blond bull that could have just crossed the North Atlantic on a Viking raid. He shakes a pair of hedge clippers at me, obviously ready to retort, then hesitates and chews at his bottom lip before speaking.

"Well, it may be, but it's all bagged there. See? Now, I gotta fish around and put your rubbish in one a them bags. No way I'm coming out clean, don'cha know." He gestures to his uniform, green coveralls pressed to a military crispness. Even the collar is starched flat. A white oval badge over the left side of his massive chest reads *Sven* in glossy black thread.

You gotta be kidding me.

"My apologies. Sven is it?"

"Ja."

"I'll get it and throw it away properly." I move to the Cushman and, luckily for me, my breakfast remnant rests right high atop one of the twist-tied bags. Sven comes up beside me. We're of a height, but those shoulders must get stuck in doorways.

"Thank you for doing the right thing there," he says, opening a bag so I can properly dispose of my semi-breakfast.

I know his lilt. "Where are you from, Sven?" I ask, just to be friendly.

"Oh, Brainerd. Ja, Mom and Dad they both came from St. Cloud, but we moved to Brainerd when I was ten. Good walleye fishing in Brainerd. Little Marta was seven then, I think. You like walleye?" The way he reties the trash bag, he could likely slap a bobber on a line and bait a hook faster than I could tie my shoe.

"I do. As a kid, Grandpa would take us to Friday night fish fries. Good stuff. Well, I gotta—"

"Really? You from Minnesota?" he says, stretching out the *o* in the way only Minnesotans can. A little boy getting a new bike couldn't crack a broader smile than Sven.

"No."

"Oh." Deep lines slowly form between his eyebrows. His jaw sets hard and suddenly giant teddy-bear Sven looks like he could snap me in half. "You're not a Packers fan are ya?"

"Um, I don't really follow football much. Say, I need to get going. Sorry again about the burrito." I extend a hand.

He shakes it warmly without crushing it to pulp. "Jeez, it's no trouble. You take care, now."

I walk off, heading toward Bennett Hall to catch Julia before her first class. But something strikes me as odd and my scar starts itching, not in the usual, watch-out way, but in a ticklish, pay attention sort of way. I look back only to see Sven has disappeared again. The soft sound of snipping shears is barely audible amidst the chatter and hum of a weekday college campus.

I look around and see the campus afresh. There is a lot of space and a lot of people. Everyone walks past the custodian and cart without so much as a second glance. It's as if he's there, but not there.

An idea starts growing. A crazy idea.

"Hey, Sven," I call. He pops up from behind the shrubs, shears in hand.

"Ja?"

"Quick question, is it just you out here today?"

"No. Da whole crew is on. Jake likes having all the guys on during the week. Says empty trashcans make the bosses happy so, you know. Why?" He tugs off a glove and flicks an errant leaf trimming from his chest.

"I'd like to meet them."

"Huh? Really? Why?"

"To thank them for a job well done. This campus is beautiful."

Sven tugs at his neat beard. "You know, I don't think anyone's ever done that."

"You're kidding?" I walk back to the big greensman in green. "Well, it's about time somebody did. Do you guys ever sit down together? Gather in one place so I can thank you all at once?"

Sven is still unsure. He contemplates me to distraction, so much so he ignores a big streak of brown dirt smeared across his hip by his work gloves. "Well, we do meet up for lunch and a round of cards..."

"Poker?"

Sven's eyes lose their distant wondering and zoom into alert, almost feverish focus. "Yeah. Every day from eleven to noon. Why, you play?"

I give my best sheepish grin. "On occasion."

Sven extends a hand and cracks a broad grin. "What's your name, mister?"

I grip his hand, "Larry. Larry Lawson."

Chapter Eighteen

JULIA is in no mood to talk when I catch her hustling out the Bennett Hall door, canvas bag slung across one shoulder.

"Hey, Jennifer," I call, trotting to catch up. "No purple pants today?"

"I'm late for American Lit," she snaps, not slowing down.

"I need to talk to you." I struggle to match her pace despite having legs a good foot longer than hers.

"Well, you've got until I reach the humanities building." She points an unlit cigarette at a red brick three-story across the way. Lighting the smoke doesn't even break her stride. She just flicks her Bic and keeps on trucking.

My legs haven't loosened up after all as my right calf suddenly cramps. "Ow, ow," I say with a wince and a hop.

"What is it?" Julia turns, blowing a jet of smoke from the corner of her mouth.

"N-nothing. Hey, just stop for a minute." I bend over to rub out the sore muscle.

She halts, taking a quick drag and readjusting her bag. "What did you do?"

I straighten up with a grunt. "Something I'll probably regret in the near future."

"Did you take my advice?" she asks with a raised eyebrow.

"Huh? What do you mean?"

She tilts her head with a devilish look. "You know what I mean. You strain yourself bouncing Marlene against the headboard last night?"

"What? No! That's not—You shouldn't be talking about—"

Julia stifles a chuckle.

"Look," I say, collecting myself and raising a defiant hand. "Nothing happened with me and that waitress. And nothing *will* happen."

Julia looks me over again. Her delightfully amused expression shifts closer to disgust. "Don't tell me you and the Professor... Did you and Chisholm actually—?"

I wave my hands as if waving away her train of thought. "Dammit, no! That's not wha—Holly and I, we— I'm not here to talk about that."

Her jaw drops open as if I'd just told her the moon landing was fake. "You? And that-that termagant? Aak!" She spins and stomps away, fists clenched, grumbling.

"Jennifer." I tug her to a stop. "I need to—wait...*termagant*?"

"It means bitch, Larry. You and that bitch."

"Hey, she's just— Don't call her—Termagant? Really?"

"So *did* you?" she snaps, her eyes tiny, fuming slits.

"No." I say deliberately. "I did not." Not since 1979. Not that thoughts of it don't spring to mind on random, inconvenient occasions, like now. Thanks for that, kid. "I strained something during my workout."

Julia gives me another once over with her eyes. I can't tell if my answer satisfies her. She simply blows out another stream of smoke and asks, "So what do you want?"

And the day started out so well.

I pick my thoughts back up off the floor, then check that we're out of earshot of the other hustling students—something I should have done thirty seconds ago—before starting this conversation over. "Okay. I want to talk to you about this campus protest stuff you've been doing."

Julia tosses her cigarette to the ground and grinds it out under a booted heel. "It was a one-time thing, Larry. Not too smart, all right? Won't happen again. Anything else?"

Her blunt, affirmative response catches me off guard. How is it this girl I've known for over six years can still bump me off my game?

"Well," I mumble, stuffing a hand in my pocket, "a copy of your work schedule would help. It's easier for me to keep you safe if I know where and when to expect you."

"You my shadow, now? Thought your agency or whatever didn't work that way." She swings her bag from her shoulder, pulls out a scrap of paper, and begins making hasty notes.

Her bag lays open on the ground, a few small cards inside catch my eye. I reach for them.

"Hey! Those are mine." Julia makes a grab for my arm.

Too late.

"A Sears credit card, an Amoco card, and a driver's license. Sandra Guttridge? Did you steal these?"

She grabs again. "No. Now give them back."

I pull free and examine the ID. It's good. Damn good. Only expert eyes would notice the little line by the photo or the slight change in type font for her name.

"Little wishful, don't you think, saying you're twenty-six?" I give her back the cards.

"Shut up." She tosses them back in her bag.

"So?" I wait. False identification has been part of her life since we met. It doesn't surprise me that she has some. The fact that she's gone out and got some on her own? That does.

"So what? Just being prepared. Like you taught me."

I did teach her. "Whoever you had do it knows their stuff."

"That whoever is me."

No words. I have no words.

Julia scribbles on the paper then folds it in quarters and thrusts it at me. "I gotta go. That's today's schedule. Catch me at work tonight and I'll have something more detailed."

I take the note, but she doesn't let go. Her look is intense, a blend of frustration and understanding that she seems adamant I grasp her full meaning.

"This is my life," she continues, vein in her forehead throbbing. "*Mine*. I know the drill—head down, don't make waves, all that. I get it. But, please, leave me some room to actually live, okay?"

Right now she's asking me, but she's one push away from switching request to direct order.

God I love her spunk.

"And I still don't like her, Larry."

I let out a resigned sigh. "You have your life, kid. I have mine. A few more days then I promise, your life gets back to normal."

She searches my face and lets go of the paper. "Whatever that means." She throws the bag back over her shoulder.

"Hey," I say, "I'm doing my best here."

She gives a tight smile and scuffs the pavement with the toe of her boot. "I know." She jogs away without looking back.

I unfold the paper while watching her leave. Once she's passed inside the building I glance at her note and give an explosive laugh. I do love her spunk. In the margins she's written today's shift at work. The rest of the paper is dominated by a rough but obvious sketch of a penis and a vacuum cleaner.

Chapter Nineteen

JULIA'S class load takes her to only three buildings on campus. I walk those in a couple hours, checking exits, basements, and any hidden nooks where someone could abscond with her in secret. The whole process serves to ease my sense of duty and reinforce Jack Underwood's definition of our protection efforts as third-rate.

At best.

I need more eyes in more places. That's why I'm strolling through the bowels of the student union, heading for a date with the staff of BHU Campus Custodial Services.

The cinder block corridor is dim and gray, decorated with hissing pipes and ductwork. The air is dank, tinged with ammonia, Old Spice, and pot smoke. A door sits open at the end with men's voices coming from just beyond.

I step inside without announcing myself.

Metal lockers painted with a crude likeness of Jimmy Hendrix line one wall. A smiley-face magnet holds this month's centerfold to a battered, pastel green fridge that could serve as a fallout shelter in a pinch. A wheeled chalkboard stands in a corner, its hand-drawn chart assigning today's duties to the pertinent staff. Atop a dented steel countertop, a brown percolator gurgles away.

Five men in matching green coveralls play cards at a stained Formica table. Beer cans, half-eaten brown bag lunches, and loaded ash trays are arrayed before them like spoils of war. Sven of the breakfast burrito has his back to me.

"Ja, so I call already." Sven gestures at a small pile of singles and grocery coupons dumped in the center of the table.

Across from the Minnesotan, a twitchy man with feathered blonde hair, mirrored sunglasses, and a bushy caterpillar mustache leans forward in his chair. His name badge reads *Russell*.

"Now just hold on, I'm not done with my story," he says with teletype speed.

"Your story is bullshit, *Cabron*," interrupts a heavyset Mexican with enough Butch Wax in his hair to lube Pop's old Chevy. Miguel, if I'm to trust the chalkboard list.

"Swear to Christ, it's true," rattles Russell. "Saw them plain as day."

"No way. The Coach, he is married and Miss Candace, she's a very nice lady," says Miguel.

Russell leers over his mirrored glasses. "She looked pretty damn nice bent over that desk."

"Aw jeez, I said I call." Sven's chair creaks as he shifts his bulk.

The other two are a shaggy, gray-haired beanpole sporting a tie-dyed head band and a bronze-skinned, dark-eyed fellow with braided black hair nursing a Styrofoam cup of coffee. I assume it's coffee. According to the board one is Jake, the other Earl.

I listen to them dicker a few seconds more then clear my throat.

"Aw shit." Shaggy rocks forward in his chair and stubs his joint out on the table.

"Damn it, Earl," yells Russell, "not on the table."

Earl coughs out a lungful of greasy smoke and points at me, "It's a fucking narc, man."

Okay, that settles who's who.

The room quiets. All eyes are on me, save braided-haired Jake who sits unfazed, calmly drinking his coffee.

Sven grins and stands. "Say, glad you could make it there. Oh hey guys, this here is the fellow I was telling you about."

"You didn't say he was a narc." Earl hurriedly wipes ash from the tabletop.

"He's not a narc," says Sven.

"He kind of looks like a narc," says Miguel with a soft burp.

"Are you a narc?" Russell snaps, brushing that oversized mustache.

"I'm not a narc."

"See, he's not a narc." Sven makes an appeasing gesture with both hands.

"A narc ain't going to tell you he's a narc, man," Earl whines.

"Shut up." Jake's words suck the air from the room. The immediate power of his quiet voice reminds me of a drill sergeant I once knew. Sergeant Ross could step onto a live fire range with mortars erupting and M-60's banging away and silence the chaos with one word.

"You come to play cards?" says Jake.

"I came to say you guys have done a great job making BHU beautiful. But I'd love to play cards, if that's okay?"

Jake shrugs then gets up to fetch more coffee, tossing his used cup in the dented trashcan and tugging a new one from a stack beside the pot.

Sven adds a chair to the table. "You drink beer then?"

It's just past noon. "Coffee is fine."

All heads quickly shake. Russell mouths "no." Sven's eyes widen. Miguel draws a finger across his throat. They quickly assume positions of casual indifference as Jake returns to his seat.

I reconsider my decision. "Um, tell you what...a beer does sound great." I sit.

Sven grins and gets me a cold Hamm's from the fridge. "We gotta finish this game first," he says.

Everyone picks up their cards.

"So what do you do, *señor*?" Miguel asks.

"Call me Larry," I say, cracking open the beer.

"Larry," Miguel repeats. "What do you do?"

"Government contractor."

"A fed?" Earl bolts up. "I ain't going back, man. No way!"

"Shut up, Earl!" everyone shouts in unison.

Earl meekly returns to his seat. "Not going back. Just saying..."

"Save the acid for the weekends, can't ya?" says Russell with a twitch and a push on those sunglasses. "Freakin' hippie."

Earl's gaze flicks from the table to me and back. He mutters something then picks up his cards.

"Pause in the action. Gotta hit the head." Russell makes a fast break for the one-stall bathroom in the back slamming the door behind him.

Jake says flatly, "Don't forget to flush."

Sven and Miguel share knowing smiles.

Flush.

I turn to Miguel. "I consult on internal security issues for the U.S. government."

Russell returns from the john. "So you at the air base, then?"

Ellsworth Air Force Base sits east of Rapid City. It's a SAC base—bombers and missiles. The only other thing I know about it is those stationed there don't complain much because, hey, they could've been stuck up in Minot. Nobody wants Minot.

"No. I'm here on family business."

"You missed some, Russell," Jake says.

There's a dusting of white on the man's furry upper lip

"Goddamnit, you know I hate being called that," Russell snaps.

"Sit down, Russell." Jake punches the name.

Russell sits, wipes his nose with a paper napkin, and readjusts those mirrored aviators. "The name's Pornstache."

Of course it is.

"Are we still playing cards?" asks Miguel. "Sven called."

"Yep." Pornstache sniffs and then lays down his hand. "Two pair, Jacks over sixes."

"Screw you, man." Earl plops his cards down and chomps into what looks like bologna on white.

The others show their cards in turn. Miguel comes out on top. He gleefully sweeps in the kitty, neatly stacking bills and coupons while Jake takes up the cards and starts shuffling with a steady, even rhythm.

Brrrp. Shfff. Tap-tap. Repeat.

I'm in. The ante is a dollar, except Earl uses a coupon for fifty cents off Huggies diapers. Again, no one says anything, so I don't.

Jake shuffles, fans and flips the deck with street magician dexterity, tossing cards to precisely the same spot before each player.

"You ever work Vegas?" I ask, taking up my hand.

"Jake?" sniggers Pornstache, rubbing his nose before rotating his cards as if they were upside down. "Nah. He ran a table in Monte Carlo."

I can't tell if he is shining me on. Jake stays mute and none of the other guys touch it.

We play cards. Poker is a great way to assess the room. I'm not focused on their tells or habits. I'm keying in on their conversation. Twenty minutes in and I know goings-on ranging from drug deals at the north end parking plaza all the way down to who's been caught mid-coitus in the storage shed.

Brilliant.

Chapter Twenty

EVERYONE talks, except Jake. He plays cards and drinks coffee, and gets more coffee, using a fresh Styrofoam cup for each refill. He isn't ignoring what's being said, that's obvious. He listens like me. His face stays cold and stoic, but I catch calculating looks from time to time. Gears are spinning and I'll lay even money on Jake as the one man who knows everything that happens around BHU.

Earl wraps up a paranoid tale of being surveilled by undercover law enforcement while he mopped the cafeteria.

"You worry a lot about the police, Earl. They on campus often?" I ask, dealing out our last hand. Time to check on Julia. Plus watching these guys consume their junk food lunches reminds my stomach that four hours have passed since the wretched burrito.

"The local fuzz only come around if someone calls 911. Campus Nazis handle most stuff." Earl adjusts his head band.

Pornstache sorts his cards. "They dress like fucking SS. You can't miss them."

I had seen a few young guys in black with red arm bands and radios. Guess BHU hires students to police their students.

"*Si*, they are all over campus, but they cannot make arrests. They have to call the real police when there is trouble," Miguel says, eyes on his cards.

"Yeah, like when Sven broke up that fight," Russell says with excitement. "Just tossed the pricks to the ground and sat on 'em until the cops showed."

Sven shrugs apologetically and slides a pair of cards at me. "Two, please."

Pornstache continues in rapid fire, "Eight fucking security kids stood around doing nothing while Sven squatted there like a bear taking a dump."

I fold my last hand on a three-of-a-kind.

"You didn't do so well, my friend," says Miguel, "You should come back tomorrow."

"Thanks for the invitation. I will."

These guys are a gold mine, working in plain sight, ignored by everyone, and yet they cover the entire university in the course of twenty-four hours.

I shake hands all around then step back out into ducts and pipes. I'm a dozen strides down the hall when I hear the heavy door *whuff* shut behind me.

Jake calls out, "What do you want?"

I turn around, keeping my face unexpressive. "What do you mean?"

He walks up, eyeing me with the compassion of a moray eel. "Three hands you could have won but gave away. You caught onto Russell's tell the first deal."

Maybe Jake did work Monte Carlo. "He flips his cards when he has more than a pair."

"Makes no attempt to hide it," he snaps.

"Miguel goes for his food when he's confident—"

"And drinks when his hand is shit, I know. You didn't come to play poker." He keeps his arms crossed on his chest. "Well?"

These guys are ideal. I need them. What's going to win over Jake?

I stuff my hands in my pockets, look at the ground, and put on my best desperate face. "I just really wanted to say thanks to you g—"

"Nope. Try again."

A bang and pop as pressure shifts in an overhead pipe. I clap my mouth shut. His dark eyes dig at me. "Okay, I have a bit of a gambling prob—"

"That's not it." His next words come out slow and intense. "Last chance. What do you want from us?"

The man can sure read a lie. Can I risk showing my hand? My scar doesn't itch. That means something. I clasp my fingers before me like a guilt-riddled penitent and mumble, "Help keep an eye on my daughter."

Water slowly drips somewhere behind me, echoing.

He takes a deep breath and lets it out slow then rubs his leathery jaw. "Tell me about her."

"Freshman, but older, twenty. Kind of a punk look, spiked hair, likes to wear an old field jacket. Lives in—"

"Bennett Hall."

Damn.

"Has a narcoleptic roommate who moonlights as a beautician. Boyfriend leads rallies against corporate farming." Jake's eyes slowly move from left to right, as if reading an entry in his own mental journal.

Double damn. "That's right."

He blinks from his trance. "She smokes, but it's all show."

"Yeah. How do you—? Look, I need your help because she has...history," I say, a lump rising in my throat as I ride the knife-edge of truth. "Something we are trying to leave behind, but certain folks won't let her. She likes it here and doesn't want to move again. I've done all I can to give her a normal life. But now...I can't do it by myself. Not anymore."

I stand locked in surprise at my own words. I hadn't known until I spoke them just how real they are. My mouth's gone dry.

Jake steps up to me, his face a foot away, those dark eyes probing. He tips his head slightly, then makes his decision.

"Show me your hands," he says.

I do as he asks.

He rubs a cracked thumb over my palm. "Not soft. You know hard work."

I shrug, still confused at the turn in conversation.

"Fine," he says. "We can use an extra man on grounds and Earl still can't run a buffer without leaving footprints up and down the halls."

"Wait. What?"

"You don't get something for nothing. You want my guys to keep an eye on your girl, you throw on a pair of coveralls and lend a hand."

"But my job? I have commitments."

He lifts an eyebrow as if to say, "Do you really?"

"Right," I mumble. My original plan to gain help was a bit different. Still... "I'd have to be done by five each night."

"Okay."

"I'm only in town this week. That's the truth."

"I know," he says. "Don't worry, we'll get our money's worth out of you by Saturday."

I exhale hard and reach to shake his hand. "Thank you."

"Save it." He says, not taking my hand. "Tomorrow. Five A.M."

With that he turns back to his office.

I head for Julia's dorm chewing on my exchange with Jake, daze and doubt dissolving with each stride.

A grin breaks out all on its own.

I just gained access to the perfect network of campus spies.

Chapter Twenty-One

JULIA slips into her dorm before I can catch her. I wait on a bench outside, pretending to read a newspaper I found discarded at the student union. No hurry. I can snag her when she leaves for work. When quarter to six rolls around and she hasn't come out, I jog over to the parking lot and see her sputtering Reliant motor out onto East Saint Joe.

Well, I'll be damned. She gave me the slip.

Her with her spunk and her brains.

Is that pride niggling at me? Still, ditching your watchdog isn't smart when you're on The Opposition's most wanted list.

The record store she works at has an odd name.

"Who or what is an Ernie September?" I mutter aloud outside a corner phone booth. It's occupied by a girl making no efforts to hide her teary-eyed call home. After ten minutes of toe-tapping and false smiles of "take your time," I get in and ring a cab, the same cab company that picked me up at the airport. Not brand loyalty, mind you. They're first in the listings.

A familiar Crown Vic wagon pulls up, I jump into the back seat and catch a wave from Mr. Aviators himself.

"Hey stranger." He grins. "What's with the hair?"

So much for the changed look hiding my identity.

"Lost a bet," I say.

He shrugs, sniggering to himself.

I tell him my destination and that I'm in a hurry.

"Got it."

He cuts two blocks over and motors west on Main. We ride in silence for all of thirty seconds before he pipes up. "Just an observation: you don't look like an Ernie September's kind of guy. I peg you for more Golden Oldies or the Barry Manilow rack at Sam Goody's. Ernie's carries some pretty weird shit, pardon my French." He slows for a couple crossing the street.

"I have a niece. Seventeen. Dyes her hair. Black fingernails."

Aviators shrugs. "Sounds like their clientele. That why you're at the U, visiting your niece?"

It's an innocent question, one any cabbie might ask of any fare. The way he asks it is a little off, like it's something he's been waiting to ask. Perhaps mister customer service here is more than he seems. Perhaps I'm reading too much into it.

My scar tingles.

"No, I'm conducting research for a book."

A grumbling Harley-Davidson cuts in front of him then brakes hard for a red light. Aviators stays cool and smoothly slows this land yacht to a halt. Nice reflexes. Cop reflexes.

Or he's just a good cabbie.

He accelerates. "Really? What kind of book are you writing?"

"A history of mechanical engineering studies. Their growth and diversity in western technical schools and universities." That ought to motivate a switch in topics.

"Oh. Sounds neat. You see Rushmore, yet?"

Success.

"Not yet. On my list, though."

EXCEPTIONALS

He nods and goes quiet. I feign looking out the windows, using the reflection to observe Aviators. I could be paranoid. Still, my scar hasn't been wrong before. Though this isn't an itch, it's more of a pay attention twinge.

We roll through the town's modest downtown, passing three- and four-story store fronts, the towering Alex Johnson's, and not a few bars with neon signs gleaming.

"The Brass Rail," I mutter.

"That place is a local institution. No dive serves better bad beer."

A Volvo sedan not much bigger than a golf cart comes up on our right. It's marked Rapid City Police Department. The officer behind the wheel in his khaki uniform short-sleeves nods our way, then turns on West Boulevard.

"Christ. Did I just see what I think I saw?"

Aviators answers with a laugh. "Yeah, cops have driven those little boxes since '80. Must have gotten a sweet fleet deal 'cause they're goofy as all get out."

I smile, picturing a cop big as Rockentanski or a perp the size of Sven squeezing into one of those clown cars. Goddamn clowns.

"Here you go." We turn into a small gravel lot beside an equally small red building. A black billboard with orange letters rises high over the front door, *Ernie September: Music and Paraphernalia*.

"This here is The Gap," my tour guide gestures to the landscape. "It's kind of the invisible boundary between east and west Rapid."

119

Julia's record store sits in a narrow gateway between two big hills. The town continues west to roll up into the higher pine forest terrain beyond.

"You need me to wait?" Aviators asks.

A pair of girls pierced like National Geographic tribesmen exits the store. I'm going to stick out like a square in a circle factory in that place. I tug on my jacket collar and push up my sleeves for a more Don Johnson-esque look. Don's a pretty cool guy. I mean, he *is* on TV.

I hand Aviators a five. "No. I'll call again if I need a ride."

"Cool. Here's my number. I'm on until midnight. There's a phone about ten minutes' walk if you need it." He points up the road. "Ask for Kevin."

Kevin. I never would have guessed. He doesn't look like a Kevin. I'll keep an eye on you, Kevin. You're my driver for the duration. I pocket his scribbled scrap of paper and head for the record shop, doing my best to stay nonchalant.

Chapter Twenty-Two

A clanking cowbell sounds as I step inside and get hit by a smell as pungent as the BHU Custodial Office. I prefer the tangy undertones of men's cologne and cleaning product supporting the skunky, herbal essence versus Ernie's choking recipe of heavy incense and pine candles mixed with the stink of cheap ganja. Wooden bins and plastic racks run the length of the room holding vinyl LP's and cassette tapes. The few customers hunch lower in their jerga hooded shirts, milling about the aisles beneath posters of Janice Joplin, Cheap Trick, Frank Zappa—all names I at least know. There are also four crazy looking kids calling themselves Red Hot Chili Peppers and some sad boys named R.E.M. I get the impression that a night of drinking and listening to these bands would drive me to assault random postal workers.

Julia, in her full hedgehog glory, perches behind the cashier counter mid-store, a three-foot high bronze Buddha smiles beside the register as if saying, "Peace be with those who pay full price." She glances at me as I walk in, then continues ringing up a pimply kid with camouflage pants and greasy hair in bad need of a shampoo.

I play casual and edge toward them, listening in as I feign interest in the music selection.

"You should see it on shrooms," Camo Pants says to Julia. "My cousin's got it on BetaMax. Maybe you can come over when you're done? We can trip out and watch Luke blow up the Death Star."

That's not gonna happen, kid. You're barking up the wrong, punk rock girl tree. I flip through the *R*'s.

"Sorry. Not really my thing," Julia says, showing a tight, customer service smile.

Told you so. I stop flipping through vinyl at The Ramones and pull out *Rocket to Russia.*

Camo Pants doesn't give up his quest. "We don't have to actually watch it. Just come trip with me. It'll be fun."

Credit for boldness. But the set of Julia's jaw is a flashing sign to the world that his greasy come-on's will lead nowhere.

"Sorry, Dwight. I don't trip in places I don't know with people I don't know." She opens a small brown bag, slips in a cassette tape and receipt, and holds it out for him. "And I have a boyfriend."

Ah, the closer.

That's my girl.

Camo Pants Dwight takes his purchase and his change and steps aside as I walk up to place my album on the counter.

Julia's eyes narrow.

I play the disoriented customer, saving my lecture about not ditching me for when we're alone. "I'm looking to branch out from Buddy Holly and the Beach Boys. Is this something I'd like?"

Julia looks at the record. "Actually yes. These guys build on classic rock sounds like the Beatles, the Beach Boys, and yes, Buddy Holly. They're true punk rockers, using straight forward rhythms and melody to underplay anti-establishment lyrics."

Wow. Okay. My girl knows her stuff. Point Julia.

"Sold. How much?"

Julia folds her arms. "You don't have a record player, Larry." She violates our little stage play, but I roll with it.

"Yes I do. At home." Actually, it's in a storage unit I haven't visited in two years.

"This guy bothering you, Jenn?" Dwight steps back in, making a weak attempt at playing the hero.

I look down from my six four height and draw a deep, chest-expanding breath.

He starts to wither, eyes darting from Julia to me and back.

She finishes him off. "I'm fine. You can go now."

He bobs his head in that indecisive way of a coward convincing himself he's leaving because he wants to, not because he'd piss himself if I lifted a finger.

"Whatever," he mumbles.

Dwight slinks out the door and the bell clangs. I smile at Julia. "You have interesting friends. Say, that was quite a sales pitch on The Ramones. All that true?"

"Listen and find out. But not here." She motions to the front door as the trio of jerga-wearing teens try to slip out without notice. "You're spooking the cattle." They leave. The store is empty.

"Funny. That's twice today somebody thought I was a cop."

"Popped collar and sleeves pushed up on your sport coat? You scream cop trying to look cool. Jesus, this is South Dakota, not Miami."

"Point taken." I return my look to normal. "You were going to give me your work schedule?"

"Right." There's a metallic squeak as she pushes back from the counter revealing she's resting cross-legged on a unicycle. Not the slightest wobble as she rolls to the shelf behind her and tugs a slip of paper from beneath a psychedelic painted frog paper weight. She pauses to flip over the cassette in the boom box and click play then coasts right back as a blend of sitar and synthesizer drones over the shop's speakers.

"Here," she says.

I pocket the paper and shake my head. "Christ, Jennifer."

"What?" she shrugs. "I pedal this thing around the shop. Customers get a kick out of it."

"We talked about this," I hiss. "The protest? Drawing attention?"

"Oh give it a rest. Riding a unicycle doesn't make me a freak. It's not gonna bring Opposition clowns knocking down the door." She taps a cigarette from a shiny pack of Kools.

And my day was going so well. I snatch smoke and pack from her hand.

"Hey!" She makes a grab but misses.

"Damnit, Julia, people are dead," I say in a whisper, shaking the cigarettes in front of her. "*They* know you, know what you can do, know what to look for. You can't go ditching me on a whim or showing off because you're bored."

"We're in the middle of nowhere! Jimmy the Fist isn't cruising Eighth Street. Why the hell did you bring me here if it wasn't the last place on earth they'd find me?"

The chances of The Opposition having a team in this flyover town are slim to none. I know she's right. It doesn't counteract years of looking over my shoulder and it doesn't make me any less worried that her giving the locals a peek at her exception won't bite her in the ass. I let out a resigned breath and smooth out the pack of Kools before handing it back.

"I'm sorry. I just want you to be safe." I want them all to be safe. With Julia, it runs deeper. "And I don't like you smoking."

She tucks the cigarettes away in a jacket pocket and steps off the unicycle, her face shifting from defiance to acceptance. "I know." She leans across the counter and takes my hand. "You've kept me safe for six years. You've taught me how to assume a new life, how to blend in and disappear...how to make a fake ID."

"Don't put that on me. You figured that all on your own."

She smiles. "I did. That's my point. Oh, and if it weren't for you, I'd have never learned the true joy of a good cheeseburger."

I chuckle and we share a rare, quiet, happy moment.

"The cigarettes are all show, anyhow. I cough for five minutes if I take a real drag. Still, there is something calming in lighting up and blowing the smoke around."

The background music switches to rhythmic drumming and wailing vocals as she lights a new cigarette, blows the smoke sideways, and leans close with that devilish look on her face once more.

I'm still mad, but there's no fire to it.

"So, what is it with you and Professor Chisholm?" she asks. "What's your sordid history. Spill the beans already."

"Holly and I, that's...complicated. She—Oh shit, that reminds me." I check my watch. "Damn."

"What?" she asks, letting off another puff of smoke.

"I'm supposed to be someplace in twenty minutes." By the time I get Kevin back here, race to the hotel for my gear, then to the dojo, I'll be late. I don't need her class punishing me for disrespecting the school on top of my already low standing. Gut-twisting thoughts of Holly shaking her head in confirmed disappointment seize my focus. I've said enough here. Julia gets the point.

"Hot date?" She crosses her arms.

"No. Not, um...not exactly. Can I borrow your car?"

"What?" She leans back and mashes out her cigarette in an ashtray that looks like a kid made it in third grade.

"Please, I don't need any more of a beating than I'll already get." I hold out my hand.

"You're into some weird shit, Larry," she says, fishing in a pocket then tossing me her keys. "Fill it up."

"Will do." I head for the door.

"Unleaded," she shouts. "And be back by ten!"

I wave. The cowbell clangs at my exit.

Chapter Twenty-Three

HOLLY'S adult class is stepping on the mat as I arrive. Lady Luck stays with me long enough to bow in on time, then she sits on the sidelines and watches for the next two hours. It's no repeat of last night. I succeed in making Dr. Bill lose his smile for once after I drop him with a leg compression that buckles his knee and has him yelping in pained confusion. It's a move I'm fond of but which Holly tells me is illegal in competition. She's laser focused on ensuring her students are at their trophy-winning best for the Black Hills Invitational Karate Tournament this Saturday.

Her decision, of course, leads to my downfall. I'm so used to taking what opening I can get that I hesitate, unsure if I'll hit too hard or connect with an off-limits target, like some black-belt's nutsack. It simply means more bruises for me, this time on my ego as I really try giving it my all. And for Holly's prize student, my all is barely enough.

Fighting Chad is exponentially harder than sparring anyone else in the room. I know for a fact that psychics don't exist—perk of the job—but I swear this kid is reading my mind. He has a counter for everything I throw. He tags me when I think we're out of distance. He closes when I step back for a breather. I finally manage to catch him, smother his arms, and toss him down with one of the ugliest throws ever. I'll take any point I can get.

None of the pain or embarrassment matters as much as the quirky smile on Holly's face. There's a pride there, obviously for Chad but also for every single student including me. It warms me to see it and, at the end of the night, I depart with a "Goodnight, Sensei" that has no subtext. She is one hell of a teacher.

Julia's closing up shop when I putter back to the record store. She introduces me to her boss—a squat, long-haired gorilla with a crooked smile and a Megadeth t-shirt. He doesn't make my scar itch, but he looks at Julia like she's some sort of prize to be proud of. Thankfully, after a minute of conversation, his total lack of aggression, continued praise of Julia's music savvy, and his ability to fit "dude" or "bro" into every other sentence puts me at ease about any machinations toward my spunky girl.

I don't think he could spell machinations if it was written on the Ernie September billboard.

"Well, gotta roll, dudes." He slaps a hug on Julia then mauls me. He steps back, wiping his hands on his jeans. "Whoa, bit moist on the backside there, bro."

"Sorry, just came from the gym."

Julia cocks her head, "Really?"

I shrug.

Her boss waves off, lumbering to a rusty yellow Camaro. I hear wailing guitar as he peels out on the gravel and motors up West Main.

"The gym, again? You needed my car for an emergency workout?"

I can tell she won't drop it, even if I ask her to. "I need the exercise and yes, before you ask, Holly was there. In fact, it's her gym — er, dojo." I unlock the driver side door then hold it open for Julia.

"Oh." She cranks the engine. When I'm seated next to her that curious look hasn't abated. "So you went to get sweaty with my professor?"

I'm about to reply when she laughs. I laugh, too. Then wince at a cramp in my side. "Stop. It hurts."

It's fun, having a conversation with her that does not focus on my job or her abilities. I want it to last, so we swing by a Burger Time on the way to her dorm. She offers to drop me at the hotel, but I refuse. "I can walk back. It will give me time to cool down and keep my muscles loose. And you can tell me about your day."

So we do it. We devour our burgers and fries in the car and slurp on our Cokes as we stroll up the well-lit path to Bennett Hall.

I'm enjoying her tale of the eyebrow-plucking roommate, my guard at ease as we share an hour resembling what normal folks enjoy, when there's movement in the shadows. A second look confirms someone parallel to us, creeping toward her dormitory entrance through the trimmed shrubbery.

My scar goes crazy.

Happy thoughts vanish.

Damnit, how did they find her?

I grip Julia's forearm and whisper, "Keep walking. Head straight for the door. I'm right behind you."

She doesn't ask questions, just strides forward, keys in hand the way I taught her. As she enters the pool of light in front of her door, the shadowy figure makes his move. I charge, the pain of a two-hour beating forgotten as adrenalin kicks in.

Julia gets her key in the lock.

The shadow raises an arm, pointing her way. There's something slender in his hand. I can't make it out.

He speaks, voice thin. "Hello princess, you're—"

I spring, wrench my forearm across the assailant's neck, and I lift him from his feet. I squeeze the choke tight.

The attacker is slim. The way his neck sits in the crook of my elbow I could strangle him with a single hand. My cheek is pressed to a head of hair that is surprisingly soft and smells of lilac.

"Don't struggle, bud," I growl.

He wriggles, grabbing at my arm.

I twist my wrist, crushing the carotid.

He's going limp when Julia glances over from her efforts at the door. Her brief look becomes a hard stare then blatant shock. She stops working the lock.

"Get inside. I'll handle this." I squeeze even tighter. The choke won't kill him, but he'll have a hell of a headache when he wakes.

And a lot of questions to answer.

Julia runs up. "Holy shit, Larry let him go!"

I almost have him unconscious. Ten minutes alone with this prick is all I need. I'll get what he knows about stolen Exceptional secrets. I'll get how they found Julia.

"Damn it, Larry. That's my boyfriend!"

Chapter Twenty-Four

"What?" I don't loosen my grip, just let my eyes drift down the assailant's form—black jean jacket, black jeans, black Chuck Taylor All-Stars, red socks. Red socks?

Well...shit.

"S-sorry."

Inside her dorm, I lay the moaning Trevor Morrow on Julia's futon. Turns out the thin, bulbous headed object Trevor clung to was a rose. I felt it best he wake up to Julia's ministrations, rather than the face of a large man he doesn't know. So, while she mops his brow with a damp washcloth, I rummage through her tiny shelf of snacks and sundries and find a tin of General Foods International Coffee. I plug in her hot pot to make a cup, figuring it as a sort of peace offering along with my inevitable apology. Pop didn't grant me any folksy wisdom for events like this.

Julia's roommate pops from beneath a threadbare Sean Cassidy comforter on the other bed, gives us a bleary once over, then slaps on a pair of headphones and rolls back to her pillow.

"Trevor, I am so, so sorry. Are you okay?" Julia soothes.

"Ow, damn," Trevor groans. "My neck... What happened?"

I intercept the conversation with, "You shouldn't be hiding in the bushes, kid."

"Dad." Julia shoots me a look to shrivel my guts.

Misfire on my part. I check the water. Still not boiling.

"Everything's all right, honey." She smoothes back his satiny hair. "My, uh, father here, thought you were a mugger. He's a bit *over* protective."

"A mugger? What? No, I brought you a rose...where's the rose?" He struggles to prop himself on a skinny elbow.

"Shh, it's okay. I got your flower and put it in an old Cuervo bottle with some water. It's lovely." She wipes his brow with the cloth.

Trevor has a distinct femininity—flowing hair, full lips, sad blue eyes, and a frame that a decent breeze might carry off. I can't see the attraction, but Julia hovers at his bedside like a battlefront nurse.

I turn away and rearrange the spoon in the mug, stirring the powder of the instant coffee as if it might speed time. Finally, steam drifts from the hot pot spout. I snatch it up and pour.

"Coffee?" I thrust the cup at Trevor with the best smile I can muster.

"He doesn't need coffee, Lar—er, Dad," Julia says with unmistakable get-lost undertones.

"No. No, coffee would be great." Trevor feebly takes the mug and sips. "Mmm. Thank you, Mr. Reardon."

The kid has manners.

"Sorry about the neck," I say.

"You nearly ripped his head off," scolds Julia.

"I was protecting you." I spread my arms in surrender.

"Jenn, I'm fine." Trevor slowly stands, leaning on Julia. It rubs me weird, this kid saying her false name. "Your dad was just being a dad, that's all. It can be dangerous for a pretty girl alone at night. This coffee's delicious by the way."

I can't tell if the waif is sincere or buttering me up. The voice in my head suggests the latter. And I know damn well that if Trevor had been a mugger, Julia could kick his scrawny ass.

"Well, uh, you're welcome. Sorry for choking you." Seems I've done nothing but apologize these last couple of days. I take the washcloth from Julia and drape it over the room's small sink. "Jennifer hasn't told me much about you, Trevor. What's your major?"

Julia gives me that look again. "Now? Really?"

"I'm just trying to get to know your boyfriend, sweetie." Jake was right. I suck as a liar. I need to take an acting class, or political science.

"After you nearly kill him?" Julia hugs Trevor close.

To his credit, the boy downplays the situation. "It's fine, Jenn."

"I wasn't going to kill him," I mutter.

Third time's the charm with her look. I wipe my hands on my pants and start thinking of a dignified way to exit.

"Honestly. I'm fine," Trevor says, brushing away Julia's protective hands. "Your father saw someone in the shadows and reacted to keep you safe. I can't fault him for that."

Damn, the kid's logical *and* amenable. Not fair.

"What were you doing in the bushes anyway?" Julia asks sweetly.

Trevor flushes red and looks at me, as if I'd sympathize with his story. "Well, I'd been waiting for nearly an hour, hoping to surprise you when you got back from work and...nature called. My dorm is across campus and all the class buildings are locked up, so I slipped into the bushes... then you came home."

Julia shakes her head and hugs him. "I'm sorry. We stopped for burgers."

He pats her hand and looks at me again. "Scientific agriculture, Mr. Reardon. I'm studying the long-term sustainability of current large-scale cereal production."

Okay. What am I supposed to say to that?

"Trevor's writing his senior project on the ecological and financial devastation caused by commercial corn farming," Julia instructs with evident pride.

"Do you know anything about Big Corn, Mr. Reardon?" Trevor rests his mug on one of Julia's plastic milk crate bookshelves. The mouse of a moment ago is gone. Before me sits a terrier, intense and, were I a young woman starting out in the world, strangely magnetic. A sudden fire burns in those blue eyes that makes me just a bit uneasy. The way I get when a homeless guy tries telling me about Jesus. Julia's door is only eight feet away. I can make it in two strides.

"Hear him out, Dad. It's the least you can do after assaulting him." Julia's death-to-me look shifts to you-aren't-going-anywhere. So, I drag over the little room's one chair and prepare for a long night.

God, I need a shower.

Chapter Twenty-Five

RAPID City is dead at four thirty in the morning. So am I, practically. Exhausted and battered, I trudge ahead like a grim soldier bringing bad news. What moves on the streets are leaves from last fall and an empty Big Mac clamshell tumbling along the curb. A chill north wind reminds me spring and winter haven't parted ways just yet. A morning like this calls for a sweater and knit cap. I'm hunkered against the cold in a sport coat and twill pants. The walk to campus is all that's keeping me warm.

By the time I throw open the door reading EMPLOYEES ONLY, I'm blowing into my hands to keep my fingers from going numb and hopping on my toes to keep them from doing the same. The dimly lit, pipe-lined hallway pings and hisses—ominous sounds that in a slasher flick would have the audience screaming for the inept heroine to turn around and run. I'm happy for the steamy warmth and that I'm on time for my appointment.

Jake and Miguel are already at the table when I enter. Miguel has his head down, scribbling something on a clipboard. Jake's leaning back in his chair, Styrofoam cup in hand.

"You need to change," says Jake. "Hang your coat in locker seven. Spare coveralls are in the last one. Should be something in there to fit you. Gloves are here." He points at the cupboard behind him.

I nod and follow instructions, rattling open the locker that cuts painted Jimi Hendrix in half.

"I have added the student union and the Bennett Hall," says Miguel looking up at Jake. "Is there anywhere else?"

Jake shakes his head. "No. The rest we play by ear."

I find a set of heavy green polyester coveralls that fit well enough. Sven and Earl arrive as I zip up. Pornstache trots in while I'm rummaging for work gloves.

Jake shows me the ropes with the courtesy of a Los Angeles motorist. By noon I've scraped litter from under bushes, emptied trash cans reeking of stale beer and fresh vomit, mopped beige hallways, and scrubbed down bathrooms (men's and women's) with splatters and streaks on the wall of unknown origin. The work is both mundane and revolting, but while doing it, I've become a fly on the campus wall. Students and staff pass by without a glance. Conversations ranging from complaints about pay to who got it on with whom after closing down Patty O'Niel's pub last night happen within easy earshot and not once is an effort made to keep me from hearing. The crew is so blatantly invisible that when Julia trots past, unlit Camel dangling from her lip, even she doesn't acknowledge me. Good.

At lunch Jake pairs me with Sven to vacuum the campus bookstore. Pushing around the heavyweight Kirby becomes a numbing therapy of repetition and concentration. Time shifts and I find I've completed the clothing and memorabilia section as well as the aisles of used texts filled with last year's scribbled notations and not once thought of threats to Julia. The discovery is so revelatory I nearly announce it to Sven. I try to catch his attention in time to note he is subtly trying to catch mine (as subtly as guy his size can be running a ten-horsepower suck machine between racks of number two pencils and college ruled loose leaf).

He tilts his head, rolling his eyes toward the entrance. I click off my machine and casually wheel it in that direction, looking past hanging banners of Mick the Miner, BHU mascot, to see what Sven sees.

Julia and Trevor are in the store, and they brought a crowd with them. A dozen people, a couple of which look more like faculty than students, shuffle along together, enthralled by whatever Trevor has to say. Julia, too, watches him with soft-eyed infatuation as he emphatically slams a fist into his palm, sinews in his slender neck straining.

I straighten stacks of *Basic Macroeconomics* while observing. The group takes over a corner nook holding sofa and chairs. Trevor stands while the others sit or lean or crouch on the floor at his feet. Julia perches in one of the chairs, chin propped on her fists, bathing in her boyfriend's presence.

It's not that I hate the kid. How can I? Hating the fine-boned little man would be like hating a puppy. It may be a damn Pekinese, but it's still a puppy. From our forced introductions last night, Trevor seems a smart, polite, kind young man with the fortitude of wet bread. Still, I can't deny the kid's charisma. His followers are rapt, caught up in a way I've only seen portrayed by actors in movies about Jesus. The passion of his talk—phrases about capitalist greed killing the family farm and corn flakes soaked in crushed dreams—can't be denied. The boy's practically foaming at the mouth.

Julia was bound to find someone someday. It's just that the first is rarely *the* one. What I hate is the thought of that kid breaking her heart because that thought breaks mine. Julia's never been a job for me. From day one she's been more. I want her safe. I want her to thrive. I want her to find a passion and follow it. I want her to seize a dream and achieve it. I want her happy.

If I were the professional I'm supposed to be, the one Jack Underwood recruited me to be, I should have recused myself from protecting her the moment he and I shook hands across that hospital cafeteria table back in '79. Should have. Could have. Would have. Doesn't matter. I didn't.

"You okay there?" Sven claps me on the shoulder.

I grab his hand with the speed of instinct, locking up wrist, elbow, and shoulder, shoving his head down by his knees.

"Hey, ow!" Sven whines, voice cramped and muffled from being bent in half.

Reflexes are still sharp (thank you, Holly and Mountain High Kenpo). Too bad they got tested on such a nice guy. I let go and pat Sven's arm in apology. "Sorry. You scared me."

"Ja, remind me not to do that again." He rolls his shoulder. "How'd you do that?"

"I've been taking some lessons. Didn't hurt you, did I?"

Sven shakes his head as he shakes his wrist. "We should go. Russell's alone mopping hallways at the gym. He always stalls around the lady's locker room entrance."

"I'll be right there." I start wrapping up the Kirby's long power cord.

Julia, Trevor, and the crowd are deep in a group discussion, him wedged in beside Julia in the chair. His fingers are entwined with hers. She laughs. She smiles.

EXCEPTIONALS

She's happy.

Damned if I won't do everything to keep her that way.

Chapter Twenty-Six

TAPTAPTAP.

I wipe soap from my eyes and listen.

Taptaptap.

Someone's at my hotel room door.

Sun's barely up. I didn't order room service and maids come later in the day.

My scar kicks into full battle itch.

Shower still running I slip into the main room, tugging on a complimentary bathrobe and searching for a weapon.

Taptaptap.

Damn this not sanctioned to carry crap. I need a gun. Instead, I snatch up the bedside bible and duck beside the doorjamb, getting as skinny as my frame allows. Opposition goons wouldn't kick down the door and come blasting in, not without a warrant, not without the protection of their FBI cover story. No, they'll jump me as soon as I open up.

"Who is it?" I silently slip off the security chain and raise the book, spine first.

A voice beyond responds. Muffled by the door, words come out, "Speck-tail liver-reed."

"Just a minute." I grasp the knob, willing myself calm.

Three.

Two.

One.

I throw the door open and spring, poised to crush the assailant's throat with one hard, theological thrust.

EXCEPTIONALS

A tiny woman in a prim hotel uniform screams, "Special delivery! SPECIAL DELIVERY!" The brown paper-wrapped box she held drops to the floor with a heavy *thunk*.

I stop mid-bible thrust, the good book suddenly heavy in my hand. I hide it behind my back and smile my most apologetic smile.

"Sorry. I didn't mean to frighten you. So sorry. Just, got really, really into Leviticus. May I help you?"

Her eyes stop bugging and her heaving chest slows.

"M-Mr. Lawson?"

"Yes."

She scoops up the package. As she straightens, her gaze lingers low on my body. "This was left for you at the front desk."

The package bears no postage. No return address. The name written in block letters on top reads, "LAWSEN."

"Are you sure it is for me?" I ask.

She gives a jerky nod. "I believe so. You are our only guest registered under this name."

This misspelled name. "Any idea who left it?"

"I'm sorry, I don't know." She glances at the ceiling. "It was at the desk when I came on shift." A warm rose hue spreads across her cheeks. Her lips tighten.

I take the package. It's heavy for its size.

No ticking. No rips. No stains on the outside.

"Thank you," I say.

We stand in an uncomfortable quiet, the woman avoiding my eyes, red creeping from her face to neck. Her lips press even tighter.

"Oh, let me get your tip." I set package and bible aside and grab a few bucks from my wallet on the nightstand. Behind me, a snigger. When I hand her the cash, she's crimson, eyes wet.

"Here you go," I say. "Thank you."

She trots away at high speed. As I lock the door, a high-pitched laugh erupts down the hall, fading away slowly.

"Weird."

Who sent this? "Who" helps me decide whether to open it or chuck it out the window.

Julia giving me an unannounced present? Not her style. And even if so, why "LAWSEN"?

Did I tell Holly I was staying at the Alex Johnson? No, I'm sure I didn't. And, again, she knows my name.

I sniff the box.

No chemical odor save for the tang of permanent marker still lingering above the letters. This was wrapped hours ago, not days.

Julia *is* the only one who knows I'm staying at AJ's.

No wait. She's not.

A cabbie in aviators knows where to find me.

I look down from my window for any sight of a Crown Vic cab motoring away. No luck. Then again, my window doesn't face every road accessing the hotel.

I set the box aside, rifle through my pants pocket for that piece of paper Kevin gave me, and grab the phone. A nasally dispatcher answers.

"Good afternoon, Hay Camp Cab, what is your location?"

"I'm not calling for a ride."

"Then how may help you, sir?"

"Do you have a Kevin driving for you?"

"Is this a complaint about your experience in a Hay Camp Cab, sir?"

"No. The driver gave me this number and said to ask for him by name should I need a pickup."

"How nice. You said Kevin? Do you have a last name? Cab number?"

"I don't." Were this Chicago I'd have checked the ID number and driver's badge before we pulled away from the curb. Small-town charm has got me soft.

"Yes sir, we do have a driver named Kevin. However, he is off today. May I send another driver to collect you?"

"No. Thank you." I hang up.

The Opposition has never used cabbies as operatives. Could be he's on the take, collecting finder's fees, running deliveries. Could be I'm barking up the wrong pine.

A delivery when I'm more under the radar than I've been in a long while. Misspelling. No postage. The math doesn't work.

My shower hisses away, insisting I take action.

I call Tabor. Seven rings. Eight. No answer.

Okay, Pop, what have you got for me? No time like the present? No, that wasn't one of yours.

Fine.

I put out the Do Not Disturb sign, kill the shower, and place the box atop the room's small table.

I hold my breath and peel off the packing tape.

Nothing happens.

I pull away the paper.

Nothing happens.

It's a shoebox. Reebok.

Hands unsteady, I look inside...and breathe out.

Well. Isn't that something? So much for my Cabbie-is-Opposition theory. Still leaves the who and how unanswered and why spelling my name was a challenge.

Everything inside I've seen before and used at one time or another for purposes both professional and recreational. One item in particular steals my attention. It's a beaut—my preferred model—right down to the dull gunmetal gray. Those shiny, nickel-plated jobs are for Roy Rogers buffs and douche bags who think they're Patton. Serial number hasn't been filed off, either. The piece is legitimate. Maybe Tabor's overcompensating on the IOU?

After inspecting the box's contents, I slide its more attention-grabbing items behind the room's vent return. A single, folded sheet of legal paper rests at the bottom of the box. Block letters match the wrapping paper.

The few clipped sentences ease my tension a hair's breadth. Mysterious originator aside, the words address a fear I'd put off after my last meeting in D.C.

"A protection agent copied the files?" I slump in the chair. The prick confessed, said The Opposition had it right—sacrificing Exceptionals was for the good of the species—then ate a bullet before our side could stop him.

How the hell does that happen?

Again, the CIA we are not.

If I trust this little care package, the mole problem has been handled and I can submit my reports, let Tabor know what I've done with Julia and the rest.

If I trust it.

My fingers remain twitchy, but my scar doesn't itch. That says a lot.

Pop might not have had something for the present, but he often talked about gift horses and their mouths.

A foe wouldn't leave me a box full of tools to ease my trade. Does my hidden benefactor know something is about to happen and wants me equipped to act? If so, what? Julia's as safe as I can make her and I promised I wouldn't move her again. Not now with her studies and her sorority rushing and her job and her (ugh) boyfriend. Besides, if I can be found this easily here, three days in, what good is it to start over someplace else? Maybe this package suggests I stop the runaround and dig in. Maybe it's time to say a silent thank you and get ready for a fight.

The last sentence reads, "Burn this." I take the metal trash bin into the bathroom, click on the vent fan, and burn the letter. When that page is ash, I rinse out the bin and flush the gray water.

Shower steam and paper smoke dissipate, leaving an odd sense of clean yet corrupt lingering along with the scent of Ivory soap. The mirror clears. I shake my head at what stares back: big me in a hotel bathrobe fit like Barbie clothes on a bulldog. Certain parts hang out on display. That explains the package lady's red-faced reaction.

I throw off the pointless garment, crank the sink's cold water, and grab my toothbrush.

Next time, shorts on before opening the door.

Chapter Twenty-Seven

USUALLY it's the actions and attitudes of the Exceptionals under my watch that grind my teeth. This week, phone conversations with Juanita, Archibald, and Tiffany prove restorative sessions of mental healing in comparison to my Rapid City-related troubles.

The countdown to my proposed departure and Holly's Black Hills Invitational Karate Tournament is a mess of emptied trash cans, buffed hallways, willful beatings, and force-fed re-education on both the lasting influences of early nineteen seventies pop rock as well as the growing villainy of corporate corn. Highlights include used condoms in the cafeteria women's room, watching Julia fawn over Trevor at a vegetarian buffet, and Holly laughing every time Chad dumped me on my ass. Holly laughed a lot.

The daily poker sessions are a release from worrying over my duty (Julia) and my vice (Holly). Plus, the guys reassure me of Julia's whereabouts when I'm not watching her and fill me in on the latest news around campus. Earl openly rolls his own and puffs away. Russell continues grooming his ridiculous lip wig (occasionally dusted with white powder). Miguel, Sven, and I stick with beer while Jake never strays far from a Styrofoam cup of his special brew. No one else drinks the coffee. Ever.

No adult kenpo class is scheduled for Friday night. Holly announces she'll open the dojo to competitors for some last-minute pointers before the next day's competition. Julia drops me off early on her way to work, so I sit out front watching cars go by and enjoying the crosstown view of a hilly, pine-studded horizon.

"You really are a glutton for punishment." Holly's heels clack on the concrete as she strides up from the parking lot. Her hip-hugging skirt and sleeveless black turtleneck convince me there is not a finer looking woman anywhere on this earth.

I stand, putting on my best smile as she reaches the door. "I paid for the week. I'm doing a week."

She gives that crooked grin I love so much and rifles through her purse, fishing out keys. "Alright then. Come inside. I hope you washed that godawful sweatsuit."

A solid week's training has knocked the rust off. I hold my own damn well if I do say so. Dr. Bill no longer smiles when we spar. I even fight Chad to a draw, though he wins in sudden death throwing an uppercut I swear came from a hidden third hand. Applause as we bow to each other.

Holly ends the session with pointers and a pep talk. "Remember, tomorrow is about you, not about anyone else. Don't worry about beating the other guy. Find the best within yourself, pull it out, and use it. And don't worry about winning. I could care less if any of you brings home a trophy. This tournament is about daring yourself to be better than you ever were before."

Damn is she good at what she does.

The class breaks up and students head home to rest before tomorrow's early start. After rinsing off, I catch Chad preparing to leave.

"Hey, champ. Can I talk to you for a minute?"

He neatly folds his uniform and slips it into a sleek green duffle. "Sure."

"I just want to say, training with you has been a pleasure. You've got something special. I've seen guys train for decades and not get half as good."

"Yeah. Thanks."

He's heard this before. Maybe he hasn't heard the rest.

"But you're not invincible. Good as you are, you do tend to throw your spin techniques without checking your target."

He tugs hard on the bag's zipper.

"And you let your left hand drift after you jab. If you're not careful, somebody is gonna snatch that or come over the top."

He chews on my words a moment. We're interrupted by Holly, clean and fresh and back in that stunning outfit.

"Time to go boys. I need to close up shop." She takes in the scene between Chad and me, parental concern shaping her face. "What is it?"

"Nothing," says her star pupil. "Mr. Lawson was just giving me some pointers."

Holly shoulders her purse. "Really? And?"

He looks at me. At first I think he's going to balk, but the kid is full of surprises. "They make sense. I'll check my target and control my left. Thank you." Chad bows and I return the respect. He turns to Holly and bows, "Goodnight, Sensei."

"You need a ride?" she asks.

"Nah." Chad shakes his head. "Grandma's shift ends at nine. I'll meet her at the store. She shouldn't be driving after dark anyways."

Holly smiles, a deep, heartfelt smile. "Well, take care of her and get some rest. Tomorrow's your day." She pats him on the cheek.

"Every day is my day, right?" He smiles.

"That's right," she says, eyes shiny with pride. "Keep that attitude."

The dojo door shuts with a weatherstripping *whuff.* She watches until he is out of sight from the big front windows. I see myself in Holly's concern, when I watch Julia walk to her dorm or up the steps to a class.

Then I'm alone with the most amazing woman on earth—taking in her look, her smell, her power to floor me at every turn—and I can't tell her how I feel. I'm about to ask for a ride to Ernie September so I can clear my head and learn more about alternative rock when she floors me once more.

"I'm too jazzed about tomorrow to head straight home. You got time for a drink?" she asks without a hint of nerves.

Holly wants more time...with me? Squeaking out a mousey, "Sure," takes more effort than fending off Chad's punches. I'm a lonely little puppy and my owner just got home.

Chapter Twenty-Eight

TURNS out Holly is a regular at The Clock Tower, Rapid's answer to *Three's Company*'s Regal Beagle. Walking in I get a hit of Milwaukee déjà vu. Again, I'm an odd duck wading into dangerous waters. The bar has dark wood paneling, mood lighting, and a collection of glaring patrons that let me know right away I don't belong. However, any resemblance to my incident with clowns and TASERs stops there. This place is quiet and subdued, and The Opposition isn't right on my heels. Somehow, I was more comfortable with the lesbians and squeaky shoes than I am alone with Holly and the risk of lengthy conversation.

Seating choices are either at the bar alongside over-preened guys doused with Hai Karate or at small, votive-lit tables where couples converse while sipping wine coolers. She guides me to a corner table beside a raised baby grand. A dude in pin stripes and skinny tie tinkles away, droning out a semi-decent *Copa Cabana* cover.

Holly nods to the pianist then waves at the bartender. "Freddy's not bad at the keys and Anton makes a mean Harvey Wallbanger. You want one, or are you still a Michelob man?"

"I'll have what you're having," I say, tickled she remembered about the beer and trying to recall what goes into said Wallbanger. Not Diet Pepsi.

Two bright cocktails arrive. Holly takes a long pull and I do the same. When she said, "mean" she meant strong enough to sterilize surgical gear.

"Damn," I sputter between coughs.

"Told you."

It takes a few seconds to get my breath. Holly stirs her drink, ice clinking as she rotates the cherry-ladened plastic sword in lazy circles.

My breath returns. "I gotta say, I didn't think you would ever want to share a quiet drink again."

Her face is shadowed, but I see the smile. She takes another sip, then sets the glass aside and leans forward. "Stop it."

I return once again in my normal, confused state of being.

She says, "Every time you do the 'I'm not worthy, please forgive me' shtick it takes me to a place I don't want to go. Got it? I'm past all that. It's old."

I swallow.

She smiles. "Let's just talk. You and me. Like two friends meeting together after years apart. Can you do that? If not, I'll call you a cab right now."

"No, please. I want what you want. More than anything. I promise, I won't self-deprecate or apologize again. I'm sorry."

She raises an eyebrow.

"No, wait. I mean...shit." I retreat to my cocktail, sipping this time, feigning interest in the assorted bills in Freddy's fishbowl tip jar.

A few couples three tables down start up a slurred sing-along. Freddy smiles and sings louder.

"Okay, two friends long separated," I mutter, then take a deep breath, slap on my best so-happy-to-see-you face and exclaim with all the joyful exasperation of a high school actor doing his first audition, "Holly Chisholm! How long has it been? Six years? Look at you. You look amazing!"

God bless her, she downs what is left in her glass and plays right along. "Why Larry Lawson, dashing as ever and still working the charm. What have you been up to?"

Games are fun. "Traveled a bit. Changed jobs a couple of times. That sort of a thing. No moss on a rolling stone. You?"

She's game. "Went back to school. Started teaching. Opened my own business."

I nod and take a sip, checking her out as if for the first time. Something about that turtleneck really revs my motor. Holly's driving along a different route, though.

Her drink is down to rattling ice. "I wrote a novel. Got married. Got pregnant. Lost the baby. Got divorced." She waves at the bar. "Anton! Another."

I swallow hard, no longer pondering curves in stretched black cotton. But the elephant will have to stay in the room for now. I'm not ready.

"A novel. Really? What about?"

"It was a coming-of-age story. A big-city girl finds love in a small town after the death of her abusive father. That sort of thing."

"You get it published?" I finish my glass of sweet fire with one gulp. "Make that two, Anton," I shout.

The bartender is grinding away, muddling oranges. The loud table has settled down.

Holly shakes her head. "No. I put it away after my tenth rejection letter."

"Oh," I mumble with an empathetic nod, her elephant looming over me, insisting on being recognized. "Is what you said true?"

"Yep. Took a year to write, a year to edit, and I'll never do it again."

"That's not what I meant."

Anton delivers our drinks. Holly pats his shoulder, and he leaves to fetch more wine coolers for the back-up singers now mauling Freddy's smooth *My Way*.

"I know." Holly plays with the glass but doesn't drink. "Yes, it's all true. We met about a year after you left. I was in a lonely place. After a few months, we eloped. A few months after that I got pregnant. We bought a little house. Two car garage, big back yard, picket fence, the whole shebang, plus all new Kenmore washer and dryer."

The room hushed as if it, too were listening to her story. She stares glassy-eyed at the table, her mind somewhere darker than The Clock Tower Lounge.

"I got the flu during my second trimester. The doctors said there was nothing they could have done. But Sean... We divided our assets fifty-fifty and last I heard he was living in Portland with some ceramic artist." She lifts her glass in mock-salute and downs the contents in one go.

Wow. Men suck.

She rumbles out a small burp. "Excuse me. Oh, nice job helping Chad. I've caught him throwing his wheel kick blind but hadn't noticed him dropping the left."

"Just trying to help." What else can I do?

"Well, it means a lot. Thank you." She looks up at me, eyes saying more than her words. That kid really is at the center of her busy, busy world.

"Might be good to have you mat-side tomorrow," she says. "You see things I don't. That is if you can fit it in before your flight."

She's serious and her tinge of loneliness has me ready to jump at the chance before I recall my cover story.

"I didn't tell you? There were some issues with the security program I'm checking. My stay has been extended. So, sure, I'd love to join you." For such a big lug, I can be quick on my feet.

Holly continues to give me what I least expect, instead of hedging her statement or laying out ground rules, she simply touches my hand and says, "Thank you."

My smile arrives all on its own.

"Now, are you gonna drink that? If not, slide the glass over here. I'm always nervous before fight day."

I raise the Wallbanger to my lips as she turns to Anton for number three and Freddy starts in on *Brandy*. Such a fine girl. This just might be one of my top ten dumbest decisions, but the warm, happy part of me doesn't care.

Chapter Twenty-Nine

MY response to Saturday morning's alarm clock is a delicate tap to the off button followed by a guttural, headache-induced, "Crap."

Last night, Holly managed to pour another throat searing cocktail into me before I switched to Michelob. I did my damnedest to keep our conversation on the tournament and not stray into "Your eyes are beautiful in this light" territory. Her eyes were beautiful, filled once again with a sparkle I'd hoped to forget after all these years. Only now the glint in her eye came from nervous excitement at Chad's prospects and leading her club in the area's largest martial arts competition, not from any designs on asking me to stay over. Despite the raging, heart pounding efforts of my every sinew to reach across the table and drag her close, I sat and listened and talked to my lost love turned friend.

And it was torture.

So, this morning, alone in a hotel room I've only booked for one more day, I take out my hungover frustration on the adjacent pillow. It yields nicely to my fist but offers me no answers about Holly or how I am going to say goodbye, again, and move on, again.

I'm as confident as I can be about Julia's safety, other than the romantic machinations of a certain waifish agriculture activist. Between my heart's desires and my brain's directives, I'm treading water in a whirlpool. The morning's one saving grace is that the Denver omelet at

Sally's is uninterrupted by waitress Marlene's suggestive gyrations.

A non-Kevin cabbie gets me to the BHU Athletic Center a couple minutes before eight. Holly's not waiting outside. After standing in a surprisingly long registration line, I find she has already checked in, marked me down as an assistant coach, and paid my floor fee.

"You don't look the part," says the wiry black gentleman running the table.

I'm in my usual sport coat and oxford's. Everyone else wears a *gi*, sweats, or some variation of snug t-shirt and shorts. The unifying element is a bulging duffle bag somewhere in the ensemble. I give the guy my best car salesman grin. "My school's a bit less traditional. Sensei Chisholm brought me on as an advisor, so to speak."

He smirks. "Well, whatever. Sign this." He slides a mimeographed insurance waiver across the table. "And no shoes on the competition floor." The form is standard stuff about competing at your own risk, the Black Hills Invitational is not liable for competitors getting teeth knocked out, ribs cracked, or their gonads mashed like boiled potatoes. I sign and follow the crowd into the main arena.

From the rumbling, liniment-tinged air of the place, several things become immediately obvious. One, BHU put all its eggs into one basket here, encompassing in a single facility space enough for track meets, football games, and, after unrolling several thousand square feet of vinyl matting, huge martial arts tournaments. I count at least two-dozen competition squares marked out with tape, each taking as much space as gymnasts use in a floor routine.

Two, either there wasn't much else going on in town this weekend, or I wholly underestimated the Rapid City area's love for karate. These bleachers can hold maybe five or six thousand and they are two-thirds full a good hour before competition starts.

Three, a tournament floor is no place for a big guy carrying his shoes who doesn't know where he's going.

"Excuse me. Sorry. I'm sorry. Oops. My mistake." I bump and jostle through the crowd of white uniforms and colored belts, clusters of them forming tight knit groups, staking claim to pieces of padded real estate with the tenacity of land rush Sooners.

I tap the shoulder of a nice looking, middle-aged fellow bending his own wrist at odd angles. "I'm looking for Mountain High Kenpo? Any idea where I can find Mountain High?"

I get a smirk not dissimilar from that at the registration desk. "Nope."

Roaming about the floor gets me nowhere, so I head up the bleachers a few rows, figuring to spot Holly by her hair. Instead, I find myself sniffing a familiar skunky fragrance as I look over the sea of karateka.

My pony-tailed custodial chum works ten feet away, shaking a dustpan into a trash bin rocking on rickety casters.

"Morning, Earl. You pull the short straw?"

He starts at my words, dropping his whiskbroom. "Christ, man, you nearly gave me a heart attack." He clumsily hangs his implements on the side of the bin. "No short straw.

We get time-and-a-half for stuff like this." He leans close, "Hey, you want to go out the loading dock and light up? I got some sweet New Mexican. Lays on real smooth. Last time, I got some skank ganja made the whole tournament like the slow-mo bit in that Bruce Lee flick. You know the one I mean?" He slowly circles his arms in front of him.

"I know which one. But no, no thanks." I turn to sweep the arena for Holly, again.

"Your loss. Say, what are ya looking for?" He shuffles up next to me.

"A friend of mine runs a karate club. I'm here for moral support. She's down there..." I still can't spot her. "Somewhere."

"Oh, thought maybe you were looking for your daughter."

"No. Why? Have you seen her?" He has my attention.

"No, man. Not me. Sven spotted her at the student union about thirty minutes ago."

"Really? How do you know?"

Earl hefts a clunky black walkie-talkie.

"Oh," I say, and lean against the railing. Part of me really could get used to having a team.

"So, what's the name of your friend's karate school?"

"Mountain High Kenpo," I say over my shoulder. One would think that auburn hair would stand out in this salt-white sea, though a few folks in black *gi* do add a dash of pepper to the mix.

"Hey guys, anyone spot where Mountain High has camped out?" Earl says into his walkie-talkie. He pulls it from his mouth and gives me smirk number three on the morning. "Mountain High. I dig it, brother."

The radio crackles and Pornstache's speedball voice barks out, "Yeah-yeah. I see them. Behind mat five. Damn, that redhead's got a nice rack. You see those, Miguel?"

"Yes, *cabron*. I see her. She is looking very nice."

Their randy comments on Holly's anatomy get my blood up to the point that the look I give Earl is nowhere near the smirk category. Based on how quickly he turns off the walkie and scoots away with his wobbly-wheeled trash receptacle, it more likely fits under the umbrella of looks that mean your spleen will soon be ripped from your body if you don't get the hell out of here.

Chapter Thirty

HOLLY has Chad and the rest warming up when I work my way around the competition space to them. "Hello."

"Look who finally got here." Dr. Bill takes a break in his shadowboxing to flash that annoyingly wholesome smile.

"You guys said eight..." I jerk my thumb at the front entrance, half a football field away and obscured by a sea of excited karate buffs.

"It's a tournament, Mr. Lawson," Chad says, tapping my shoulder as he passes en route to dig something out of his gym bag.

Dr. Bill goes back to throwing jabs at nothing. "Eight never means eight on fight day."

Holly is bent over, pressing a young student whose name escapes me into the straddle splits. "...and one, two, three, breathe out." She lets the girl return to a normal human posture then walks over to me. "Early bird gets a good warm-up spot. And gets to check out the competition as they roll in."

I follow her gaze, surveying the gathered competitors and landing on a team of angry-looking fighters sporting hair dyed to match their belt colors.

"Denver," Holly says. "They left with a dozen trophies last year."

"But not the championship." I incline my head at Chad.

"No." She leans conspiratorially close, "Screw what I said at the dojo. I want to kick their asses."

EXCEPTIONALS

I help limber up Chad and a few others before an official comes over to announce the start times and brackets. After a rousing speech by a guy who could pass for a street corner Santa Claus were it not for the stars-and-stripes uniform and black belt around his girth, the tournament gets under way.

Holly's students disperse to their competition mats. I tag along with her, listening as she inspires and advises, throwing in my own two cents where I think it may help. At each mat, she gives her students her undivided attention. But, as we transition between them, she's always looking for Chad, checking on him the way a hen might check on a chick at play in the yard. As the day wears on I find myself cheering and consoling alongside Holly, as if we were long-standing partners. I give hugs to the losers and high fives to the winners. It feels organic. It feels right.

Morgan, Holly's flexible teenaged green belt whose name I'd blanked earlier, works her way to the under eighteen quarterfinals. Dr. Bill holds his own in the over forty division. Chad is far-and-away the standout, moving and countering like he knew every strike coming his way before it was ever thrown. In his first match, his opponent doesn't score a single point. The second is the same. Opponent number three gets so frustrated he launches a rugby tackle and is disqualified. Holly is beside herself. Yet, with each cheering win, she checks the bracket boards. The Denver team is progressing, too.

"Don't worry about it," I assure her.

She tips her head dismissively and we head to the next match.

The fights are enthralling, almost personal. I'm so wrapped up in the action that when the tournament breaks for lunch, I don't recognize a familiar, demanding voice yelling behind me.

"Larry! Larry! Larry!" Julia waves at me from the bottom row of bleachers. The purple pants are back along with her now customary field jacket. I'm glad she's here, that she's close, but her and Holly under one roof gives me pause.

I slip over through a gap in the milling crowd. "Hey kid, what brings you here?"

"Aren't you supposed to know?" She winks.

I have no comeback.

She gestures to the room. "Well, my options were a livestock show or this. So…"

"Ah. And the boyfriend?"

She lights up in a way that makes me uncomfortable. "He'll meet me later. He's with his academic advisor about getting published in some professional journal. Isn't that amazing?"

"Yeah. Sure is." Sure isn't. I should care. It means a lot to her. It should mean a lot to me. I smile back.

"Journals are for graduate students. Trevor will be the youngest they've ever accepted. I'm so psyched." She's practically bouncing.

I muster up some excitement. "That's great. Are you staying for the rest of the tournament?"

"Probably." She ducks conspiratorially beneath the railing. "I see you're still hanging out with Chisholm."

Telling her it's none of her business will only fuel the imagination. "I've told you. Just old friends. She's been letting me train at her dojo this past week, so I'm lending a hand."

"You know, my car still smells like man-sweat."

"Hey, I shower."

She rolls her eyes. "Right. Anyway, I'm sitting up there." Her absent gesture lets me know I'll find her if I look hard enough. "I'm grabbing a hot dog before they start up again. Join me?"

"Larry!" Holly this time.

Julia clicks her tongue. "The shrew calls."

"Stop," I say in my dad voice. "I gotta go. Dinner after?" I start moving back to the Mountain High group.

She frowns in Holly's direction. "Maybe. I need to be at work by six."

I shout over the growing distance, "I'll swing by. We can get ice cream once you're done."

"Ice cream?" What is with that smirk making the rounds today? "Am I twelve? Beer and a shot."

With that she heads for food. As she turns down a stairwell, I see her bump into a large guy coming the opposite way. Not large, huge, with a block jaw set tight, cropped hair, and shoulders so broad everyone he passes turns sideways to let him by. He's dressed in the blue uniform and heavy-laden belt of a cop, but there's something about him that doesn't read right. The uniform doesn't quite fit and he's not scanning the crowd, not looking for areas of trouble. In fact, as soon as he tops the stairs, his gaze fixes on one point. Curious, I check what he's looking at and find he's locked on to the Mountain High crowd. Holly, who's left

Chad to his stretching, is striding toward me. When I look back at the cop, he's gone.

My scar itches.

Shit.

Chapter Thirty-One

"Larry, come on." Holly puts a hand on my arm. "Slip on some mitts and work Bill's timing. He's fighting one of those Denver pricks next."

"Sure." My gut's gone liquid at the sight of that cop. Pop always told me the gut sees truth the eyes miss. The officer could have been pulling a figurative Pornstache and was just checking out Holly's bust line. But that's not it. There's something else I can't put my sparring-gloved finger on.

"Let's go, then." Bill pops me with a one-two.

"Okay, okay," I say, rubbing my jaw. I file the cop under paranoia to later examine and focus on Bill. "Don't drop that right. Remember, mix up the timing, mix up the range, mix up the opponent." We work for a few quick minutes before Patriot Santa returns to announce the start of the second half.

Excitement ratchets up as the afternoon presses on. One of Holly's yellow belts with only six months at the school gets second in his division. Morgan wins her first match against a rotund Denver competitor touting a green-on-green color scheme but is eliminated in the semis by a girl kicking with legs longer than Morgan is tall. Dr. Bill's first match is a draw, but when he bows to his opponent at the end, the angry Colorado ponytail across the mat lets slip a bit of profanity that eliminates him for unsportsmanlike conduct.

Dr. Bill stuns me by coming over and whispering, "Dickhead didn't know to keep his mouth shut." And then he slaps on that Boy Scout smile.

As Chad moves up from the quarterfinals to the semis, I notice the bracket board. No Denver has made the championship picture, but another name is working through the competition on a collision course with our young prodigy.

"Who is Simpson?" I ask Holly during a break in the action.

"What?" She replies, obviously confused.

I point to the boards. "Simpson. From..." I can't quite read the school's name. "Eton hippos Ito? Is that Latin?"

Holly is just as perplexed. "Not any Latin that I know. I've never heard of them. And it looks like Simpson is their only fighter."

"He's supposed to be at mat twenty-one right now."

We look down the arena. Holly points. "That has to be him."

At the far end of the complex, a one-sided bout is under way. The one she fingers as Simpson fights in black pants and a white t-shirt clinging to muscles so well-defined we can make out bicep veins from here. For a moment the other fighter rallies with a furious kick punch combo, but Simpson slips around unfazed and drops the poor guy on his back with a move I don't catch.

"Damn." Holly mutters.

"Yeah." What the hell was that?

She shrugs, but her voice is tight. "Well, Chad's faced all kinds. Let's focus on the fight in front of us."

The fight in front of us is Dr. Bill versus a shorter, balder, happier version of himself. The two go at it with a playful air that has those gathered around cheering and clapping with each point no matter who scores. In the end, Dr. Bill succumbs to the other guy's goofy footwork and a light tip-tap kick to the head. They bow, shake hands, and walk off chatting like old friends.

As I follow Holly around, I catch sight of my custodial team and glance into the crowd to check on Julia. It takes a couple tries, what with the ups and downs of a throng unafraid to vent its disagreement with any referee decision. I first spy her blue-tipped blondness munching on popcorn, booing and cheering in synch with her neighbors. She is joined by Trevor, whose animated talk does not distract her attention. All is right with the world, then she turns to him and lays on a long, hard kiss.

I turn away, not sure I ever want to see that again.

Far below them, standing against the rail, the behemoth cop is back. So's my itch. He's still not looking around the crowd but staring at one spot. Holly has gone ahead of me to watch Chad's last semifinal match. That's where he's looking. What is this guy's deal?

As I strain, and survey the crowd, it hits me that he is the only uniformed cop in the place, the only one I've seen all day. No campus security, either. An event like this demands a police presence, at least for managing traffic to and from the Athletic Center.

Holly calls me but I give her the "just a minute" finger and duck down an access tunnel to the concession stand concourse. I find who I'm looking for sweeping in front of

Pretzels & Cheese. The tile floor is slick under my stocking feet, and I curse as I catch my balance.

"Damnit. Hey Earl, can I borrow your walkie?"

"Don't know about that, man. Regulations." He presses his palms into his lower back and sighs after an audible pop. "Ah, that's it."

I get uncomfortably close and form my words with hard-edged intent. "It is important." Then in a gentler tone, "Please."

He blinks several times. "Uh, sure man. Here."

I click the mic. "Guys, it's Larry. Any of you spy Rapid City PD around the arena?"

Pornstache clicks back first. "I see one. Jesus, Sven, he a cousin of yours?"

"No," Sven replies slowly. "No, I don't think so. But I got eight uncles, don'tcha know."

I cut in. "Anyone see a cop besides the giant in the stands?" I look questioningly at Earl. "By the bathrooms, in the crowd, the front door, anywhere?"

Earl shakes his head.

Silence. "What about campus Nazis?"

"No." Miguel joins in. "That is not right. Last year, there were like, six or seven in the place."

I toss the radio to Earl and run back, trading reefer and stale popcorn stink for the arena's locker room nerves and lineament. Fans mill about, leaving their seats at a pause in the tournament action. A pair of giggling coeds brush past me the other way and then a human tide rushes for snacks and potty breaks.

I worm my way through, toes getting mashed more than once. The bracket board displays today's final match—the open division championship—with Holly's Chad Ellis versus Simpson from the odd-named school. A countdown clock reads four minutes twenty-seven seconds, twenty-six seconds, twenty-five.

After jockeying my way back to the competition floor, I shoot across, spying Julia and Trevor still in their seats. The big cop is talking into a radio not unlike Earl's and looking once more in Holly's direction. He gives a familiar menacing grin and a deep, sickening feeling churns inside me.

I yell, "Hey cop!" over the crowd noise and pray I'm wrong.

He looks to my shout. When he finds me, he lowers his hand-held and narrows his eyes. The crooked nose is new. So is the split in his right eyebrow.

Goddamn. Special Agent Bartholomew Rockentanski.

He looked better in clown makeup.

Chapter Thirty-Two

NO doubt. It's Bart.

The brute turns from his perch and disappears down the stairs.

I spring forward. How had they found Julia? No one knew she was here. No one. Is this the work of my package-delivering benefactor? Some unknown evil prick playing both sides? The how would have to wait. I need to get Julia out of here.

Fans flow back in as I hit the steps leading up the bleachers.

"Ladies and gentlemen," Patriot Santa's voice booms over the speakers.

I keep shoving my way past, stubbing my toes, stepping on some others. "Excuse me. Pardon me. Excuse me."

Santa carries on as if a kidnapping attempt wasn't imminent, his words barely registering as I fight to get to Julia. "Now we come to it. The final match of the day. The bout to crown our 1986 Black Hills Invitational Tournament Open Class Champion..."

He announces Chad. Spectators jump to their feet, many holding their ground and giving me dirty looks in case I'm some asshole jockeying for a better view. I lose Julia amidst the masses in the upper bleachers, but keep charging on, praying she's where I'd seen her last. Also, hoping Bart's big frame doesn't pop up in the same space. A raucous crowd is great cover for abducting a small blond freshman.

Simpson is announced as I scrunch past a young mom with babe in arms.

"...fighting from the Eton hippos Ito school. With a record of..."

Such an odd name. Like something from a Saturday morning cartoon. So odd, I can't stop chewing on it despite my laser focus on reaching Julia.

I catch sight of Simpson bowing in. He looks early 30s and chiseled from granite, now wearing all black right down to his sparring gloves—a fully embraced bad guy stereotype.

Across the mat, Holly is talking advice to Chad. Every once in a while she checks over her shoulder, frustration plain on her face.

Sorry I can't be there. Again.

I still don't see Julia. But I don't see Bart, either. A thing or two from that care package would do well to ease my current anxiety. My rod and my staff, that sort of thing. Unfortunately, I left rod and staff in the hotel room. That won't happen again.

Eton hippos Ito. What the hell does it mean?

"The first to score five points wins and will take home..." The announcer's voice continues to roll over the crowd. Then, a familiar, but rarely heard laugh, rings out close by.

There, in the middle of Row K, halfway between the fight floor and the steel rafters, stand my Exceptional and Trevor. Both are on their feet, holding hands, staring down at what is about to unfold. They're packed in, but the row above has an open space. I apologize my way to the vacant spot and note the unchecked body odor of a flabby woman in worn-thin U.S. bicentennial t-shirt and Coke-bottle glasses. That explains the free chair.

"Jennifer." I say, trying to keep my voice even as I crouch behind Julia from above.

She looks over her shoulder. "Hey...Dad..." The words stretch out unconvincingly.

Trevor turns, too. "Oh, hello there Mr. Reardon."

"Trevor." I nod to him. "Jennifer, can I talk to you for a minute?"

The arena's quiet becomes an eager hush. Chad and Simpson are at their marks, bowing first to the ref, then to each other. Julia turns back to the action.

"It's important." I add some commanding fatherly emphasis.

"Not now," She shoots me an angry look. "They're starting."

"Hajime!" the referee shouts, outstretched hand chopping the air. And two fighters go at it.

The crowd gasps as Simpson feints with the left then throws a looping right roundhouse. Chad slips away unscathed. Holly stands stoic at the edge of the mat, willing her student to victory.

"Jennifer, I need to talk to you." I grab her shoulder.

She shrugs free. "No," her voice an angry whisper.

Trevor gives a girlish whoop as the action ramps up. Crowd noise swells to a nervous rumble and I glance back to the mat. Chad is something else—bobbing, weaving, countering. His opponent is cool and slick, moving like a black snake on the hunt. Holly presses her hands together, fingers to her lips.

"Kick his ass, Ellis!" the smelly lady next door belts out.

"Jennifer!" I bark. Time is short.

"Dad!" She throws her full, back-off-right-now glare at me. "After the fight."

Kids. I clench up in frustration. Looking around, I can't see Bart. Maybe us slipping out with the departing crowd is better than leaving on our own.

Eton hippos Ito...Two p's. Two t's.

I scan for any other clues in the thundering arena that might tell me what The Opposition is up to. Exits are free. Nobody's waiting at the stairwell, no one walking the catwalks above me.

I grind my scar against the chair back.

Scoreboard reads two-zero Ellis.

Simpson huddles on the edge of the competition mat with a weasel-faced man in a gray tracksuit.

Chad kneels before his mark, breathing easy.

Holly yells encouragement, but still glances around the crowd.

Where the hell is Bart Rockentanski?

Julia has Trevor's hand in both of hers, squeezing it in delighted excitement.

Dammit, we need to go.

When they start again, Simpson is a different fighter. He narrows his stance, dancing on the balls of his feet Mohammed Ali-style. Chad adjusts without a hiccup. He launches a straight right and Simpson grabs it, sending him tumbling with a quick flip of his wrist.

"Fuck!" blurts smelly lady.

Chad takes out Simpson's legs and the bigger man crashes to the mat.

"Fuck yes!" she cheers.

Chad pounces for the follow-up but Simpson hits first, kicking from his back straight into Chad's gut.

The whole crowd groans as one. It is the first time someone has scored on their champ in three years, and kicks earn two points.

Two-two.

Holly steps in, looking concerned. Chad smiles and waves her off. The kid doesn't seem fazed. If anything, he looks strangely energized.

All is still as they reset once more.

I can't get sucked into the fight. There's movement in the access tunnel behind Holly. My scar flares. An angular shadow obscures the man's face, but the sheer size and police blue shirt give Bart away.

"Jennifer. It is exceptionally vital that you come with me. Right now."

She's about to chew me a new one when she catches the cue. I point across the arena. In a confused huff she follows my aim.

"What is it, Jenn?" Trevor asks, shouting to be heard over the crowd.

Julia's shoulder's arch like a frightened cat. She doesn't look at me. "Is that?"

"Oleg. Strongman of the Caucuses," I snap.

To Trevor's credit, he's concerned by the change in his girlfriend. "Who? Jenn, what is it? What can I do?"

"N-nothing," Julia says with a fake smile. "We just, need to go."

"Hey!" croaks my stinking neighbor. "Take your family drama outside, would ya? I'm trying to watch the Black Hills Bruce Lee kick some ass here."

Bruce Lee. Second reference today.

Two p's. Two t's.

"I'll be goddamned."

"What?" Julia asks, getting up from her seat, eyes wide.

It can't be. The Opposition operates through the FBI. That's their method. Jack's training and my experience proved that. This is something new. And I missed it.

"Stay here," I order.

"What is it?" Julia's voice quavers.

"He's not here for you," I growl and jump up. I fought Chad myself. I should have seen it.

"What do you mean?" Julia yells after me.

"Just stay with Trevor," I command, and barrel my way out of the row.

Smelly lady bawls at me, but her shout is lost in the arena's vibrating cheer as Chad connects once more. The kid has exceptional reflexes.

Four-two Ellis flashes on the scoreboard.

Eton hippos Ito. Just The Opposition in anagram. The ballsy pricks.

Chapter Thirty-Three

I take the stairs two at a time and am nearly to the arena floor when a flailing fan arm clocks me in the nose.

"Oh, dear goodness me. Are you all right, my friend?" A tender hand touches my arm.

I blink away tears to see a gentle-faced black man in black pants, black cassock, and white collar. "I'm fine, Father. Fine."

"My humblest apologies," he says as I try to extricate myself and get to Holly. "My son, where are your shoes?"

"Long story," I say. "Go with God." I wave and move away.

"And you as well," he shouts after me.

The whole arena goes suddenly quiet, but not because of our exchanged blessings. The priest's eyes are wide in horror.

Chad is on the mat clutching his throat. He's sputtering, fetal, fighting to breathe. Simpson turns from looming over the downed champion and quietly kneels at his mark, poker face back on.

Chad's head lifts and falls feebly back to the mat. He blinks and gasps but doesn't get up. Holly races to his side, tears streaming, crying for help. A half-dozen others rush to join her, yelling in panic.

"Give him room!"

"Get the paramedics!"

"Who knows CPR?"

An angry whisper rolls through the crowd. A boo calls out. Then another. A recognizable voice from the Row K vicinity shouts. "Fucking bastard!" Everyone begins yelling. Patriot Santa snatches the mic and nods to the panel of referees.

"...Simpson is disqualified for illegal and deliberate contact..."

More shouting.

I push to get on the competition mat. A brusque Denver blackbelt with a dyed black ponytail steps in front of me.

"Hold on there tough guy."

"I'm with Mountain High. Excuse me." I step around him, but he shuffles back in my way.

The blackbelt plants his feet wide. "I've seen you around. You a doctor?"

"No. Look, just let me—"

"Only family, head coaches, and medical personnel are—gah!"

I hit his solar plexus quick and hard. He wasn't being a dick, not really. He was just trying to help control the situation. And he'll be able to breathe in a minute or two.

Behind him, two white-shirt paramedics race onto the mat with a gurney, pulling Holly off Chad and shooing the others aside. They don't even stop to check the kid's vitals before lifting him on and wheeling him back down the access tunnel. The whole thing is done with the comedic expedience of circus clowns running in and out of the center ring.

Clowns aren't funny.

Holly is sniffing back tears as I finally bowl my way to her.

"Are you okay?"

She wipes her eyes then slaps me hard in the face. "Where the hell were you?"

I halt my, "I'm sorry" and force my words out with deliberate calm. "I'm here, now. Are you all right?"

"No. I'm not all right. That—that asshole punched Chad in the throat."

That asshole is gone. I look around the arena. No Simpson. No coach in a tracksuit. Bart Rockentanski is gone, too.

Holly is in no mood to listen and there's no time to explain. I want to grab her by the shoulders, plant a hard, desperate kiss on her lips, then make a grand departure, promising to return and tell her everything. I settle for grabbing her by the shoulders.

"I need a favor."

"What are you—." She shakes her head as if clearing away confusion. "What?"

"Please. I need you to do this."

Holly grips my wrist.

"Run up to Row K. Jennifer is there with her boyfriend. Can you take her back to your place? Just for tonight. I'll come get her soon as I can."

"What? But Chad? They—"

"Please!"

"Larry, she and I...we don't get along." Her muscles tense against my forearm.

"I'll explain later. Just keep her safe for me," I beg.

She gives a slow, considered nod. "Okay. But... Chad?"

With a lump in my throat, I sprint for the tunnel, tugging off my socks as I go.

"Where the hell are you going?" she yells at my back.

"After your champ!"

I bolt down the echoing concrete, weaving through people that should have damn-well stayed in their seats. At concessions there is no sign of Bart or the paramedics. My fifty-fifty chance of which way to turn improves when I spot Pornstache, standing amidst scattered wrappers and cups, gesticulating at an upended trashcan.

"Russell!" I rush to him.

"The hell—It's not Russell, okay? It's—Where are your shoes?"

"Did the paramedics come this way?" I point past him.

"Huh? Yeah. Who do you think made this goddamn mess? Assholes blasted right into me. Didn't even apologize. Just kept trucking." He thumbs the same direction I'm pointing.

"What's that way?"

"Service elevator. Loading dock." He yanks the trashcan upright. "Assholes."

Paramedics position the ERV where it will have the quickest line of egress, which is out the front. The loading dock was the furthest from the main road, on the opposite side of the building.

"Do I need a key?" I ask, panting, adrenaline ramping up.

"For what?" He replies wiping his nose.

"Do I need a key for the damn elevator?" I bark at him.

"Yes. Christ. Why?"

I snatch the key ring dangling from his belt. "Which is it?"

"What?" His coke-addled mind can't keep up.

I press forward like an angry bear. "Which key, Russell?"

"Th-the little brass one." He cowers in surrender.

"Thanks." I bull past him and shout over my shoulder, "I owe you one."

"Damn right," he yells. "And it's Pornstache!"

At the elevator I jam the key home, twist, and punch the down button. My bare feet tap in nervous broken rhythm. My hands clench and unclench as sweat trickles from my temple. I pray I'm wrong, but my scar tells me I'm dead right.

The steel door grinds open. Grinds closed behind me. As the whole thing grinds down to the loading dock, I consider my options. At least two unknowns, possibly four, possibly armed. Four unknowns and Bart Rockentanski. Damn, I wish I had that care package right now. I wish I had shoes.

Chapter Thirty-Four

WHEN the door opens, I charge out hoping to catch them by surprise. Instead I ram smack-dab into an unmoving wall of muscle. The impact sends me ricocheting back into the open elevator. The hulking mass of FBI Special Agent and Opposition heavy Bartholomew Rockentanski fills the doorway. Beyond him the phony paramedics slide strapped-down Chad into a brown cargo van. Bart's cop outfit is fake, but it sports a real enough sidearm and holster.

"We gotta stop meeting like this, Bart. People will talk." The elevator is empty, no weapons for me.

Bart cracks a one-sided grin and that split brow puckers together. He doesn't say a word, just reaches around the door, pushes the up button, then steps back and crosses his arms.

The shiny steel panels begin to grind closed.

No choice.

I launch myself at Bart. His hands move to catch me, feet set wide, braced to take my best shot. Only, instead of driving my shoulder into his gut, I feint high then drop low, tumbling between his legs and punching his groin on the way by. There is no soft give of mashed testes. What I get is the hard, hollow knock of knuckles on plastic.

I roll to my feet, wincing as bits of gravel jab my tootsies.

Bart turns, rapping on his cup with a holiday-ham-sized fist. "Learned my lesson. Now I come prepared."

A heavy slam of car doors. The van's closed up. The driver (Simpson's track-suited coach) sticks his balding head out the driver side window and lifts his chin at Bart.

"Go," the big man replies. "I won't be long."

Baldy cranks the ignition.

I run three strides after them before a mammoth paw digs into my shoulder and drags me to a stop.

Tires squeal and the van speeds away. I miss the plate number, gasping with pain at Bart's crushing grip. He adds to my hurts with a hard thrust of a pistol barrel in my spine.

"You and me are going for a little walk." Bart shoves me forward.

"No." I spin and stand my ground, hands raised. "You...big ox."

Ow, my shoulder. Does he crush golf balls as a hobby?

"Why would I go for a walk? I used to carry the badge, remember? Crisis situation 101: never leave a public space with an assailant. Survival rates are highest if victims keep the situation from changing locations. Plus, there are a thousand people within earshot right now."

Bart's eyes narrow and he shifts his grip on a revolver far too small for his big mitt. "Shut up, Lawson. What are you doing here anyway?"

Holy shit. He doesn't know. It's a small relief despite having the barrel of a short barrel Ruger Security Six pointed at my chest.

"Oh, you know, taking in the sites."

"Yeah. I don't think so."

"I'm surprised, Bart." I shift into my fighter's stance, ready as I can be for what is about to happen. I hope there's no broken glass. Even clown shoes would be welcome right now.

"About what?" He thumbs the hammer but doesn't cock it.

"That you think."

Bart snarls and lifts the gun to face level.

"Hold on there, Bart. When the crowd hears shots they'll head over here—oh, they will. You're going to look mighty suspicious as the cop walking away from gunfire. You can't shoot me and stay either or your little costume party comes unraveled. What's the world's biggest dumbass to do?"

Tendon's bulge from his neck to his temples. "I'll show you." He strides forward, bringing with him an odd dry, dusty smell. He draws back the gun to pistol-whip me into putty.

Moron took the bait.

He throws force enough to crush my skull, but it never lands. I slip outside the blow and capture his gun hand in both of mine. Then step, pivot, and twist. I hear a slight popping sound followed by a gasp of brutish pain, and Bart is ass-over-teakettle on the ground at my feet, his gun in my hand.

"Christ," he hisses, then slams a melon fist atop my bare right foot.

I hop back. Damn that hurts.

Bart sits up, wringing the wrist of his gun hand.

I hobble away and level the weapon at Bart's chest. "Where are they taking Chad?"

"Fuck off." He moves to stand.

"Uh-uh-uh. Stay down." I click the hammer back.

"Same logic goes if you shoot me. Only then you get to explain shooting a cop with his own gun." He rises, shaking his maimed limb. "By the time the dust settles, that karate kid will be long gone, and you'll be on death row. This state is fine with capital punishment."

I can only stand in stunned impotence. Because the dumbass is right.

"Now then, lets you and me have some fun." Bart smiles a broad, demonic smile. His big fists come up, ready to pound me into the pavement.

I uncock the pistol.

"Larry!"

Somebody's always calling my name.

Holly, Julia, Trevor, and a twitchy Pornstache stand at the service elevator. With my shoes.

Bart seizes the moment, wrenching the gun aside and slamming a frozen turkey fist up under my ribs.

I collapse like a limp pillow.

That dusty dry smell—reminding me of younger days and old barns—hits me again as he bends down, growling into my ear. "We'll finish this later." He shoves me hard to the pavement, holsters the gun, and walks away without so much as a glance at the assembled witnesses.

The asphalt is rough but welcoming. It doesn't bite my side the way it did my feet. I rock as I fight to drag in air without spewing out my lunch.

Running footsteps. Holly stoops to help me up.

"What the hell was that? Where's Chad?" she asks.

Julia joins her in grabbing my shoulders and they roughly sit me up.

184

"S-slowly," I wheeze, my gut aching, shoulder tender, foot throbbing, legs slow to respond.

The world keeps shifting beneath me as the pain peaks. It's all I can do to sit and not to collapse back to the ground.

Trevor stands to one side, flabbergasted. "That cop hit you! Hit you, then ran off. That's police brutality. I'll call the ACLU. I'll call—"

"Trevor," I cut in, jaw clamped tight. "Follow him."

The kid blinks twice. "F-follow him?"

"Car. License plate. Anything." My vision is going dark around the edges. Sounds are getting fuzzy, distant. I haven't passed out from pain since...ever.

"What? I don't—"

"Just do it," Julia snaps, then gathers herself and places a hand on her boyfriend's chest. "Please, I'll explain later. Do as Lar—as my dad, says."

Trevor looks Julia over. In a breath, resolve replaces timidity. "I'll be right back." He sprints off.

Good kid.

"Dad?" Holly gives me a teary, querulous look.

"Long story." I groan.

"I'll bet there's a short version. Where's Chad?" Holly insists, sniffing.

I shake my head.

Pornstache hovers around the edges, hugging himself and yammering, "Oh Jesus. Goddamn. Oh Jesus."

Julia grabs my chin. "We need to get you out of here."

Holly sets aside her questions and gingerly probes my stomach. I wince and gasp only to wince even more. "We should call an ambulance," she says.

185

I shake my head again.

"He can't go to a hospital." Julia has her determined look.

"Why not?" Holly asks, hot hands under my shirt making me, with the most inconvenient timing, recall sunny afternoons together by a mountain stream.

Focus, damnit! They have Chad.

Julia stands and crosses her arms. I can see the torture on her face as yet again her world is turned upside down. "Too public. They'll find him."

Holly's brows scrunch together. "What are you talking about? Who will find him?"

"Bitch," Julia snaps, "you have no idea what—"

"Hey!" I smack Julia's leg, my abs throbbing with the effort. "Enough."

Pornstache paces and rubs at his nose. "Jesus, that fucking cop. Jesus, Larry. Jesus!" I wave the janitor over.

"Office. Get Jake."

He stares wide-eyed for a moment, then nods like a dashboard bobble-head. "Right. Right. Got it." Pornstache fumbles for his radio and steps away to make a call.

Julia and Holly bend down by me. Spiked hair grazes my right cheek, silky strands tickle my left. Both ladies grumble, their arms rigid around my ribs.

"I-I'll get Chad back," I mumble. "I just...need a minute." My gut aches. Only shallow breaths will come.

Julia is grim-faced, but steady. She knows what this means.

Suspicion edges Holly's eyes. She whispers, "What do you mean get Chad back? What have you gotten him into, Larry Lawson?"

Chapter Thirty-Five

TREVOR returns out of breath. He spotted Bart getting into a Buick and even caught the license plate number. He mumbles it aloud over and over like a mantra, trying to get his mind around the speed of events. Julia grips his hand, talking sweetly, easing him down. She's a rock while Holly is a firebrand, demanding answers I'm not prepared to give. Sven saves me the inquisition, squealing up in his little Truckster. Everyone climbs on and he speeds us to the campus custodial office. At least the jostling ride of zips and beeps along the sidewalk reassures me no bones are broken.

We trundle along the now familiar dank basement corridor and through familiar metal doors, to the familiar mélange of man-smell, stale coffee, and reefer. The rest of the gang is already inside.

"Why here?" Holly asks, refusing a chair proffered by Miguel. She stands, arms crossed in the middle of the room.

"In a minute," I reply.

Jake comes up. "You don't look so good," he says without a smile.

"I've been better."

Earl offers the newcomers some Kool-Aid from the fridge.

"No, thank you," says Holly with tight-lipped courtesy. "Larry, why did we come here? We should go to the police."

"No police," Julia says, then points to the open fridge. "Is that beer?"

Trevor looks at her sideways. As do I.

"What?" Julia shrugs.

"Um, yeah..." says Earl, bobbing his head like a chicken winding up to peck. He gets a can of Hamm's from the fridge and passes it to Julia. He gestures with one at Trevor who waves it off, still a bit wide-eyed.

"You?" Earl tries again with Holly.

"No," she grumbles, courtesy all but gone. "Thank you."

"Does your phone call long distance?" I ask Jake, not immune to Holly, but focusing on the task at hand. I need information.

"This one does not," Jake says, nodding to a rotary dial mounted next to the time clock. "The one in my office does." His office is a walk-in closet back down the hall.

"I need to use it," I say.

Jake doesn't hesitate, simply nods. "Answers will wait until you return."

How he grasps the gravity of the hour without my saying a thing, I don't know, but it is appreciated nonetheless. I turn for his office.

"Dammit, Larry," Holly snarls. "Tell me what's going on."

I rub my tender gut and face her. Her anger comes from fear; fear about Chad and about being in the dark, about being lost. I see it in her because I've seen it before. I saw it in 'Nam. I saw it when I was with the Bureau. I've seen it on the face of every Exceptional I've uprooted these past six years. I see it when I look in the mirror and think about Julia on her own.

"I need to make a call. When I come back. I promise." The metal door closing behind me cuts off her huff. I step into Jake's office and pick up the phone.

Tabor doesn't answer. An assistant picks up, offering an alternative number as soon as I tell her who's calling. It's not a D.C. area code. I dial. The dial tone is weird.

A buzz and a click and then a hissy, "Tabor" shouted over background noise. Disco? The beat is hard and pounding. Exuberant screams, too. High pitched, like a roomful of ladies cheering their lungs out.

"It's Lawson. Can you hear me?"

"Just a minute," she yells so that I must hold the receiver a foot from my ear. She tells someone she'll be right back. More hissing static.

A mic'd voice where she's at calls out, "Ladies! Give it up for Henry the Eighth Wonder of the World!"

More screams. The music shifts. Then street noise.

"This is Geraldine Tabor."

"Tabor. It's Lawson. Listen, I need—"

"You were told to keep me in the loop. Four days without a peep is not keeping me in the loop. Now you call right as Henry the Wonder is swinging it up on stage? We need to work on your timing."

"I lost a boomer."

"Shit." Her voice lowers and the street noise dissolves. "Which one?"

"Not one of mine. Another. New. Happened today. I didn't see it until it was too late." The admission aches like Bart's punch.

A car horn honks on the other end of the phone followed by a guttural cry of, "Outta the road!" Whatever Tabor does, an engine revs and I hear the swift, retreating sound of a car departing at high speed.

Things go quiet, again. "You, okay?" she asks.

She's not inquiring about my physical condition. Six years under Jack and that question was never asked. How things change.

"Pride took a pounding, but I'll heal. The problem is the snagged boomer. I need information."

"Don't know what I can give you, seeing as how you haven't told me where you are."

"Rapid City, South Dakota." No reason to hide it anymore, not with The Opposition on the ground already.

"Wow. You do like going off the beaten path. Let me think." A long quiet on her end ticks by with every heartbeat. Then, "There was something in Wednesday's brief about taking down a smuggling operation in that neck of the woods."

"What was getting moved where?" Black market goods in the least populated region in the country? That doesn't make sense.

"Adult paraphernalia." She says it dead serious. "Some group was shipping crates of porn and vibrators cross-country by rail. Hid them in grain cars or something. Apparently there's a demand in Canada for certain things only available stateside, so—"

"Where was the bust?" No Fed wants to get involved in the smuggling of marital aids through flyover country. That sort of thing tends to be kept quiet. Any agent looking to make his or her way up the ladder and avoid career-long heckles in the locker room would keep away from a dildo smuggling collar. Damn if it doesn't offer The Opposition a dark line of communication and, depending on the site, a safe base of operations.

"Some grain elevator or feed mill. It was on the rail line, that I remember. Any help?"

Grain elevator, of course. That explains why Bart smelled like a hay barn. His crew smuggles Chad out of the country on a train that bypasses border checkpoints and will get rubber stamped by the RCMP. "Yes, it is."

"You know for sure your boomer has gone walkabout?" she asks, voice genuinely optimistic.

"No. In fact I'm pretty sure this one they'll play with for a while." I don't grasp my own reasoning, but the kid is alive, and the hard, unmoving nugget at the center of my being won't hear otherwise.

"Then there's hope." A pause on the other end of the line. "Look, Lawson, I'll do what I can on my end. Just don't take any chances. Save the ones you can." She stole that from Jack. Still, sounds good coming from her. Puts me in a thankful mood.

I say, "By the way, I appreciate the care package."

"What are you talking about?"

"The box of goodies delivered to my room, that wasn't your doing?"

"No. You only just told me your location. What was in the package?"

The mystery continues. I'll have to solve it later. Chad is the task at hand.

"Most of my Christmas list. Listen, thanks for the information. I've got to go. There's a boomer to round up."

"Fine. Secret Santa gifts are a problem. You watch your back, you hear me? And call within twenty-four hours or I'm sending in the Marines."

"Funny."

"I'm not joking. Good luck, Lawson. Now then, if I hurry, I can still catch Henry before he takes his royal package off stage." A click and the line goes dead.

Marines? She just might do it, too. That won't happen. I'll have Chad home before sunrise.

I hope.

Chapter Thirty-Six

BACK inside the office, Julia and Trevor huddle together at the table, still holding hands. He seems calm, gently sipping a cup of red Kool-Aid. She takes a long pull from her beer. Jake is making coffee and the others are standing around in uncomfortable quiet. Even the usually chatty Earl and Pornstache are mute, leaning against the Hendrix lockers. Holly, however, is seething, glaring at me as I enter.

"So?" she snaps.

How to begin? I know Jake and his guys can point me toward the right grain elevator. How do I ask them? How do I handle Holly? They've all got so many questions. Too many. I'm tempted to throw Julia over my shoulder and march out the door. That doesn't save Chad, though. What can I do?

"Just tell them," Julia says, burping into her sleeve.

I stare at her, my throat tight, mouth dry as I ponder options.

Jake turns from the percolator. "Yes, tell us all. Tell us the why behind an elaborate scheme to kidnap a teenager. And the real why behind having us watch this girl for you."

Julia thumps her can on the table. "What the hell? You've had these *creeps* watching me?"

Oh, shit.

"Hey," grumbles Pornstache looking insulted.

Miguel rubs a mocking finger under his nose and sniffs. "She is not wrong, my friend."

"Screw you, bean—"

"Shut up!" Holly shouts. She's in my face with two strides. "Now, either you come clean with what's going on, and I mean all of it, or I'm on the horn to the cops." She jabs a finger at the wall phone. Her lips quiver. Her whole body wound tight enough to snap. "And I'll crack the nuts of any asshole in this room who tries to stop me."

I get it. I totally get what she's feeling and why. There just isn't much to give her.

Julia scowls at me. Trevor has a hand on her shoulder, all gentle support. I should be that gentle hand. I should be there for her, always.

"I can't answer all your questions," I say to Holly. I look past her to Julia. "You know I can't."

Holly's face darkens. The weak foundation of respect, trust, and friendship I've rebuilt with her this week is swept away like a sandcastle at the stroke of a wave. She gives a curt nod. "Fine."

She shoves past me for the phone.

"Holly, please don't."

I grimace as she snaps my halting hand into a tight wrist lock.

"Larry, I swear..." Her eyes are wet. Once more, I've let her down. She stands in a room full of people, all alone.

"Please," I say. "Making that call won't help you find him."

Her nostrils flare and a single tear tracks down her right cheek. She shakes her head then let's go my wrist with an emphatic twist, leaving a sting as she reaches for the phone.

Screeeech!

I wince.

Holly stops.

Everyone else shrivels at the sound.

I turn to see Julia, standing beside the table, metal chair drug across the concrete to the middle of the room. She has that fuck-it look, again. She gave that look to Jimmy the Fist at the Rubyfruit Jungle. She gave it to me when I got here—Jesus, was it only five days ago?

I shake my head at her. "Don't."

Julia shrugs. Then, in one smooth move, rocks the chair onto a single leg and springs atop it, feet to the ceiling, weight balanced entirely on her right hand.

She doesn't even wobble.

Sven's eyes go big as golf balls. Earl stops rolling a joint mid-roll. Pornstache and Miguel pop forward off the lockers. Even stoic Jake raises an eyebrow over the rim of his Styrofoam cup.

Julia switches to her left hand with a skillful hop. The chair shivers, then rests stock-still.

Holly clears her throat. "What the hell is this?"

"Um, Jennifer?" Trevor shrinks into his chair.

I reach to get Julia down, a spinning Rolodex of excuses for her behavior flipping through my mind, the most obvious and the most farfetched both resemble the truth.

She stops me with an adamant finger in my face. "No. Don't." Her field jacket rumples around her armpits. Torn back pocket on those purple pants. Not the tiniest, unbalanced wiggle of a limb. Perfect.

I drop my arms. "Jennifer, this doesn't help."

"Really, Larry? It sure makes me feel g—"

She's cut off by the snapping, crinkling grind of buckling metal. The chair's aluminum leg collapses, dropping inverted Julia to the concrete floor like a cut anchor.

I spring to catch her before her skull cracks open on the pavement, but she's faster. One clean, twisting flip and she lands on her feet with impossible grace, impossible for someone in jackboots and field jacket, impossible for anyone on this planet other than her. My momentum carries me forward and I embrace her. Hugging my girl tight, knowing that what she's just done changes everything, changes us, changes me. I want to shake her with rage, at the same time whisper that it will be okay. I don't know what to do other than keep her safe, so I hold on.

She pushes away and gives me a hard, loving, defiant look.

She whispers, "No more lies."

Chapter Thirty-Seven

"Well," says Holly, "That was...interesting." She returns to the phone.

Julia shouts past my shoulder, "Hey, it's why they took Chad."

Holly pauses, receiver just off the cradle.

"It's also why you can't call the cops," says Julia.

"Young lady," Holly snaps. "Goddamn it, if you know something, spit it out. Because if somebody doesn't produce some answers—and I mean now—I'll throttle every last one of you starting with that chest-ogling shithead there." She thrusts her chin at Pornstache.

"Hey, what'd I do?" he whines.

I shake my head at Julia. "Jennifer, please, don't make this worse."

"First off, stop calling me Jennifer."

"Okay...daughter?" Pitiful.

"She's not your daughter," says Jake. "That's obvious."

Julia shakes her head and turns to Trevor, eyes soft. "My name is not Jennifer Reardon."

"Enough." I grab for her arm, but she shrugs me off.

"Larry named me that," she steamrolls on, "when he relocated me here. Jennifer Reardon is the third name I've had since high school. My real name is Julia Rourke. For a while I was Julia Richards, but..." She lifts her hands dismissively. "And yeah, Larry is not my father."

Trevor's face is a cartoon of disbelief. My gut drops to the floor. There is moving fast, and then there is rally car insanity.

Holly's unmoved. I'll bet Julia's story smells of Larry Lawson bullshit. The same stink I left her with six years ago. Back then I had been nearly two years in the FBI. I always hoped she connected my abrupt departure to the necessities of the job. That job, not the pot of beans Julia's spilling.

"Why did Larry give you a new identity?" Holly asks, fiery anger replaced by cold curiosity.

Julia looks like a long-suffering patient happy the doctor's finally pulling the plug. There's no stopping her.

"For protection from the group hunting me...and hunting those like me."

"Those, like you?" Holly asks, training shoe tapping on the concrete.

"Wait." Trevor bolts up from his chair, hands raised, fingers twitching as he tries to grapple with the compounding revelations. "So...ah, Julia. Are you in some kind of witness protection something-or-other?"

My girl addresses her young man with steady calm. "Not witness protection. More, something-or-other."

"And that cop? He was after you?" Trevor asks, voice thin.

The kid catches on quick.

Julia shrugs. "He's come after me before."

Trevor slumps back in his chair. "This is heavy."

"Which is when Larry brought you to BHU." Holly says, still resolute, not looking at me but at the one giving the answers.

199

Julia nods and shoves her hands deep in her pockets.

"Only today he wasn't after you, was he?" Now Holly gives me the full force of her attention. "He was after Chad. Why was he after Chad, Larry?"

Julia tries to answer but Holly raises an interjectory hand, stopping her response before it can start. "I want to hear it from him. What exactly is going on?"

Sorry, Jack. You taught me better. And Pop, go ahead and slap your forehead one more time.

"Julia and Chad are what we call Exceptionals."

"Who's we?" Holly asks. "The FBI?"

"No." I place a hand against my nervous stomach. "I haven't been with the Bureau since, well, since us. Not since her." I look at Julia. "I work under the authority of a congressional subcommittee. We protect the identities of Exceptionals within the United States. Like a witness protection something-or-other."

Trevor's gone pale.

The custodial crew avoids eye contact, save Jake, who's locked on me.

Holly chews on my words. "What is an Exceptional?"

"Exceptionals are people, like Julia, who have special abilities that set them apart. That make them...exceptional."

Pornstache cocks his head. "So, they're like superhe—"

"No!" Julia and I bark in stereo.

I continue. "We don't use that word. Too much baggage. Besides, nobody's wearing capes and fighting crime. They just want to be left alone to live their lives like the rest of us." Julia's been telling me that all week. I thought I understood. But I'll never be in her shoes.

EXCEPTIONALS

Jake picks up his cup. "And her ability is, what? Acrobatics?"

"Perfect balance. As long as she can move her limbs, she can't fall down." I let a note of pride slip into my voice.

Everyone looks at Julia.

Her cheeks grow pink. "In the circus I would balance atop a broomstick, atop a basketball...in a dunk tank."

"You were in the circus?" asks Trevor.

Julia shrugs, meeting his eye with a sidelong glance.

I continue, "Six years ago they came for her. I stopped them, but not until after they'd killed her entire family just to cover their tracks. That's when I started protecting her."

"And they are?" Holly insists.

Oh boy. "The bad guys. Look we really don't have time for this."

Holly drags out a chair and plops down, crossing arms and legs to control her roiling frustrations. "Give us the abridged version."

Julia sits, too, tipping her head in anticipation. We'd never really had a deep heart-to-heart about The Opposition.

Chad is out there. He should be the task at hand. Yet here I stand, bound by love, duty, and the inability to see how I'm going to get the kid out of this jam. So, I jump in where Jack first hooked me.

"What do you know about Bruce Lee?" I ask.

Holly cocks an eyebrow. Trevor is blank faced. Julia's attentive, looking to see where I'm going. The janitors, except stoic Jake, wriggle as if it's a game show question.

201

Pornstache pipes up, "Made some kick-ass chopsocky flicks."

"Ja," says Sven. "he beat up Chuck Norris in one of them."

Miguel shakes his head, "Ay-yi-yi."

"He played Kato on that show, um..." Earl snaps his fingers in a pointless effort to recall.

I stop them. "Bruce Lee's murder was the first time we took notice. We, the federal government, I mean."

"I thought Mister Bruce Lee died from an overdose of drugs," Miguel says.

"No, man," says Earl, drawing a flat hand across his throat, unlit doobie still dangling from his fingers. "He crossed the Chinese mob."

I pace a few steps. "Just rumors. How much do you really know about him?"

Holly sucks in a short-tempered breath, "Chinese American. Founded his own martial art, wrote books, and became a movie star."

I lift a finger. "An action movie star, the fastest ever on film. His moves were so fast, the industry created a new recording speed so audiences could at least glimpse what he was doing. For years the standard held at twenty-four frames per second. That wasn't good enough. Even when they bumped it up to thirty-two frames per second his moves still looked impossible. For anyone other than Lee, they were."

"Okay. Fine," says Holly. "Lee was fast. The guy trained a lot."

"So did I," says Julia. "Six days a week since I was seven. I was headed to the Olympic trials before..." she trails off, ending with a gesture at me.

"Exceptionals like Julia and Bruce Lee start out at a level it would take comparable athletes years, even decades to reach. Add in training, and they can achieve things impossible to replicate."

"This group that murdered Bruce Lee..." Holly gestures for me to get on with it.

I stop pacing. "The Opposition."

"The Opposition," she continues. "Also took Chad?"

"Why?" asks Jake, eyes narrowed.

"He was fast, too," quips Holly.

I consider that a moment. "It's not his speed. His blows are fast, but not Bruce Lee fast. It's his reactions. He can read what's coming at him as if his opponent were trapped in Jell-O. It's really quite..."

"Exceptional?" quips Julia. Her turn, I guess.

"Anyway, we used to think The Opposition just wanted Exceptionals dead. That's changed. In recent years they've been kidnapping them. The way we figure, they're looking to replicate the abilities of Exceptionals, distill and market them, if you will."

"For medical advancements?" asks Trevor.

I shake my head. "Enhancement drugs. The black-market kind."

"Like steroids?" quips Pornstache. "That shit's everywhere already. Hell, I'll bet half our football team is juiced."

"And if they pop hot on a piss test they're off the team. What The Opposition is pushing is undetectable." I look to Holly. "It alters the user at the base level."

"Changes their genes," she says.

"Their pants?" asks Earl.

Holly ignores him, eyes still fixed on me.

I wrap things up. "The Opposition is well-funded, covert, and international. They are damn hard to find and even harder to stop."

Jake rocks forward in his chair, setting aside his cup. His focus, too, never left me. "I did not ask why they took Chad. I asked why the government would take notice of Bruce Lee's death?"

Leave it to Jake to not miss a trick. "Again, rumors. Lee rubbed elbows with movers and shakers, and not just in Hollywood. Eventually the blend of high-profile hearsay and concerns reached congressional ears. They set up a subcommittee to dig deeper. What they found was a pattern, one that suggested a single hand at work. By late seventy-seven we had an agency, of sorts, seeking out Exceptionals to keep them secret and safe."

Holly lets out a tight breath. "So, that dirty fighter, that Simpson, was he part of The Opposition as well?"

"I don't know Simpson. Maybe." It makes sense, what with the disappearing act after the fight. "The phony cop is one of them."

Bart Rockentanski would have to be dealt with once and for all. While I pray for the chance, I'm not looking forward to it. Add in Simpson, a guy who can really fight? And the others? Lucky I have a few things at my hotel room to even the odds.

Chapter Thirty-Eight

"So," Holly says, "A group out of James Bond has kidnapped my best kenpo student to turn his reaction time into an illicit drug, is that what you're saying?"

I can't argue. "More or less."

"I'm calling the police." She brushes past me for the phone.

"You can't," I say, reaching to grab her shoulder but pulling back when I see her flinch.

For the past six years she's become a master of self-discipline and control, building walls to protect herself from ever being hurt again, at least by me. Here I've gone and collapsed a tunnel beneath her defenses. First, by coming back into her life and second by being connected to the abduction of someone she deeply cares for. I want to comfort her, to whisper into her hair that it will be all right. I've only ever loved two women in my adult life. Both in entirely different ways. Both are here, with me, in this room. Yet, I can't reach out to either of them.

Holly bridles. "All this crazy Exceptional crap you and Miss, Rourke, is it? have told doesn't change the fact that Chad's been kidnapped. You saw him put in a brown cargo van and Trevor there can ID the car of the costumed cop."

"The Opposition has infiltrated law enforcement," I say.

"This is Rapid City, South Dakota." Holly clenches her fists. "Why in the hell would some international drug lords sneak spies into the police department of a middle-of-nowhere town in a middle-of-nowhere state?"

"I meant federal law enforcement. FBI. I know The Opposition has moles there because I've met them, sometimes more than once."

"And?" Holly barks.

"And kidnapping is a federal offense. You report an abduction and you immediately grant The Opposition a window to come in and cover this up."

She's unconvinced. And reaches for the phone again.

"There were no real cops at the tournament. None," I say. Holly pauses.

I push on. "An event as big as that would warrant at least a pair of uniforms walking the venue plus a patrol unit out front to manage traffic flow. None of that was there."

"So what?" she says, back still turned. "Maybe the organizers failed to coordinate with police."

"Is that likely?" I ask.

From the easing of her shoulders, she doesn't buy her own argument. "No. That tournament has been on the same weekend, at the same place for years. And police were always there."

"Do you see?" I ask.

The room is eerily hushed, as if it and everyone inside held their breath, waiting to see whether Holly came to reason.

She turns. "Are you saying they sent a ringer to the tournament, set up an elaborate getaway scheme, and even...leveraged cops, just to get at Chad?"

"Maybe. They've done worse." I reply, looking at Julia.

She paces away, shaking her head, only to turn right back in a circle of frustrated anger. "Christ, Larry. This is insane! I don't believe all your secret squirrel bullshit. There isn't some nefarious organization sneaking around snatching folks that win karate tournaments."

Her disciplined walls are crumbling. The same happened to me when Jack Underwood gave me the rundown two days after I'd found Julia's family and put four feds in traction. I try calm logic. "And yet you just saw a girl in Doc Martens do the impossible...and Chad is gone. Unless we do something to get him back."

"About that," Julia says, inflection rising.

"Yes," I say, relieved to get back to the task at hand. "About that."

Holly mutters, "This is crazy." But she doesn't go for the phone.

"Jake, I need your help," I include his whole crew in my request. "Best intelligence suggests The Opposition may be using a local grain elevator as a base of operations. One outside of town."

Jake doesn't pause for a breath. "Makes sense. Lots of coming and going. Easy to slip a single guy onto a line-haul rig."

"Or a train," Sven says.

"Probably a train," I say. "I think The Opposition has taken over a smuggling ring used to bring contraband into Canada."

Jake nods. "There are three local elevators. One off Sturgis Road up north, another south of town, and one out east."

"Three?" I grumble. That's two too many. Checking three will take time. Scouting the site, determining points of ingress, tracking security, all take time. Time I don't have.

I turn to Julia, "I need to borrow your car, again."

"Where are you going?" she asks.

"To find Chad," I say, holding out my hand for the keys. "Jake, can you get me the addresses of those elevators?"

"Now hold on," Holly says. "You're going to drive around until you find someplace you think The Opposition might be holding him?"

I give her an incredulous look. "So now you believe me about The Opposition?"

"Shut up," she says. "You can't just head out like you're looking for a lost dog."

I step up to her, keeping my voice soft. I'm in a rush, but part of me still hopes to salvage some of this week's gains. "This is what I do, Holly. If you have a better plan, one that doesn't involve the police, I'd like to hear it."

We challenge each other with our eyes for a moment. Then, another mechanical squeal breaks the tension.

Jake wheels the scheduling chalkboard away from its corner. "Well, I have a better plan, if either of you care." What he reveals behind it is something I would never have looked to find in a custodial office, nor ever thought to see outside of a secure government facility.

A tidy bank of small TV screens sits against the wall. Below is a single computer console and keyboard—top of the line Commodore from the logo. A shortwave radio and CB base station are mounted beside the screens. Everything is powered down, but as Jake flips a single black switch, the assembled electronics hum and flicker to life.

"That's the quad," I say, pointing at one of the screens. I look at another. "And the cafeteria." The dozen little screens show a dozen different locales around campus. Suddenly, all the knowledge Jake and his boys have concerning campus goings on makes a bit more sense.

"That's the door to my dorm room," Julia exclaims. She glances around and locks on Earl. "You! You were there this week...replacing the hall light."

Earl shrugs, unlit J still dangling from his fingers.

"Miguel," says Jake "Why don't you reach out?"

Miguel nods. "Si." He puts on a headset at the CB, rotates a couple dials, and repeats a brusque phrase in Spanish.

Jake says, "Miguel has...cousins."

Miguel cracks a knowing grin. "Si." He clicks a few keys on the computer and three of the screens show new images.

"Give him what you've got on these guys," Jake says to me.

Trevor stands, a bit wobbly and pale, but earnest. "I can ID the car and license plate."

Jake nods. "Fine. Get over here." To me, "Give us twenty minutes."

Holly raises a questioning hand. "Uh, just exactly how many cameras do you have around campus?"

Pornstache chirps, "Eighteen. Thirty-two if you count the feed we pull off campus security."

"Excuse me but isn't all that—" She gestures at the equipment. "—illegal? Invasion of privacy alone?"

"Not the CB, now. Nor the shortwave," says Sven. "The closed-circuit security feed?" He waggles his hand in the air.

"Chill out," says Earl, fumbling for something in his pocket. "It's not like we put 'em in bedrooms or the ladies loo or anything."

"Yeah," sniffs Pornstache, "We're not pervs."

"My question is where you got this stuff," I inquire. "I mean your shortwave has signal hopping and uses a six-digit keypad with digital readout. That's state of the art. I didn't see stuff like this in the Army."

"It *is* state of the art," Jake says.

"Plus a few modifications to keep cops and FCC off the scent," says Pornstache.

"Yes," I persist, "but where'd you get it?" I'm pretty sure a janitor's salary couldn't pay for something like this, even if he saved up for a couple years.

"You ever see *Press Your Luck*?" asks Pornstache.

"The TV game show?" asks Julia.

Pornstache looks smug. "No Whammy. That's all I'm saying. No Whammy."

Holly steps closer. "You went on a game show and won enough to pay for...this?"

"Among other things." Pornstache sniffs and rubs his nose.

"Christ," mumbles Holly shaking her head.

"Why?" I ask Jake.

For the first time since I've known him, Jake smiles. "Because it's fun."

"And I got a granddaughter here with a restraining order on her ex," says Earl, stone cold serious. "Kill that a-hole he comes within fifty feet of her again."

Sven clears his throat. "There used to be a rash of car break-ins and burglaries. Ja, that's been stopped." He cracks his knuckles.

"And pricks from South Dakota Sate kept sneaking in and stealing the mascot," chimes Pornstache. "That ain't happening no more."

Miguel raises a hand for quiet. "Si?" he says into the microphone. "Estás seguro? Gracias." He pulls off the headset and turns to me. "My cousins, they found the car and the van."

"Where?" I ask. Task at hand here I come.

"They are parked at the Duddard Feed elevator."

"Which one's that?" I ask.

Sven says, "It's out east, by the airport."

"Great." I say, stomach tight, nerves gone, thrill of the hunt overwhelming.

Chapter Thirty-Nine

THE room is quiet, interrupted only by the gurgling percolator. Julia lets go Trevor's hand. Sven drops into a chair, frame giving a worried groan beneath him. Earl looks at me with expectant, bloodshot eyes. Pornstache pops first one knuckle, then another, his lip rug twitching. Miguel pulls what appears to be a ham on rye from the fridge. Jake sips his coffee.

"Okay." Holly interjects. "What next?" She's antsy, eager even, foot tapping once again.

I know where Bart's got Chad. But I don't know anything about where I'm going. "First off, what the hell is a grain elevator and what does it look like."

"Ja, it's a series of storage silos where grain is brought in, stored, mixed, and shipped out again—off the trucks and into the train let's say." Sven cracks another Hamm's as he speaks. "Duddard's is on the rail line. My nephew Gustaf, he works for the Burlington Northern and he took me through one time." His Adam's Apple bobs as he drains the can in two seconds.

Nephews? Cousins? Thank God for janitors and their large families. Whatever I did to earn this luck, Lord, thank you. Oh, and if it's not too much trouble, can you have Bart Rockentanski come down with a sudden case of bloody dysentery?

I ask the big Minnesotan, "How well do you remember it? Can you knock up a sketch? I don't need a wiring diagram, just rooms, hallways, doors in and out, that stuff."

"You betcha." He gets up, chair screeching its relief, and commences scratching a rough diagram on the chalk board.

"What are you thinking?" Julia asks, coming up to lay a hand on my arm.

I step around the table. A plan comes slowly, edges fuzzy. Bart's men will be armed, but they'll avoid gunfire—tends to draw problematic attention and, heaven forbid, honest cops. A glance at Sven's chalk drawing and it's obvious that I'll have my hands full getting Chad out.

"Shit," says Pornstache. "They could be holding the kid anywhere in that place." He rubs a knuckle under his nose.

"It's like one of those needle in a grain sack things, man," drawls Earl.

"Haystack, Earl. Haystack," says Miguel. "Idiota."

I raise my hand for quiet and Sven takes us through what resembles a matchbox married to a couple of tallboy six-packs. "Ja, so, they got an office next to the main elevator. First floor is reception, sales and receiving, that stuff. This here is the bathroom. The second floor has storage, break room, showers, and a couple of places for truckers and engineers to catch a nap. Third floor is operations, where the whole elevator is controlled, weights and volumes recorded, all that jazz."

For someone who consumes malted barley the way most folks breathe, Sven has great attention to detail. The office is too exposed to hold a prisoner, too much coming and going. Dense as Bart Rockentanski is, he wouldn't use a place so vulnerable that any yokel could stumble on his prized Exceptional bound and gagged in a broom closet.

"Tell me about the elevator itself. What's in there?" I ask.

214

"Well, each of these cylinders is a storage silo. Down here is the work floor where the trucks come and dump grain."

Jake chimes in. "Anyone use the work floor at night?"

Sven looks at the ceiling, then rocks his head slowly side-to-side. "No. No I don't think so. Da trucks come mostly in the daytime hours. Night is when they load the trains."

"And where do they do that?" Holly asks. Frustrated tension vibrates off her in waves.

"Here." Sven points to what looks like an odd playground slide sticking out from the structure. "This is where the mixed feed is fed into the grain cars."

"That's where the action will be tonight," I say.

"Ja sure. Though, most of it is automated now. The operations room, that's where it's all controlled from. Might be a fellow or two on the ground for eyes on, though."

"What is this?" I point to an odd sort of cupola atop the structure's middle.

"Oh, that's the headhouse. The whole place is called an elevator because this bucket conveyor pulls grain up from the pit here below the work floor to the headhouse. Then the head machine pumps it into the correct silo through these pipes. This elevator is a feed mill. It stores and mixes different grain types, so this machine—"

"Got it." The headhouse is roomy enough, noisy with working machinery, and sits a hundred and fifty feet above any prying eyes. That's where they'll have Chad. "Is this the only way up?" I point to a staircase at one end of the building.

"No. That's the fire escape. Here there is a little elevator." He points to a slim shaft leading up from the work floor. A system of catwalks runs from elevator to headhouse to fire escape, making two ways in, neither very conducive to a speedy extraction.

"Damn, that's where your karate kid must be." Earl says, finally lighting his J. "Only place that makes sense." Fingers of smoke accompany his words.

"You're right, Earl," I say.

"I am?" He coughs out a gray puff.

"It is the logical place." I point to little circles drawn around Sven's main sketch. "What are these?"

"Lights," Sven says. "The grounds are lit all night there."

Again, great attention to detail. Still, how do I get across a well-lit expanse of open ground that may or may not have men milling about, then get up top, get Chad, and get out without guns going off or someone calling in the cavalry? The night's bound to get rough, and while I don't mind trading blows with The Opposition, I'd hate to put some grain-slinging stiff in the hospital for simply being committed to his job. "God, I wish I knew how many are inside."

None of us have an answer for that particular problem. The faces of Jake's crew screw up with thought. Julia purses her lips and squints hard at the board. Holly looks ready to burst. I stare at the drawing, chewing over possibilities. Then Trevor, meekly huddled away all this time, steps up.

"What if the numbers inside don't really matter?"

"What do you mean?" I ask.

"I mean, what if we cleared the building?"

"Si," says Miguel, snapping his fingers. "We trip the fire alarm. When they all come out, we—"

"No," says Trevor. "Not the fire alarm. That would bring everyone out in a cluster, making it impossible to snatch Chad from the crowd and, if anything, give your Opposition guys a perfect opportunity to smuggle him onto the train. Plus, the alarm would bring police and fire, and as I understand it, we don't want that."

Damn if the kid isn't bright. I think I see where he's going. "We need to draw them out, but in a way that does not bring immediate outside attention."

"Exactly," he beams like a teacher having a breakthrough with a student. "I propose a protest."

Chapter Forty

ONLY Julia and I catch Trevor's drift. She smirks. I don't. I'm weighing the risks.

"A what?" snaps Holly.

Trevor pushes on with his scheme. "Hear me out. I know a dozen campus radicals that would jump at the chance to protest." He shrugs. "Some for the party piece, some for the cause—"

"Amen, brother." Earl raises his roach in salute.

"You mean a demonstration?" Holly kicks in. "You want to picket the elevator?"

"Yes. Between whom I can reach in the next hour and who they can get through the grapevine, I'll have a chanting mob clogging those train tracks by the ten o'clock news." He steps back and Julia wraps a proud arm around his waist.

"That's my guy," she says with a wink.

So much for the meek bundle of milquetoast. This is the charismatic leader from the BHU bookshop. This is a go-getter who's convinced me he can deliver everything he just promised. I can see why she likes him.

"Good," says Holly.

"Won't that still bring the cops in?" Pornstache asks with machine-gun speed, then sniffs. A familiar dusting of white clings to his lip ferret.

"Must you do that now?" Holly snaps at him.

"What?" shrugs Pornstache.

"Not right away," says Trevor. "Calling in the cops will be a last resort for these guys."

I nod. "Because calling the police to quell a demonstration brings reporters on scene."

Trevor's beaming, "And these corporate farm jack-holes don't want a student protest leading the local headlines. Stories like that get picked up by national. Do you know that for every acre sowed and harvested by a corporate facility, an equal number of—"

"Great," says Holly, before Trevor's tangential train gets rolling. "You set up the protest. That draws them out. How do we know there won't be any left inside."

"That shouldn't matter," I say. "Anyone coming from the office will be regular mill workers. Those in the headhouse will be Opposition. When they grabbed Chad, it was a team of six. Opposition runs squads of four to six, no more than six."

"How can you be sure?" asks Holly.

"I've spent the last six years battling these clowns. A full-blown protest on site when they're trying to move an Exceptional? That draws out three at least." I count off on my fingers. "Two to investigate and one to guard the elevator. Plus, I'll bet they've got someone in the operations room conducting overwatch. Leaving at most two up top." This just might work.

"Fine." Holly crosses her arms.

Sven stifles a rumbling burp. "Hrrp...um, ja, and if three are coming down, they'll be packed like kippers in dat little elevator."

"Even better." I clap Trevor on the back. "Good work, kid."

Julia gives him a proud squeeze. He goes stiff, then gently pulls away and swallows hard. "Thanks."

A bit of color leaves Julia's face at the cool reception. Topic for a later conversation.

"So the protest draws attention away from the work floor." Holly joins me at the chalk board. "We sneak over, take out the elevator guard, then it's up top, deal with the other two goons, and get Chad out lickety-split. Is that it?"

I nod. "Basically. Wait a minute. What do you mean *we*?"

She stands her ground without so much as a glance in my direction, every ounce of her adamant. "One, a second pair of eyes always helps. Something I learned counseling you after Vietnam. And two, there is no way in hell I'm not going in there to rescue someone closer to me than family."

Yes, were it Julia up there, nothing would stop me going in. But bad guys and bullets are nothing new to me. "Holly, this isn't sparring in a dojo. These guys are pros at what they do."

"And I had a full-contact record of eight wins, zero losses," she says, still eyeing the sketch. "I'm going in. End of discussion."

"You will need eyes and ears on the ground as well," says Jake. "Sven knows the layout. I can work the gear. He and I will take the operations room."

"Ja," says Sven, flexing his thick arms and cracking another beer. "I like dis plan."

"And my cousins, we can run interference with the police," chimes Miguel, licking his fingers. "Lead the gringos on a little chase."

220

"Hey man, and like the rest of us will be at ground zero sticking it to the man." Earl blows a greasy cloud and stubs out his roach.

"Yeah, we'll make sure nobody follows you up the elevator," Pornstache snaps with a grin, mustache clean.

"That's what I just said," Earl mutters.

Pornstache sniffs.

These fools don't understand the danger. "No. I go in alone."

Holly turns, one eyebrow raised as if daring me to come up with a better plan. Why does she do things like this? Things that make me love her and so damn aggravated with her at the same time.

Julia cracks a grin and shrugs. "Face it, Larry. You need us."

Hell no. I pull her away from the group, to huddle in mock privacy before a pin-up of Miss May 1984. "Absolutely not. You are staying here. What if they recognize you? They haven't stopped looking for the girl with perfect balance, you know. I've kept you one step ahead of them so far. I'm not about to deliver you to their front door."

"Look, you've done a bang-up job, moving me from place to place, resetting my life every few years." She grasps my arms tenderly. "But I'm not some doe-eyed teen anymore. My life has been for shit ever since junior high. Tonight I have a chance to stick it to these assholes and I'm taking it. Don't worry. I'll have Trevor to protect me." She winks.

Damn, I do love her spunk.

I run a hand through my hair. My throat's tight, mind racing to counter her argument—*their* arguments. No wisdom for me, Pop?

"Please, stay here. I can't lose you. I just... can't."

Flat fluorescent light reflects in her eyes. She's not my kid. I can't stop her outside taping her to a chair. And it hurts more than Bart's goliath punch. The tightness shifts down to my chest. "If I lost you..." My voice catches.

"You won't. Besides, any of them get past my agriculture activist knight errant over there, I'll hop up on a power line and sprint back home." She cracks that devilish smile.

I take one more look at the sketch. Rescue Chad. That is the task at hand. What's my best approach to achieve that? There is hell of a lot that can go wrong. A hell of a lot.

"Guys, you don't understand what you're—"

"Yes," snaps Holly. "We do."

The room awaits my answer. A stubborn, determined, unanimous, if somewhat chemically addled, room.

Here gathers my strike team, put together by the writers of *Caddyshack*.

"Kid," I say to Trevor. "Rally your troops."

Chapter Forty-One

THE soft glow of Rapid City Regional Airport sits low on the distant horizon. Each sweeping pass of its tower beacon turns tonight's persistent drizzle into rhythmic flashes of white and green stardust. A soggy night is a mixed blessing. It hides us as we move, but now I'm chilled and my shoes squeak with each slinking step. Still, glad to have my shoes.

A pair of Burlington Northern locomotives idle under a pool of light, small beneath the towering concrete structure of the Duddard grain elevator. An anaconda of train cars stretches out behind the engines, disappearing east into the inky black. Over the hissing diesel whine, a couple of men are shouting, perhaps an engineer bantering with one of the site workers.

Under a different streetlamp, parked away from the compact office building amongst a handful of other cars, squats a familiar cargo van beside a Buick matching Trevor's description. Bingo. Thank you, Miguel's cousins.

Taking in the whole complex, with haloed lights and little movement, the place seems far larger than what Sven's drawing led me to believe. The silos are not just tall—ten stories up capped by red flashing lights to ward off aircraft—but the whole thing has the footprint of a football field. Now I know how the first Mongol felt when he reined up to the Great Wall.

A dank cocktail of wet grass and car exhaust gives the night a deep sense of foreboding. Add to that the lingering memory of Bart's punch, and I'm not the least at ease with this plan. Or the risk I'm taking with Holly, Julia, and the rest.

My gut doesn't hurt. That's something, I guess.

A heavy drop falls from the open trunk lid of Holly's maroon Continental to splash cold on the back of my hand. The weak bulb within casts deep shadows across the assembled contents of my mysterious care package, hurriedly snatched from my hotel room in a race to get on site before Trevor starts his mini-riot.

"You bring one of those for me?" Holly asks, gesturing to what I'm tucking into a hip holster as she zips up a dark raincoat.

"No. Sorry," I say, checking that the safety is on. Having the familiar weight on my hip feels good but does nothing to calm my anxiety. "Holly, please let me go in alone. Stay outside with the others."

"Not happening." She steps on the bumper, double knotting her shoes.

I grab her arm harder than I mean to. "Damnit this isn't like one of your tournaments. There's no ref, no rules, no one to step in and stop things when shit goes sideways."

She doesn't pull away, just looks up at me, jaw set in brave defiance. But I can sense her fear. It matches my own.

"I know that," she says, swallowing hard. "But I'm going in anyway."

"If they start shooting..."

"I'll deal with it."

"Holly, you've never been in a firefight you don't know what—"

"Stop it." She jabs me in the chest. "You can't talk me out of this. So, unless you're going to try and wrestle me into the trunk for the night, I suggest you quit stalling and focus on the task at hand."

She chose the magic words. How did she know? How does she always know?

Holly shrugs off my grip and grabs a slim cloth bag from the trunk. From that she pulls a pair of *nunchaku*—foot long sticks connected by a short cord—and tucks them into her belt.

Okay, we're doing this.

"You bring any of those for me?" I ask with a smile.

She softly closes the trunk. "No. You wouldn't know what to do with them if I did."

Lights flash on the distant street. A convoy of cars pulls into the elevator parking lot. Doors open and in the scattered lights I can see two, three, four dozen or more bodies assemble, picket signs in their hands. I can make out Sven's big form amongst the group, but with the rain obscuring my vision I can't tell who else is who in the crowd.

The portable CB Jake lent me crackles in my jacket pocket.

"Protesters have arrived, man." Earl is mellow. A regular intake of herbals obviously generates a sense of ease despite what is about to go down.

My watch says 9:30. "Right on time."

I key the handset. "We go when the chanting starts. Radio silence until Jake and Sven are in position." For some reason I think of hushed signals sent beneath dark jungle canopies. Sergeant Ross barking at us about radio discipline.

Ross was a good man, bit of an asshole, but good. He didn't deserve to die the way he did.

Holly fidgets beside me, face pale, patting her pockets to make sure she hasn't forgotten anything.

I push memories aside and lay a hand on her arm. "We'll get him back." The words are as much for me as for her.

She flashes a weak smile. "Funny, I was just thinking who would water my plants if something bad happens."

"Nothing is going to happen to you." It's a hollow promise. We both know things are about to get dicey. Holly may not have crept through mud and blood along the Cambodian border or done any of the dark things that haunt my dreams—God I hope not—but if anyone here is up for this, it's her. I wish she were miles away, yet I need her beside me more than ever.

"I want to do this," she says, looking past me at the growing scene. "I have to do this. Christ. I have cement in my shoes and a stomach full of Pop-Rocks. Did you ever eat Pop-Rocks?"

My turn for a weak smile. "Yeah." Now's not the time for a Patton speech. I just wish there was something I could say, something quick to reassure her, to explain why I had to leave her six years ago, something to explain how I feel about her at this very moment. All I come up with is, "It's okay to be scared."

Turns out, it was the right thing to say.

Holly's fidgeting stops. Her arms rest at her sides. A rivulet of collected drizzle runs down her sleeve to drip from the knuckles of her clenched fist. She fixes me with a stare, and I see the steel in her.

EXCEPTIONALS

"I'm not scared for me," she says.

Neither am I. Still, Pop-Rocks.

Chapter Forty-Two

ACROSS the field the protest kicks in. Placarded signs pump up and down under the yard lights. Muffled chants drift across the open space between us and them. Without another word Holly and I slip from behind her car.

The prairie grass is soft and yielding, muffling our sloppy steps, reassuring me that we approached in secret. Not that anyone at the elevator could hear us over the combined noise of idling train and chanting mob. Rain bent grass brushes against our legs and soaks my pants from ankle to shin. Holly stays right beside me, crouched low.

We reach the train tracks and slip into the shadow of a big grain car. The rumble of diesel engines thrums in my chest and it's strangely reassuring.

Trevor and Julia have the crowd shouting, "Sound the horn against Big Corn!" I peek around the corner and see a crowd of teens and twenty-somethings, some in ponchos or raincoats others in BHU sweatshirts. One in a spangly denim jacket pumps a sign up and down that reads, "Corporate farms kill America," black letters starting to bleed down the damp poster board. Mingled in with them I catch Earl in tie-dye and Pornstache wearing green track shorts and a black muscle shirt that highlights his noodle arms.

I signal Holly and we crawl beneath the train car to check the work floor. It's dark and I can't see anything past the vast open bay doors. Smells of grease and soot punctuate the air.

EXCEPTIONALS

There's movement beyond the crowd. Three men in hard hats and canvas jackets arrive, trying to break up the protest. They might as well be pebbles trying to stop a river. The group circles and chants around them.

That's when a bar of light cuts into the work floor darkness. It's the door opening on that little elevator leading to the head house. Two silhouettes step out and one remains. Holly sees it too and gives me a nudge, "You were right."

I incline my head at her. The men wear jackets and hardhats like the three that came from the office. But the newcomers don't quite fit the working-class mold. Their jackets aren't frayed and stained. Their faces are clean-shaven and freshly scrubbed. Their eyes aren't focused on the crowd, but dart to the blind spots and check the corners. I ease Holly further back in the train's shadow.

Part of me held out hope that Bart would come check things personally. Get him out of the way while we slipped in to get Chad. No such luck. None of these guys throw a shadow like a lumbering grizzly. What I want to hear now is Jake on the radio telling me he has secured operations. If we move before that, some Opposition asshole will be feeding Rockentanski our every move.

The crowd keeps milling and chanting. The radio is silent. The moment stretches painfully on, but I tell anxiety to take a back seat.

Then Julia appears.

Damn it all, she's right there in the mix. Barking at the three workers. Doesn't she see the two guys moving in from her right? After all this time, hasn't she learned to blend in, to disappear into the background? Her adopted blue-tipped look should have clued me that my girl no longer gave a fig about hiding.

Then, as she so often has, Julia proves herself. She turns back into the milling crowd with casual grace as if she were simply taking her place in line and now it is the next protester's turn to step up.

Thank God.

Holly's kept her eyes on the elevator while I was distracted. "There is one guard to the left of the elevator door," she whispers. "Hard to see him now that it's closed, but he's there."

I strain to catch an outline or movement, but I've been staring at the lit protesters too long and my eyes don't adjust that quick. A hiss on the CB sends a jolt through me. I crank down the volume and press the speaker to my ear.

"Operations...secured." Jake sounds winded.

"Roger," I answer quiet as I can. "Are there cameras? Do you have a visual of the work floor or head house? Over."

Pornstache jumps in, "Was there a fight? Did Sven thump the guy?"

"Shut up, Russell." Jake beats me to the mic.

"Ja, I thumped both of them." Sven chimes in.

"Quiet on the line!" I hiss. Both of them? That evened the numbers even more. I wait three heartbeats then click the handset again, "Jake, what do you see?"

"Six monitors. Parking lot clear. Three angles of the yard show the crowd. I see five hardhats out there. I have a shot of an empty room with lots of pipes along the walls and ceiling. Something strange, though." The CB goes quiet. Holly gives me a questioning look. I gesture for her to keep her eyes out there, not on me.

"What's strange?" I ask.

Jake clicks back on. "Sven says that room is the head house, but nobody's up there."

Shit. That has to be the place. The office doesn't make sense. The three guys from the elevator are not regular joes. What is it? What did I overlook? "Jake. Does the camera show the whole room or just part?"

"Not the whole room. I'm seeing a corner and an exit door."

Holly murmurs, "Could be they've just hidden him out of view of the camera. Simple as that."

Simple as that. At this point, I'm out of options. "Miguel, you there?"

A soft radio squelch then a sudden burst of tinny music. Anne Murray? "*Si*, I am here."

I bury the radio against my chest.

"Damn it, Miguel. You trying to get us caught?" I hiss.

Holly goes pale and jerks out her nunchucks.

When he comes back on at least two other voices are muttering something untoward in the background. "Sorry, *señor*, my cousin, he just put in a twenty-inch Rockford Fosgate."

"We are set. Are you ready?"

From what Miguel told us, he has *a lot* of cousins. Between them, they have about a dozen vintage muscle cars all of which may or may not be legally registered and all of which have undergone a certain level of, as Miguel calls it *mejora*. He said it with a sly smile so I don't doubt he and his family are about to lead the RCPD on a merry chase, keeping the boys in funny white Volvos away from Trevor's diversion.

The protest chant is now, "Just say no to corporate grow!" The three workers from the office have been jostled away from the tracks, crowd squarely between us and them. The two goons from the elevator stalk just outside the light like wolves prowling a campfire. Any minute they'll turn back to report what's going on to the boss up top—to Bart Rockentanski. Always thought the guy a lummox, guess he's been promoted anyway.

Holly draws her knee up under her, ready to sprint for that elevator on my signal.

Miguel clicks back on. "We are ready."

Chapter Forty-Three

THE Opposition goons turn and walk back to the elevator.

"Here we go," I snap into the mic and slip quickly from the train's shadow into the lamplit drizzle.

Holly jumps up beside me, but I put a calming hand on her wrist. "You remember what to do?"

The muscles in her neck work as she swallows hard. "Are you sure this will work?"

"You're the one with the doctorate."

"Yeah, but not in electronics."

I give her a weak smile. "I have firsthand experience with the business end of these things. It'll work."

My heart pounds as we follow the pair into the shadow of the work floor, I keep one eye closed. It's an old army trick to avoid night blindness in the quick change from light to dark.

One of the goons mutters, "Bunch of college kids angry about corn." It's one of the two with his back to us, the one to our left.

A low voice from the shadows replies, "No sign of what's-his-name from the tournament?"

"Na. The big man is just being paranoid." This from number three, thin, with a nasally southeast twang.

The one in the shadows slides open the cage door to the elevator. "You know he hates being called that."

Nasal Twang responds, "Don't matter to me. He ain't—hey, what're you doing?"

Holly strides into the beam of light cast from the open elevator. She lays on her sweetest face and saunters right up to the trio.

Shadows guy steps up between his compadres. "Lady this is a secure area. Go on back to your little protest."

They're shoulder to shoulder, blocking the elevator.

"That's alright," Holly says, voice like honey. "Now, you hold this." She hands the guy on the left the knobby, needled end of a thin wire. "And you hold this." She does likewise to the guy on the right. The wires trail past her into the dark.

"Lady," says the middle guy in his low voice, "I don't know what—"

"Okay!" Holly shouts over her shoulder.

I flip the switch on a care package goodie and fifty thousand volts lance out of one TASER node, passing through the twitching, gibbering, conjoined bodies of the three goons, to the other node, completing the circuit. Electronics. Or is it physics? I keep the button depressed for two whole seconds then let the trio tumble to the floor in a moaning mass of tan canvas and white Duddard Feed and Seed hardhats.

I step into the light. Holly's chest is heaving hard.

"You did great," I say. Walking up to the pile and delivering a knockout punch between the eyes of one guy not as dazed as his pals. I scan the three men's faces and mutter a soft curse. One is the weasel-faced coach from the tournament. The other two were the paramedics.

Holly's lips quiver. Sweat beads on her forehead. Her hands are shaking. I start to reach for her, but on seeing me she sucks in a deep breath, sets her jaw, and flexes her hands. "It's fine. I...I just didn't expect... I'm fine."

I start going to work on the three, binding lips and limbs with BHU janitorial-grade duct tape.

"Will they be..." Holly struggles to keep her voice even.

I pause in gagging the skinny one and give Holly a reassuring smile. "These guys will live. They'll be sore for a few days, but they'll live." They'll also have unsteady vision and one heck of a hangover. I should know.

Holly blinks, then gives a short nod.

"Now, you want to help me?" I hand her the roll of tape.

A minute later the goons are trussed up like pigs at a luau. They squirm a bit, but the tape holds. A quick frisk finds FBI badges and ID—none I recognize—plus loaded, standard issue S&W model thirteens.

I offer Holly one. "Here you go."

She waves it away. "I was kidding. I hate those things."

"Has nothing to do with love or hate. Has to do with coming out alive." I proffer the pistol again.

She shakes her head once more.

Fine. I empty the cylinder of each gun into the grated feed floor then toss the weapons atop our shed raincoats. Holly and I tug on a couple canvas jackets and matching hardhats these guys no longer have need of.

We step into the elevator and shut the gate.

"Going up," Holly says, a sense of adventure back in her eyes. She pushes the button and the elevator jerks and clanks and starts trundling upward.

I radio Earl and Pornstache. "Three for the dumpster."

The elevator is slow and choked by a dry mix of grain dust and old dirt. It's what I smelled on Rockentanski. This is the place. Chad is up there, and I'm mounting a rescue alongside the only woman I've ever been in love with—the woman I abandoned a week before our wedding because a girl who can't fall down needed me to keep her safe. It's a decision I've hashed over every day since. But I wouldn't change it.

Holly's citrusy sweetness lingers, floating beside me. Beneath the feed-and-seed aroma and the dank weather, I smell her. Maybe it's the memory of what we once were, or wishful thinking, but her presence, even now amid this craziness, both calms me and puts a hitch in my heartbeat.

She clicks the ends of her *nunchaku* together, staring at the ceiling and moving her lips slowly, as if wishing the top floor to arrive, or offering a last-minute prayer.

I reach out and take her free hand in mine. "Thank you."

She doesn't return my grip, nor does she look at me. She doesn't pull away, either. I can see her processing chaotic emotions. I can empathize.

She inhales and squeezes my hand. "It was your plan. I'm just happy I didn't get zapped, too."

That's not what I mean. I turn to her, bumping shoulders in the cramped elevator, "I mean, thank you for being here. For insisting. For being so great. For," I struggle for a solid kicker but only manage, "everything."

"Thank me when Chad's safe." Holly clears her throat then laces her fingers in mine. "But you're welcome."

We stand there for a couple breaths—the elevator motor screeching, the cage rattling, the air humming around us.

Her profile is the same one I saw a lifetime ago, me waking from sweat-ridden nightmares of screaming men and gunfire and death everywhere, her caressing my forehead and telling me it will be okay. The same one I gazed at as she slept the deep, sound sleep she always slept after we made love. The same one I've missed for six years.

She meets my gaze, "What are you staring at?"

The smart thing would be to turn aside. Instead, I keep staring and croak out, "You."

She lowers her eyes. I don't know if she's frustrated or playing shy. But she's still holding my hand.

"Holly, when this is over, tonight, I mean...when things calm down..."

She squeezes my fingers hard and when she looks at me again, there are tears. There, too is something I hadn't seen this whole week—deep, deep, longing.

"Shut up," she whispers, then sniffs and straightens with a readying breath. She gestures with her chucks at the ceiling. "Chad first. Then we'll talk." With that she turns from me to the cage gate and rolls her neck to get loose.

I swallow and follow suit, patting hips and pockets, reassured by the presence of a few more care package presents.

Chapter Forty-Four

THE elevator comes to a grinding, lurching stop. Beyond the gate looms the charcoal sky, an underbelly of oppressive clouds lit by distant, downtown lights. On a starry night, under different circumstances, this could make a romantic moment. Tonight, I shove thoughts of romance to the back of my overstuffed sock drawer of priorities. With jacket collars up and hardhats pulled low, we yank aside the gate and step onto a wet, narrow catwalk. Weak rain patters on my plastic hat. Holly and I take the deliberate, weary pace of guards returning from a pointless errand.

From ground level, this grain elevator looked big. Atop it, with only sky above and a long plummet to the train tracks below, I get a stomach-squeezing sense of our true height. I fight down the vertigo and focus on getting the champ before skinning it out of here.

The headhouse sits fifty yards away atop the center of the structure. Its door stands open. Silhouetted in the frame is a single figure, legs spread, arms crossed at the chest. The orange glow of a lit cigarette moves from mid-body to the head and back, followed by a puff of smoke that disappears on a fitful wind.

The figure is not Bart Rockentanski. Three goons down below. Two in Operations. Bart makes six. They've never worked teams bigger than six. They never did before now. Meaning my one real advantage—knowing how they operate—is completely gone. Meaning the guy in front of us is...

"Shit." I'd held to a slim, vain hope that Simpson was just some ringer sent to get the job done at the tournament then cut loose.

Nope.

Above us, high on a pole, a red aviation beacon pulses. It's supposed to warn off low-flying aircraft. What it does now is give Simpson the face of a devil on a date while the headhouse backlight frames him the way his fight gear did. There stands one bad guy.

"What is it?" Holly whispers. She doesn't break stride. Luckily, the forty yards left to go will keep us from being heard.

"It's Simpson." My right hand itches for my holster. I have the drop on him. We look like his own guys, not a covert midnight assault. But I dare not shoot unless I want Julia's little soiree downstairs to turn from chanting rally to panicked anarchy at the sound of gunfire. Instead, I take comfort at having good company and the advantage of surprise.

"Great." Holly's voice is matter of fact. She shoulders past me, head bent low like she's merely in a hurry to get out of the wet. She quickens her stride with each step.

"What are you doing?" I say, jaw clenched, scar itching as I hunch over to remain inconspicuous. None of the now duct-taped elevator crew were close to six-foot four.

"He leads with his left," she says over her shoulder, both hands behind her, gripping the wooden chucks.

And here we go.

The catwalk is too narrow to run side-by-side. I move to get past her, but she blocks my way. We're lined up and

I'm trapped at the back, unable to lend a hand unless Holly drops to the floor.

"Wait." My breathy whisper is wasted on her.

Simpson lets out another waft of smoke and steps forward, out of the doorway, the light of the city highlighting his cruel face. "What's the story, Coop?" His voice is a contradiction to his dark appearance. It's light, almost boyish.

I cough, but Holly says nothing. Nor does she alter her powerful strides, gaining momentum as she closes on her target.

"Cooper," he says. "What's the hubbub?"

I admit, Holly attacks the way I would have coached her. She doesn't yell, doesn't look up, doesn't do anything to give away her intent. She closes to striking distance and lashes out, swinging her *nunchaku* with lightning speed at Simpson's exposed temple.

But Simpson either sensed something was off or his reactions, too, verge on the exceptional. He jerks his head back and the solid oak rod glances from his forehead with a soft *tok*. Spinning with the blow he twists into a tense crouch and flicks his lit cigarette at Holly's face.

She ducks aside and the orange firefly tumbles straight at me. On instinct I catch it like a little league shortstop.

"Ah!" I yelp and shake the stinging butt from my hand.

Holly pivots, bringing the chucks around to make a second cat-quick strike. I lean away to avoid her backswing. Simpson back rolls and pops up into a fighting stance, suit coat off, now gripped in both hands and twisted into a stout cord. A dark line shows against his skin, running down his cheek. Holly's opening blow left a gash.

Holly shouts, a guttural cry from deep inside. A true, resonant spirit yell.

The red beacon light pulses again, and Simpson's wicked grin flashes scarlet.

Holly lunges, chucks spinning. She opens with a feint to lift his guard. He buys it and she sweeps low to hobble his leg.

Simpson shifts stance and the weapon whistles by. He counters with a tree-felling roundhouse kick.

Holly ducks.

There's my opening. I throw an overhand right at the bastard, but Holly's firm rump slams into me mid-thigh. I wobble back, missing by a mile.

Holly's hat tumbles off in the fracas. She pivots to square with Simpson again, her ponytail whipping free.

His eyes narrow in recognition. That grin morphs from villainous to downright wicked. "The coach," he says, all boyishness gone. "This should be fun."

In her place, I'd have fired back a retort, caught my breath, and reassessed tactics. But Holly wastes no time, going straight for the kill. Her chucks whirl, flicking out at head, wrists, and knees.

Simpson shifts, blocking blows with his coat, slipping his legs out of the way.

If she drives him into the open space of the headhouse, I can join in the fight. Standing here I'm one step beyond useless. It hits me that this must be how she felt seeing Chad go down after Simpson's cheap shot.

There's another *tok* and Simpson shakes his left hand with a grimace.

Holly presses forward.

He lunges right at her, forcing her swing to overextend. The *nunchaku* tangles with Simpson's twisted coat. Giving a yank and a yell of his own, he rips Holly's weapon from her grip.

Holly doesn't panic. She leaps, slamming her knee beneath his ribs.

Simpson grunts but catches her leg. In a flash he's wound the coat about her thigh, twists, pivots, and smashes her into the catwalk's metal railing.

Holly's shout of pain ignites a flame of rage inside that's been waiting years to burn hot.

My turn, cocksucker.

Chapter Forty-Five

I snatch up Holly's discarded hardhat and hurl it at Simpson. It connects with the side of his head in a hollow plastic crack. Delightful.

He lets go his coat and stumbles backward, into the headhouse, right where I want him to go.

Ah, room to maneuver.

Simpson keeps his feet. He blinks away my opening blow and sizes me up with a grin. The streak of blood down his face making him even more sinister.

"I take it you're Lawson. They warned me about you. Bigger than I figured."

I take off my hardhat and grin right back.

Simpson bounces light on his toes. "You know what they say. The bigger they are, yada yada yada."

He fires a one-two combo with machine gun speed.

I slip the jab and bring up my left to shield the cross. My left holds the hardhat.

Hollow plastic crack.

He grimaces, shaking out his hand. "You wanna fight that way? Fine."

No more talk.

My kick is quick and low—a shot at my favorite target, just above the knee.

He checks it and counters with a blitz of chops, punches, and elbows.

I cover up, bobbing and weaving. His blows glance off. But an uppercut sneaks through and snaps my head back. I feel the force but not the pain.

We trade more blows. The bastard fights like me, going for every opening, looking to end the fight fast.

He catches my wrist and pivots lightning quick—a move to break the joint and dump me on my ass in one go.

I counter by spinning inside his momentum, slipping from his lock, and getting a grip of my own. Wrenching on his arm, I bend him over by bringing my weight to bear with a thrust of my forearm just above the back of his elbow. It's a textbook armbar.

Apparently, Simpson read that book. He twists and rolls out of my hold, somehow catching me with a shot to the jewels as he does. That pain I feel.

Should have taken a lesson from Bart and worn a cup.

Simpson flexes his arm. He's still grinning. "You'll have to do better than that. The boss said you were good. So far, I don't see—*urgh*!"

The prick forgot about Holly. With his back to the door, she'd snuck up behind him, jerked his jacket over his throat, and with a twisting two-handed heave she turned her ass to the bastard, yanking him onto her back like a farmer hoisting a sack of potatoes.

She growls, teeth clenched.

He tears at the noose, eyes bulging, face red, body stretched out like a man on the rack.

She jerks harder, lifting him off his feet.

He thrashes, kicks.

Stepping up I end his struggle with a quick, thrusting punch to his solar plexus.

He stops kicking, jaw chewing air he can't suck in. A second later his eyes roll up and he goes limp.

She doesn't let go.

"Holly."

Spit froths from her mouth.

"Holly, you can put him down."

Her nostrils flare. Her eyes are red-rimmed and wet with rage. They meet mine.

"Put him down before you kill him."

Her grip loosens but she's still got Simpson propped up.

I put a hand on her shoulder. "You don't want this. Trust me. Please. Let him go."

"Fine," she growls. She drops Simpson like, well, like a sack of potatoes. He collapses in a heap behind her. He's not moving, but he is breathing, unconsciousness resetting his diaphragm. "Tie that prick up. I'm going to find Chad."

She pushes past me further into the head house. This grim, vicious, kick-ass side of her is something I never saw in the Holly I wanted to marry. Never in our time dating. Never in our year as patient and therapist. Never. It's scary.

I kinda like it.

Now, task at hand. I rifle Simpson's pockets and pat him down—no holster, no gun, no badge, just a pack of Winston's and a gold Zippo. He's not dressed in a Fed's cheap suit, either. His black-on-black ensemble is tailored. My hired thug theory looks better and better. The Opposition is running with an entirely new playbook. The consequences of that will wait for later consideration. I hogtie Simpson with his belt and coat, gag him with a sock, then drag him to an out of the way corner.

"Over here!" Holly's shout rings with relief.

I sprint for her.

The headhouse room is a big, airy rectangle. Between me and the far end, foot-wide pipes run along the walls and across the high ceiling to meet at a cylindrical drum in the center almost as tall as the room and wide as a carnival dunk tank. I run past it to Holly.

She's found Chad.

On the floor, partially hidden by a pipe, two bound, bare feet jut out. No sign of anyone else.

The kid sits propped against the wall, restrained much like the three goons we left on the work floor. He's shivering. He wears his karate pants, but his *gi* top is gone, his thin t-shirt not doing much to shield him from the cool night air. An angry bruise rests just above his collarbone. Other than that, he doesn't look bad. Holly peels the tape from his mouth while I go to work on freeing his legs.

Holly's voice cracks. "It's okay. Everything's going to be okay. We'll get you out of here."

The kid gasps and shakes his head. He tries to reply but all that comes out is an angry croak.

I tug free the ankle tape.

Chad winces.

"Sorry, kid." I start on his wrists and the band pinning his elbows.

Holly puts a gentle finger on his throat. "Don't talk. Let's just get you to a doctor."

The last bit of tape comes free from his wrists and, instead of giving either of us a grateful hug or mouthing, "thank you," Chad shoves up to his feet.

Applause—lazy, amused, mocking applause from a single set of hands—echoes off the pipes, concrete, and steel of the head house.

I spin, hand at my holster.

Right then Jake's voice crackles on the radio. "What's happening up there? The cameras lost you when you ran past the big head machine."

I keep my grip on the gunmetal care package surprise at my hip, eyes not leaving who just walked into the room, and free the radio with my other hand.

"Not now." I switch off the power button.

Chad tenses. Holly, too.

I curse.

Strolling casually in through the near door, gun in hand and dwarfed by the trailing colossus of Bart Rockentanski, is Jimmy the goddamn Fist.

Chapter Forty-Six

"I thought you would come up the fire escape," the little killer says with a click of his tongue.

Still tweaks me sideways, that deep baritone from that small frame.

He turns and hands a crisp twenty to his fellow asshole. "My mistake."

Bart Rockentanski cracks a thin crooked smile, carefully folds the bill, and slips it into a chest pocket. I notice his right wrist wrapped in athletic tape. He's dressed in denim overalls, heavy boots, and a checkered shirt stretched tight across his barrel chest. Guess they don't make one of those canvas jackets in rhino size.

Jimmy wears a gray suit and tie, looking every bit the federal investigator, save for the glossy cane he leans on. Warms my heart to see that barkeep's beanbag round did some long-term damage. Amputation would have been preferable. Beggars can't be choosers. But suit and cane are not my focus, it's the small caliber revolver in his other hand. The gun is not trained on anyone specific; he just has it out, knowing he's got the drop on us.

"Hands," he says.

I stand, letting go the pistol holstered at my back and lift my hands. Holly and Chad follow suit to stand in line beside me.

"When Bart told me about you back Milwaukee, I knew it wasn't coincidence. Today he tussles with you again.

Patterns, Lawson. What did the FBI teach you about patterns?"

"Don't mix plaids and stripes?" If I spring away, I can draw Jimmy's fire, give Holly and Chad a chance to sprint for the far door.

"You always were a funny one." Jimmy hefts his pistol and gestures down the room with his cane. "Go see to Simpson."

Bart glowers my way then stomps off past the head machine.

That puts barriers between both exits. So much for making a getaway.

Holly clears her throat, whispering none-too-softly, "Who's the midget?"

I suck air through my teeth, praying I can shove her and Chad aside before Jimmy starts firing. In my Bureau days I saw him take a man out at the knees after the idiot let the M-word slip in office conversation.

Jimmy doesn't shoot. "Miss," he says, "I apologize. Proper introductions are not on the evening's agenda and Lawson here really should know better than to bring a civilian along."

"His name is Special Agent in Charge James Morgenstern Hopwyth the Third," I say, trying to keep the focus of animosity on me. "We call him Jimmy."

Holly raises an incredulous eyebrow. "We?"

I give a subtle, not-now head shake. Grunts come from Simpson's far corner as Bart undoes my handiwork.

Jimmy continues, "I take it you are part of this bumbling effort Congress has been playing at? That fits. Some of those files did have an odd, double-L notation." Jimmy shuffles and shifts his weight. "Those must be the ones you were supposed to protect. Funny. You were nowhere to be found when we processed one Marcus Beane."

Hope that damn knee hurts, Jimmy. Hope it hurts all damn day.

"He did put up a fight. Though, in the end, we always get our man." He smirks at his own pun.

Time to find an angle. "Something I could never figure, Jimmy. Why you, of all people, would take to hunting down those that don't fit the mold."

He taps his cane. "Oh, those like Mr. Beane and young Mr. Ellis are cast from an entirely different mold altogether. They are *more* than human. Can you not see that for someone like me, who has spent his life being treated as *less*...it makes perfect sense? You call them, 'Exceptionals.'" He shakes his head. "So misguided. People like you never see the bigger picture."

"People like me don't kidnap and kill."

Jimmy tilts his head at me. "We both know that's not true."

Sins of the past. No time to dwell on them now.

Two grumbling voices from the far corner. Simpson's awake.

Great.

I can feel Chad and Holly tense as the two men rejoin Jimmy. Simpson groans and blinks like a man waking after an all-day bender. He rubs his throat.

"Is it sore?" croaks Chad.

Simpson flips the kid the bird as he stops behind Jimmy.

Chad chuckles like a strangled toad.

Jimmy says, "The karate champ comes with us. His particular ability demands study. Stimulus response testing, that sort of thing." He gestures at Holly and me with his pistol. "You two, on your knees, hands on your heads."

Between Holly and me Chad shuffles his feet, arms dipping a bit. He's brought his right foot back—a tight boxer's stance. Shit. He better not be planning something.

Simpson watches him, still rubbing at his throat, eyes narrowed.

Bart sees it, too.

Crap. I need their focus on me.

I spit out, "You're a prick, Jimmy." Nice. Very creative.

"Maybe so," he says. "But I have the gun."

"You shoot us, and everyone down below hears it. This room is an echo chamber."

The chants of Trevor's protest ring faint but clear up here. Stalling is my only option. Stall until an opportune moment lets me get the drop on one of them. Stall and hope Holly and Chad know enough to run when I move.

"Oh, come now," Jimmy says with disappointment, "there are ways around that. Look where we are." He gestures at the head machine. On the wall beside it sits a control panel with various knobs and gauges including a big green 'ON' button and red 'OFF' one. "Now then, get on your knees."

Bart moves to close the near door. Simpson stays put, giving Chad an expectant leer over Jimmy's head.

I'm a split-second from making a gunslinger quick draw when Holly barks, "I don't think so."

Chapter Forty-Seven

WE stop.

All of us.

Bart stands like a gorilla struck on the head, hand reaching for the doorknob. Simpson's eyebrows shoot up. Even Jimmy tips his gun aside in shock.

Me? I blow this open and obvious chance to pull my forty-five-caliber surprise from its holster. I'm as stunned as the rest.

Holly steps forward, pointing at Jimmy with her chucks. "If you're going to shoot, shoot. We're not about to make it easy for you."

Holly, I love you, but what the hell are you doing?

Jimmy, quick to recover, says, "Miss, I do not know you. I do not like you. And I do not need you." He clicks back his pistol's hammer and aims at her center mass.

"No!" roars up from my throat. I yank out the modified Colt Model 1911, aiming for the little bastard about to put a hole in my one true love.

Before I pull my weapon, before I crouch into a shooter's stance, before Jimmy can even squeeze off a round, Chad moves. He throws himself to the ground, catching Holly by the collar as he goes, jerking her down with him.

Jimmy's pistol gives a sharp *kak*. The round misses, ricocheting off pipes behind us with a *ping*.

My Colt is not so quiet. The report is deep, concussive, and eardrum-rattling, bouncing around all this metal and concrete. I miss Jimmy, my shot going high. It would have taken Simpson in the ribs, had he not dived aside when I drew.

"Go!" I shout, shoving Holly and Chad at the room's only cover: the massive canister of the head machine. I blast two more shots at our assailants as we scuttle away. Both miss.

Small *kak-kak* gunshots. Dust kicks up at our feet.

We dive behind the head machine as a thunderous *BOOM* joins the cacophony.

I glance to see a quarter-sized hole in the cylinder's metal skin.

Another *BOOM*. Bart wields a semi-auto twice as big as my Colt.

BOOM! BOOM!

Kak-kak.

"Larry!" screams Holly. "What do we do? What do we do?" Her eyes are wide. Her face pale.

Has she been shot? No. There's no blood.

She's not hurt, she's scared. Chad is curled into a ball beside her, hands pressed to his ears, nostrils flaring with each short, panicked breath.

These two know fighting. They've never known gunfighting.

I don't care how you psyche yourself up, when the bullets fly and the air vibrates and the clamor and chaos have your mind screaming to run away, all your bravado means shit. I should know. I pissed myself that first day in 'Nam. What matters is the next moment.

"Stay down," I command, then reach for the radio. I need Jake's eyes to get us out of here. But the walkie is gone. I glance around and see it, broken in two parts, ten feet away. It must have popped from my belt in our dive for cover.

So much for the cavalry.

It is a straight shot back to the entrance, but it's open ground. Reaching the skinny catwalk beyond would expose our fleeing asses. No thanks.

I slip to the far side of the cylinder and peer around (sticking my head out the same place the enemy last saw it is a sure ticket to a bullet in the brain). Bart and Jimmy have backed behind their doorjamb for cover. One shoots high, the other low. No sign of Simpson.

I squeeze off three shots before they see me. Cement dust puffs around the entry and both men duck away. That gives me an idea.

I drop the near-spent magazine from the pistol's receiver and slap in the full, eight-round spare my mystery benefactor included in that gift box. The two goons seize this opening to blast away. Jimmy's fire pings with little effect. But a few of Bart's cannon balls punch through our steel shield just over my head.

"Chad!" I yank the kid's hand from his ear. "When I fire, you run."

The kid's face is blank, mouth open in terrified confusion.

I tighten my grip, squeezing his arm hard as I can.

The pain trick works. His eyes come suddenly into focus. He winces and pulls away.

I say, "Run when I shoot. Don't stop until you're in the little elevator. Got it?"

He swallows hard and nods.

"Wait there." I check on Holly. She's gone fetal, but she heard the plan. She nods.

One at a time. I'll get them out of here one at a time.

The goons are checking their fire now, not shooting blindly.

Dust and grain showers around us from the holes punched in the head machine.

Now or never. I thump Chad on the shoulder then leap into the open floor beyond the drum. My move takes Bart and Jimmy unaware. I aim and fire at my own pace. Each round slams into the doorframe, spraying cinder block chips and forcing those boys to stay hidden.

Chad springs for the open exit.

I keep firing until he's out then duck back to semi-safety, slamming against Holly as Bart's heavy fire takes chunks out of the floor at my feet.

Holly snatches me, fingers burying into my coat like talons.

I try to pry her free, but her grip is undeniable.

She stares into my face, tendons bulging as she clamps her jaw shut with adrenaline-powered conviction. Her lips part in a trembling grimace, "Don't...leave me...again," she commands, shaking me as she does.

I search her eyes. She searches mine. I put my hand over hers, trying to be tender despite the terror.

I shout over the noise. "It's okay. *We* are going to be okay."

Her death grip loosens and she takes my hand like she did in the elevator and with the force of a sucker punch, she kisses me.

It's not a chaste, good-luck kiss, but a full-on-the-lips, impassioned smacker that, for one brief moment, shuts out the riot of the room, of our situation, of the world, and lets in only the rapture of two beings connecting.

I want it to last more than anything.

Then another bullet hole blasts open right between us. I choke on a puff of grain dust and reality comes crashing back.

"Later," I bark, mouth dry despite lips wet with Holly. "We need to go."

She nods and gives me a squeeze, eyes focused and clear. "When you shoot, I run."

I scoop up the discarded magazine with its pair of remaining rounds and set myself for a quick magazine exchange. With a hard breath I mouth a countdown to Holly—three, two, one...

"Now!"

My shots are clustered in pairs. Holly races for the door as blast three and four ring out. Thin steel clatters on the cement when my empty magazine drops and I slap in the spare.

Bart peeks around the doorjamb. He levels his hand-cannon at me. Jimmy stays hidden.

I thumb down the stop and the Colt's slide slaps forward. Time for an all-out charge.

I fire, and fire again.

Bart fires, and fires again.

A white-hot pain lances up my forearm. My ears ring with the thunder of the high-caliber blasts.

Bart shouts, "Son-of-a-bitch" in mad, clipped staccato.

EXCEPTIONALS

I'm two strides from their doorway redoubt and try to squeeze off another shot, but my rounds are spent.

The room goes quiet save for Bart's curses, my halting skid on the concrete, and the hiss of grain pouring from pipes well vented by bullets. The shooting has stopped. And I can feel wetness pooling in the sleeve of my coat. A graze, but a long one.

I flex my hand and wrist. Everything still works.

The wall and floor before me are pitted from forty-five caliber slugs keeping Opposition heads down. Too bad they didn't knock any Opposition heads off.

"Ah, shame." Jimmy chides as he steps from behind cover, little pistol trained a bit too low on me to be sporting. "Count your shots, Lawson. You always want one in the chamber. Guess you forgot that rule."

I can twist and take it in the hip. There are worse places to get shot. After that, who knows what these two will do to me.

Holly's safe. And Chad is safe. That's what matters.

From beyond Holly and Chad's exit comes grunting, a woman's shout, and a throaty male yell.

I look over my shoulder. With curses and a cloud of kicked-up grain dust, Holly and Chad tumble back into the room. Simpson strides in after them, wet and exceptionally eager.

"You fucks are dead," Simpson says in that slithery light voice. "I'm gonna beat the living—*Umf*!"

Simpson gets knocked sprawling by a shove in the back from strong, gymnast arms in an olive drab field jacket. The room's pale fluorescent light makes her spiked hair shine sapphire platinum against the night sky beyond the door.

"I thought this was supposed to be a rescue," she exclaims, an odd smile on her face.

My mind sprawls like Simpson, tripping over how that bastard got around us, only to flail in horror on the fact that Julia just joined the fight.

Chapter Forty-Eight

"Oh, shit."

"That about says it," utters Jimmy, eyes wide. The little prick is too good at his job. "Julia Rourke. Well, I'll be..."

"An asshole," I quip to get his attention back on me.

It works. His lip twitches as he looks me in the eye, aims his pistol at my crotch, and squeezes the trigger.

I flinch.

Nothing. No shot. No *kak*, just the hollow metallic click of the gun's hammer striking a spent cartridge.

"What in the?" Jimmy checks his weapon.

"Yep. That about says it." I kick Jimmy square in the chest, launching him ass-over-teakettle back where he popped from.

He bounces off the great thigh of Bart Rockentanski lumbering into the room.

'Oh shit' has graduated to 'oh fuck.'

The slide is back on Bart's pistol. Blood drips from his arm, same as mine. Only my shot caught the meat of his bicep. Dirt streaks his face, eyes bloodshot from sprayed concrete dust. Jimmy racquetballing off his leg doesn't faze him in the least. He steps into the room, a juggernaut of destruction.

Bart is pissed off.

Behind me, Holly and Chad are on their feet. Simpson, too, chuckling.

Outside, continued crowd chants and faint but distinct police sirens. I pray Miguel and his street savvy cousins have them two minutes out.

"C'mon, Larry... We gotta go." Julia's voice is steady.

"I know, I know," I say, mind racing on how to get the hell out of here. We have the numbers, but Bart's a wall, Simpson is a wildcat, and I'm sure Jimmy's not out for the count. Of the three, I'll take my chances with the angry kitty.

With a shout I fastball my empty Colt at Bart's head then turn before seeing it connect to charge right for Simpson. He may be able to stop me, but that gives everyone else a chance to bolt.

"Go!" I call, waving a hand at Julia. "Get ou—*ouch*!" Hard, sharp pain hits the back of my head with enough force to carry me off my feet. I pitch headlong, belly-sliding in the dust, grinding to a stop between Holly and Chad, neither of which have moved one step toward the door.

"Laying down on the job?" Holly asks, regarding me with one raised eyebrow. Her voice is calm. Her hands tremble.

"Thought it time for my union break."

She shakes her head.

The back of my head throbs. Stars orbit my vision. Pushing to my feet, I spy Bart's thrown gun ten feet away, wedged beneath a pipe after bouncing off my noggin. He's stomping toward us. Simpson stands between us and Julia, poised to fight, eager even. Julia, for her infuriating part, remains a punk sentinel in the doorway, that screw-it look on her face.

"Get back downstairs," I order her.

"Not without you," she retorts, then gestures behind me. "Turn around."

I spin to face Bart, two strides away, angry veins bulging.

My right hand slips into my pants pocket. That care package offered one more useful present, the brass rings of it cool as my fingers slide in.

"Get them out of here," I shout to Holly.

Whether or not she heard me I don't know, because she whips out with her *nunchaku* and leaps for Simpson.

Bart points at me with a kielbasa finger. "I'm gonna snap your goddamn spine."

"Well, I plan to shatter your knees and crush your larynx. So...touché."

The big guy's eyebrows furrow and he pauses in his stride. "Shut up." A Christmas ham fist swings for the fences.

I slip sideways, hitting him a hard one-two in the floating ribs.

Bart doesn't wince, he snarls and throws a crushing backhand. I catch it with a stiff, brass-knuckled bullseye on his bandaged wrist.

He steps back, shaking out his gimpy limb, and grins. "Ow."

Ow? I gotta do better than that. Bart is one big target but so is an oak tree.

He lunges for me.

I dance, circling and pressing him, throwing body blow after body blow. He covers up, then cannons a right to my chest that knocks me back three steps.

"Ow." Damn, that hurts.

Bart barrels in like a linebacker, shooting a high tackle at my chest. Too high. I use his momentum to my advantage—snatching his suspenders, rolling backward with him, and thrusting a foot in his gut as we tumble. I launch Bart to the center of the room. He slides ass up against the Swiss cheese head machine cylinder with an echoing brass gong *bong*.

Holly gets knocked against him by Simpson. She's right side up. She and Bart exchange looks—hers one of pain and determination, his sheer rage.

He swipes at her with a big mitt and she scuttles out of the way.

I pull her up.

"How you doin'?" I ask.

"I've been better. Chad, get out of here!" she yells.

Chad refuses. He's holding off Simpson. The villain is smiling. Not a good sign.

Julia isn't in the doorway which I pray means she's already down the elevator. Then I glance up and there she is, crouching like Tarzan on a pipe suspended from the ceiling.

"Damnit," Holly and I say in stereo, only she's not looking up.

Bart's on his feet.

"Julia, get out!" I thrust a finger at the open door.

She cocks an eyebrow and shakes her head.

She damn well better stay up there then.

"Simpson's mine," says Holly, pulling my attention back to Bart.

"No!" A rasping bark from Chad. He holds both hands up to halt Holly where she is. He thumbs his chest then points at Simpson. "Me," he croaks.

Holly and I exchange glances.

"This isn't a tournament," I say.

Holly gives a tight smile. "He knows."

Chad rolls his shoulders, lowers his chin, and waves Simpson to him.

"Two fights aren't in my contract, kid," says Simpson. "But this lesson I'll teach for free."

Holly faces Bart and whips her chucks in a vicious display.

"Alright then, big guy. Let's see what you got."

I move away from her, opening more angles of attack.

And we're at it. All of us. All at once.

Bart rushes Holly. She slips sideways and counters. I go low. Bart dodges. Chad and Simpson blur into the background.

Holly and I hit Bart with a combo that leaves him staggered. The brute rolls his taped wrist, now bloody from the leaky wound in his bicep. He gives us that scrunched eyebrow look I used to call his thinking face.

Before he can make up his mind what to do, Julia drops from her perch to land two-footed on Bart's buzzcut head. She wails like a drunken banshee and dances a crazy, jack-booted jig, using the big man's skull for her stage.

Bart swats at her as Holly strikes, her chucks making a nice wooden crunch against the giant's knee. He buckles but doesn't drop.

Julia dances like she's got an audience.

I shoot in on Bart's other side, my kick landing on the sweet spot, a hand's breadth above the tibiofemoral joint of his other leg.

A normal man would collapse. Bart howls in pained rage but fights on, shoving Holly back with one hand, forcing me away with the other, then grabs for the head-hopping Julia. She jumps nimbly over his reach and comes back down hard with both feet atop his skull. Not a wobble.

Bart bends with the blow. She just stomps and stomps like she's crushing roaches.

"Little bitch!" bellows Bart, grabbing at her feet. Failing to dislodge her, he tucks and somersaults forward.

The girl with perfect balance stays with him the way a lumberjack rolls a floating log. She steps from his head to his back to legs to feet, then springs from his boots to catch a hanging pipe. An acrobatic heave and she's up high once more, well out of Bart's reach.

She never ceases to amaze.

"I told you to get out of here," I shout.

Julia cracks a smirk. "You're not my father, Larry."

She's dishing out some payback and loves it. I just wish there were a way she could do it without giving me a coronary.

"Then stay up there. Please!"

I don't know if she obeys because Bart's on his feet in front of Holly.

She lays into him with chucks, elbows, and knees. Bart swings at her with all the effectiveness of an old man swatting bees, but he's backing her up to the wall. Her third blow is a good one, a vertical knee right to the family jewels.

I wince at the thought of it, even as I move, even as I hear the hollow plastic echo of his cup taking the blow.

"Little lady," Bart rumbles, "That'll cost ya." Quicker than I thought possible for him, Bart snatches Holly by the throat, slamming her against the wall. He draws back his bloody arm for a punch to shatter brick.

Her eyes bulge. Her hands tear at his grip.

I'm there, shouting for Bart to drop her, and throwing a blow that carries all two-hundred and twenty pounds of me behind it.

The brass-knuckles land on target, connecting with a wet smack on his bicep bullet hole.

That arm drops limp and Bart releases Holly to cradle it.

"Mother fucker!" he yells, spraying blood from split lips.

I hit Bart again, straight and hard, crushing his nasal bone beneath my metal fist. He stumbles back, blinking in stunned surprise, bloody nose to match his bloody mouth.

Holly leans against the pipes, chucks dangling, struggling to get her breath back.

Chad grins at Simpson. The man in tailored black isn't smiling anymore, he's snarling, gasping, and throwing the kitchen sink at a kid who sees each move coming. Chad makes Simpson miss yet again then drives him back with a blitz of punches. Then, as if I had given him the advice only yesterday—Christ, it *was* yesterday—he spins, checks his target, and connects with a wheel kick to Simpson's temple that knocks him crashing to the floor.

Exceptional.

Bart lets go his lame arm to gingerly probe his mangled face. "You broke my goddamn nose!"

I hoped to break his goddamn skull.

Holly steps next to me, game faced and ready for one last go at the big guy.

"You okay?" I ask her as Bart flexes the fingers of his bad arm.

Holly coughs, nodding. "I'm f—"

Kak!

"Enough of this." That odd, baritone voice.

Jimmy the Fist has reentered the fray. He leans on his cane beside the head machine, pistol trained on me, gun smoke drifting from the barrel to join the grain dust now choking the room.

I knew the little prick wasn't out for the count.

Chapter Forty-Nine

JIMMY clicks his teeth. "I've never been one to hold grudges. Clinging to the past and all that. I'm more of a present moment kind of a guy. At this present moment, you have presented me with an interesting conundrum." His cane clicks as he steps forward, gun pointed dead at me. "Orders were to collect one Chadwick Ellis. But, to finally bring in *the* Julia Rourke, the girl with perfect balance? Well... When she popped through the door, I thought, 'could that be?'—nice job with the hair by the way. But then you shouted her name, Lawson."

Did I? Christ, I did. Damnit.

"So, despite orders, I'll seize this moment to clean up some old business," he says.

Sirens outside. Not here yet, but closer. The crowd's stopped chanting, too. It's riotous below, the indistinct noise of dozens shouting. Clock's ticking.

"The clock's ticking," says Jimmy. "Get down Miss Rourke or Bart here will get you down."

Bart cups his nose, scowling my way before locking eyes with Julia.

A shower of dust as she scuffles on her grain pipe perch. Julia shouts, "Both of you can fuck off."

Jimmy gives a thin smile. "Charming. Now Lawson, I'll ask you and your lady friend to step over by our young karate champ, there." He gestures with the gun. "Julia, get down here, now."

"If I come down there," Julia snaps "It'll be to kick your midget ass."

God, I love her spunk.

Jimmy stiffens and inhales, nostrils flaring.

Chad steps up—knuckles split, forearms battered, and favoring one leg—and places himself between us and Jimmy. "Take me," he croaks.

Holly gives a panicked wave, "No, you can't."

The champ stands resolute. He looks at his *sensei*, his mentor, his surrogate mom, and mouths, "I'll be okay."

"Don't. Please, don't do this." Holly's voice is choked tight.

Jimmy huffs. "Touching. You do have something special Mr. Ellis, really. However, Julia is a prize we've waited a long time to win. I'm not letting her slip away a third time." Jimmy looks to Bart and nods. "Since I seem to be short on manpower, one of you will have to do. Please, take no offense. We'll round you up in due time."

"Why you rushing off?" God, I hope Jake's caught the action on his security feed and is sending whatever cavalry he can muster. "You got a hot date?"

"You're not far wrong with the hot part," Jimmy says. "The clock *is* ticking, and I don't plan to be here when the alarm goes off. So, while we'd like young Mr. Ellis there to survive this fracas, I can't have you following me either..."

KAK!

I flinch. But I'm not shot.

A wooden clatter as oaken sticks tumble to the concrete. Then a quivering hand tugs my shoulder.

"Larry?" Holly's gone white. Her lips tremble. Sweat beads on her forehead as she grips me. Her other hand is pressed to her side. A dark stain spreads beneath her palm.

"*Sensei*?" whispers Chad, eyes wide.

She slides into my arms—something I've often dreamed of—but not like this. Never like this.

"No." I clutch her tight, cradling her against me. "No. No. No!"

"You mother fucker!" Julia leaps down, snarling.

KAK!

She stops short as Jimmy's shot ricochets off the floor in front of me.

"The next shot is in Lawson's right leg. Then the left. Then his skull. Understand how this works?"

Bart stomps past Julia to pocket his tossed pistol then gather the unconscious Simpson across his shoulder.

Julia's eyes beg me to tell her what to do. Holly grits her teeth. Her breath comes in shallow, hissing gasps. Chad hovers beside her holding her arm, whispering, "It will be alright, *sensei*," over and over.

I'm at a loss. Stuck. Overwhelmed. Come on Pop, I need your words. I need help. Somebody help! A panicked wrath builds inside me, boils—a pressure cooker with no release.

I hold Holly close and press her hand against the bleeding. It's all I can do.

"Get the girl and let's go," says Jimmy.

Julia looks over her shoulder at the looming Bart then back to me. The terrified girl is back once more, the girl I haven't seen in six years. The girl that came home from school to a murdered family and cold-blooded kidnappers. The girl that wants me to save her. Needs me to. Begs me to.

I don't know how.

"Larry? I... I...." Her lips twitch.

My hands tremble. My legs are jelly. I'm weak as a newborn. Weak and sorry. I'm so sorry, kid. You were supposed to stay down there. You were supposed to stay away.

"Bart, the clock is ticking," Jimmy snaps.

Bart shoves Julia forward.

I'm supposed to keep people safe. It's what I do. It's what I'm best at. What's the point if I can't even protect the ones I love? What good am I? Not much at all.

Fine. If that's what it comes to, then at least I'll go out giving those I love a fighting chance. I'll throw myself on Jimmy's gun, take the shots so the others can get out. I *will* save them. I will save Julia.

I tense to spring, to launch myself at Jimmy and crush the life from him with my last, bullet-riddled breath.

Then Holly grunts in pain, clutching my hand vice tight.

And I stop. The devil's choice sits before me once more: Julia or Holly. I can't have both.

Bart snorts. "Move." He pushes Julia out the far door toward the fire escape. Her face is cold, stoic, resolved. Hopeless. And like that she's swallowed by the darkness.

"Julia." Her name comes out a helpless, pathetic whimper. The very sound of it enrages me. I crush weakness and yell, "Julia!"

"*Tsk*. You get too attached." Jimmy keeps his gun on us as he backs through the door. "Now you better get the others away. Be a shame to lose young Ellis' potential because of your inability to see the task at hand. The clock is ticking."

The task at hand?

"I'm gonna kill you." I say, voice dry and sinister as a sidewinder.

"I do miss that drive of yours," Jimmy coos. "That determination. That rage I see inside you at this very moment." He looks cherubic—small, smiling, framed in the doorway before a black canvas of night sky. He's an innocent about to gleefully step into the unseen. No. He's a demon happily slipping back into the nether realms.

"I will kill you." The words grind out as if I were chiseling them in stone.

The task at hand.

Jimmy gives a mock salute, "The clock, Lawson." Then he is gone, cane clacking on the catwalk as he hurries to the fire escape, slipping further away with each passing heartbeat.

I scream.

I scream the scream of useless, wasted, impotent fury, a scream that erupts from my molten, burning center to spew out across the world, or at least across the battered and bloody room of the head house. It winds down like a French police siren, leaving me drained. Tears drip from the end of my nose.

Holly's voice trembles. "L-Larry..."

Pop did have words for me. Julia's not dead. There's still a chance. Right now, Holly is the task at hand. Holly and Chad. Save them. Focus.

I sniff and wipe my eyes. What did that prick mean by the clock is ticking? Why was he in such a hurry? The train isn't going anywhere. Not with the crowd out there and the cops en route. I glance out the far door leading to the elevator. The airport's tower light sweeps past. The room sparkles with millions of drifting grain dust flecks, then the light moves on.

The airport.

The dust.

Oh, the vicious, evil bastard.

"We gotta go. Now," I shout, scooping up Holly.

She gasps as I cradle her close.

"What is it?" asks Chad beside as we scurry to the door.

"Jimmy's covering his tracks. Run!"

We sprint from the headhouse, pounding across the catwalk. The little elevator is twenty yards away. Ten.

A deep, thumping rumble lifts the metal grating beneath us, then drops us hard.

Chad stumbles on his bad leg. My knees buckle but I stay up, holding Holly tight.

The world erupts in blinding, deafening, searing pain as the headhouse explodes.

Chapter Fifty

THE air ignites.

My nostrils sear.

My lungs burn.

I crash forward atop Holly. I feel her scream but can't hear it over the roar of the blast.

This is it. I was too slow. We're dead because of me. I only have one breath before the flames consume us. Consume Holly and leave Julia to the wolves. End me before I can tell either how I really feel.

And then, Chad.

The kid is exceptional. Faster than I can hope, before my weight has pressed Holly to the catwalk, he moves. He throws himself across my back, shielding us with his body, forcing us down as the blast wave rips across the sky.

He yells in my ear, howls in pain and terror and sheer grit as he sacrifices himself to protect his sensei, his teacher/mentor/mother, and the asshole who broke her heart.

Exceptional.

Just as fast, the fireball is gone. Bits of cinderblock and metal still clang and tumble about, falling to the catwalk, tumbling away to the ground below. My ears ring. My head spins. The night air vibrates with the aftershock and reeks of burnt cloth, hair, and flesh. My back is hot. My ears scorched. Strange then, that the steel beneath my hands is cool, almost soothing.

Holly groans.

"You okay?" I ask.

"Been better," she grunts. "You're c-crushing me."

Gathering myself hurts. Everywhere. My left arm's lost its strength, doesn't cooperate. I rock up and Holly gasps. The side of her face is dark with dirt and soot. Some of her hair is singed down to stubble. She's still pale. But she's lucid. And never in her life been more beautiful.

Chad slides off me, thumping to the catwalk, unmoving.

Holly draws a panicked, wincing breath. "Oh no...."

Wounds and blood, limbs bent and broken, I've seen all that dozens of times. I can stomach those. Burns are a level of terrible that my gut's never been able to handle. Chad's back is laid bare, the skin blistered and charred, melted away in places, the flesh beneath a raw and oozing relief map of hell. His hair is gone. One ear nothing but a misshapen lump. The smell hits hardest—sweet, like roasted pork prepped for a Sunday barbecue. I choke back vomit as I slap away low flames on his pants.

"Is he...?" She can't bring herself to say the word.

His eyes are closed, his face dirty but smooth, still unscarred by both Simpson's best efforts and Jimmy's. Breath leaks from him in a wheeze. Then his back raises and falls. The rhythm is ragged and shallow, but steady.

"No. He's alive." And unconscious, thank God.

Holly sniffs and sits up. Her smile is tight, a picture of fear and relief combined.

How do I get the two of them out of here?

"Can you walk?" I croak, probing Chad for the best way to lift him without hurting him more.

Her side still leaks, the dark stain stretching from ribs to knee, fingers coated in blood peppered with gravelly bits.

She grasps the warped railing and pulls herself to her feet. "What choice is there?"

I grab Chad under the chest to avoid terrible burns and heave. My left arm refuses. I growl and curse, but I'm going nowhere.

"I can't—"

Another tremor rocks us. Holly tumbles from the rail, screaming as the metal bar catches her side. Chad's limp weight drops me to my ass. I collapse beside Holly, and we huddle, Chad across our laps as the world rocks and rolls around us. Her hand finds mine and I clutch it for dear life.

The tremor stops.

I'm crying. Holly's crying. Chad still breathes.

Soft, cool wind touches my face, stirs Holly's remaining hair, and carries the stink of defeat away. The night sky holds a gentle memory of rain, though only shredded cloud remains to obscure the stars. The rooftop beacon flashes red and the repetitive white and green beams from the regional airport tower sweep the sky. The catwalk groans. From the ground below, shouts and sirens.

The flickering flames of the headhouse silhouette Holly like a dark angel come to carry me home. But I can't go. I still have tasks to complete.

I clear my throat and search for the right words. "Holly, we...uh...."

She gives a slow shake of her head. "Maybe," she says. "Maybe not. But...I wanted to. Since seeing you at Sally's diner. I wanted to."

My cheeks are wet. Feels good. "I can't let them take her."

She nods, eyes heavy.

"I didn't want to leave you, back then," I say.

Holly squeezes my hand. She forces her eyes open and smiles. Her vision goes distant, as if looking past me. Her grip softens then goes slack.

"Holly?" I gasp, reaching for her. "Holly, no. Don't you dare—"

"Shhh," she purses her lips then lifts her hand from mine to point.

I turn, over us looms a shadow so big I fear Bart Rockentanski is back to finish us off. I can't stop him.

"Ja, I have them," says a jolly voice with a wonderful Minnesota lilt.

God, if you are up there, I owe you. Again.

Radio static crackles. Jake's voice. "Hurry. Another silo could blow any minute."

"Okay-okay." Sven clips the handheld to his belt and bends over us. "This is no place for a sit down. Come on." He grimaces at the burnt form of Chad but lifts the kid with the tenderness of a mother pulling her newborn from the cradle.

I wrap Holly's free arm across my shoulders and we shuffle along behind him and into the cramped little elevator. During the shaky, scary ride down to the work floor Sven says nothing. Holly trembles, but stays solid, jaw clenched against the pain.

I'm focused on getting Holly and Chad to the paramedics.

Then Julia.

On the ground, pandemonium rules. Feed mill employees and protesters run about like scared chickens, pointing up at the elevator, cringing against each other, or

276

scattering into the night as flashing lights and sirens race into the parking lot.

Sven leads us from the shadows to lit ground beneath one of the yard lights, the idle train as a backdrop.

Pornstache races up, sunglasses gone, eyes like saucers, blood drawing a thin line down his jaw from a gash on his cheek. For some reason he's soaking wet.

"Goddamn!" he snaps. "You guys look like shit." He steps closer as Sven lays Chad in the grass. "Goddamn! Did they torture him?"

I don't answer, just take his proffered arm and let him help me to sit Holly beside the train. The rest of the crew emerges from the dark. Jake checks the wounded. Earl pulls up short, wringing his hands, tip of his tongue flicking across his lips.

"She's been shot," Jake says, taking a look at her bloody side.

"Not...that bad," says Holly, putting on a grim grin.

"And she's in shock." Jake is looking at Earl, one eyebrow raised expectantly.

Earl is nervous under the gaze of his boss, oddly nervous even for him. The old hippie paces, shaking his head. "Aw, man. No. I can't. It's been like ten years. I can't..."

"What do we do, Earl?" Pornstache asks, rubbing his nose.

For whatever reason, Jake has ceded all authority to the Tommy Chong lookalike whom I wouldn't trust to mail a letter. I'm in no condition to argue. My head throbs. My bullet-grazed forearm burns, and every muscle is beaten lead.

"Ja, tell us," adds Sven, crouching by Chad. "The kid here is Swiss steak and Larry is, well, just look at him."

"I'm fine," I mutter. It's a lie, but one I have to believe.

"No, you're not." In a finger snap, Earl's slack-faced demeanor is gone. A wizened man of authority stands in his place. "Russell, take off your wet shirt and drape it over the kid's back. Then go grab one of those paramedics. Tell them we have an unconscious minor with third degree burns."

"How come I'm always the one running errands?" grumbles Pornstache.

"You are good at it," says Jake.

Pornstache narrows his eyes then shrugs. "Okay." Then he runs back into the crowd.

"Jake," says Earl, "bend Professor Chisholm's knees and wrap her in Sven's jacket."

I miss his other commands. One, I'm stunned by take-charge Earl and two, his confidence bleeds into me. Chad will live. Holly will live. They're safe. With this crew around them, they're safe.

Once more Julia is my task at hand and she won't be safe until I find her.

Chapter Fifty-One

A ladder truck wails up to the edge of the yard a football field away. Any minute the RCPD will be here too despite Miguel and his cousins. There's a sound of tearing cloth. Sven rips his flannel shirt into strips and Earl wraps them over Holly's wound. Jake has Russell's shirt draped over Chad.

"Did anyone see Julia?" I ask.

Earl grabs my grazed arm. "Not since she scampered up that drainpipe. We heard shots. Then she just bolts. Quick as all get-out, she's up the side of the building like a monkey after a banana. Gone. Never seen anything like it. Your shoulder's dislocated."

"It is?" That explains it. Holy hell, the damn thing hurts.

"Sven, pull down on Larry's arm. Gently. Like you're a bucket of ice cream in his hand."

Sven does as he's told.

I gasp and grit my teeth. "You weren't always a janitor."

Earl whispers in my ear, "Combat medic. Marines. Try to relax."

"What kind of ice cream?" asks Sven.

Earl grins. "I don't know, man. I dig rocky road. You?"

Sven nods. "On the farm we made ice cream every Fourth of July. Oh ja. Vanilla with raspberries fresh from the—"

I scream.

Earl's shove is quick, sharp, and harder than I'd thought possible for the likes of him. My shoulder is back where it should be. I rotate the arm slowly, gingerly. Still hurts like hell but working.

"Thanks," I hiss.

"I should bandage that." Earl points at my forearm. Sven hands him a strip of flannel shirt and he sets to work.

The airports beacon circles the sky above us.

Jimmy, you slick bastard. I'll get you yet.

A voice in the crowd rings out, "Julia!"

My heart leaps. Did she escape?

It's Trevor. He breaks through the crowd and sprints over. Alone.

"Thank God." He stops short, eyes wide, pallor shifting more and more toward green. "Julia. Where's Julia?"

He's looking right at me.

I can't answer him.

"She's been taken," Holly says. She's scooted over beside Chad, gently holding his still hand.

"Wh-what do you mean?" Trevor stammers. "I saw her go up there. Didn't she come down with you?"

"Listen," I say, speaking soft to calm him. "She came up and—"

"She's taken?" Trevor's green-gilled look shifts to blotchy red anger. "She went up there for you. You! Her great protector. Isn't that your job, to keep her safe?" Tears glisten in his eyes. His voice cracks. "Where is she?" He shoves me hard and I stagger back.

Jake steps between us. "Boy. Look at this man." He gestures to me. "Look at him. Do you believe he did not everything he could to stop them from taking her?"

Trevor trembles in rage, glaring at me, fighting back sobs.

"Here," says Jake. "Drink this. It will calm you."

He pulls a slender, insulated flask from his jacket pocket and offers it to the kid.

Trevor takes it with mumbled thanks and swallows a quick drink. His face scrunches up in a disgusted spasm, but then he glowers at me once more and regains himself, swallowing hard.

"Now," says Jake. "Go organize your people. If any are hurt, get them to the paramedics. Those that can, should get out of here before any police arrive."

Trevor's tense anger seeps from him as whatever he just gagged down moves from mouth to stomach. His shoulders slump. His jaw loosens. And he takes a jerky step back.

"Easy," says Jake.

Trevor blinks. "You...failed her." He swings an accusing arm at me, then blinks once more, slowly, before disappearing among the crowd.

"What is that stuff?" I ask Jake.

"Old family recipe," he replies and takes a swig.

"We find it is better not to know." Miguel steps from between the rail cars. "What did I miss? What did—ooooh, *Ay-yi-yi*!" He grimaces as he catches my face in the light.

"That bad, huh?" I grumble.

Miguel nods, eyebrows raised. "Si, I hope the other guy, he looks worse."

"Guys. Plural," Holly says with a cough, holding up six fingers.

"Are we ready?" Jake asks Miguel.

"I borrowed my cousin Pedro's van. It is waiting by Professor Holly's car."

Van. Bart's crew had a goddamn cargo van. I look for it past all the milling people. As two firemen move a group aside, I catch the brown side of it parked where we'd seen it before, beneath a streetlight halfway across the parking lot. But what is missing, is Bart's car.

A wellspring of energy pops open in me like Jed Clampett's bubbling crude. "The Buick. That Buick four-door that Trevor ID'd at the tournament. The one your cousins spotted here. Did any of you see it leave?"

Earl looks up from tending to Chad. "Not me, man." Jake and Sven shake their heads.

"Was it blue?" Miguel asks.

"Yes."

"*Si.* I saw it," says Miguel. "It drove up Airport Road as I was pulling in."

Yep. The airport.

"That little prick," I spit, moving to Holly.

"What is it?" Jake asks, he and the others gathering around me.

"Please, I need your car keys." I say, reaching down to her.

She studies my eyes. Hers are dark, bottomless pools and add a new ache to my chest. "You have a bad habit of needing other people's cars. Ever consider getting a rental?"

"Tell us what's going on," Jake commands.

"The airport was always his plan," I say, speaking to everyone but keeping my gaze on Holly. "He wasn't going to use the train. This place is a distraction. He's flying her across the border."

"Ja, could be," mumbles Sven. "Da Airport Road leads to the charter terminal, not the commercial one. If the preflight's done, he could get clearance and be on the taxiway in minutes."

No one speaks. We all stare at the big guy.

"What? My uncle Ragnar, he flew for—"

"How many minutes?" I bark, smacking him on the chest.

"Ten, maybe fifteen if, like I said, he had the preflight done, which..."

Task at hand. I'm coming Julia.

"Holly, please. I can save her."

Her face softens. She lets go of Chad's hand to clutch mine. I wince at the lance of pain in my shoulder.

"Look at you," she pleads. "You're beat all to hell."

Her grip is warm and loving, tempting me to stay, to cling to her. "I'm the only chance she's got."

She studies me for a breath. "Okay. But I'm coming with you."

"No." We all reply in a chorus of concern.

"That bullet passed through both intestines," Earl states in a tender, bedside voice. "If it's nicked the renal vein.... Lady, the only place you're going is a hospital." He taps me. "The same should go for you, hero. But I see that isn't open for discussion."

I respond by pulling my hand from Holly's, laying it palm up before her. "Keys. Please."

Her lips quiver and her voice trembles. "So, you are leaving me again?"

"Please." My voice trembles, too.

"Pedro's van is better, I think," says Miguel. "Telling the police why Professor Holly's car is at the airport will be harder than explaining where it is now."

"Right," says Jake. "She was here as part of the protest. Everyone heard shots fired. She caught one."

It fits.

"Go then," Holly whispers. "But you better damn well come back. We have...things, to talk about."

She's gorgeous through my tears. If only I had done—what? What could I have done different? Kept my work a secret to stay with her? Lie, to the best, most wonderful woman? I pat her hand. "I never wanted to leave you."

She mouths, "I know."

"And I never wanted you to go in there."

She grips my wrist hard, voice cracking. "You couldn't have stopped me."

"Hey! Hey guys!" Pornstache runs this way with two paramedics in tow.

Holly smiles up at me. "Go save your exceptionally annoying little brat."

I kiss her on the forehead. "I love you."

She mouths, "Me too."

"Go," commands Earl. "I got this. If it was my daughter out there, I'd already be gone."

I nod in thanks and turn to Miguel. "Keys?"

"Oh no, *señor*. I will be the one to drive."

"No, guys, you've done too much already. I'm not going to risk—"

"You are wasting time," snaps Jake, shouldering past into the shadows of the train.

"Stop." But he's gone. Sven moves to follow. The thought of the big farm boy on the ground in a pool of his own blood steels me. I step in front of him. "No, please, I need you here with Holly. She'll need a protector. Say you're her cousin, whatever. Just, please, stay with her and Chad, help Earl and—" Can't believe I'm saying this "—Pornstache to keep her safe. I trust you. Please."

Sven swells with a shuddering breath then engulfs me in a hug.

"Ah! The shoulder!" I squeal.

Sven sets me back down with a sheepish apology. "Sorry."

With a nod to Holly, I follow Miguel into the dark, slipping between rail cars, loping back across soggy fields to cousin Pedro's van.

Chapter Fifty-Two

THE van's diesel rumbles. Streetlights zip by faster and faster. Their manic rhythm shoves aside worries about the mess I left behind and focuses me on the mess I'm tearing headlong into. Task at hand, right Pop? Task at hand.

Miguel steers around the grain elevator chaos of gathering fire engines and funny Volvo police cars. Airport Road stretches north through prairie grasses that blur at the edge of our headlights. The glow of amber light around the charter terminal grows as we close. Even from here I see activity. Someone walks beneath a light to disappear in shadow. A tanker truck moves from one hangar to another.

"My thanks to you and your cousins," I say to Miguel.

He concentrates on the road, only tilting his head in response.

I lean back in the jouncing passenger seat of Cousin Pedro's converted postal service cargo truck and run my fingers through a bit of the orange shag carpeting that lines walls, floor, and ceiling. Jake sits behind us on a red Naugahyde couch bolted to the truck floor. A multi-faceted glass disco ball sways over his head. We thump across a pothole and the whole rig creaks.

I want to say something, talk these guys out of risking their lives yet again for someone they've known a week or at least convince them to hang back out of the line of fire. But the words get stuck somewhere behind my teeth.

Miguel swerves around a bolting jackrabbit.

"What's the plan, *señor*?" he asks.

EXCEPTIONALS

The chain-link perimeter is thirty seconds away. The gate we're speeding toward stands open under a lone light. I don't see Bart's Buick. No planes are on the taxiway. Nothing on the flight line. Jimmy's ride is still inside a hangar. This time of night, it should be the only one open.

"A gun would be handy right about now," I say.

Jake slips up to crouch between us. Shadows roll over his face and linger in the deep creases around his mouth and eyes. He looks tired and old, older than I'd ever guess.

"I don't do guns," he says.

He may not have a choice.

Miguel points at the glove box. "Check in there."

Inside the small compartment are a stack of roadmaps, some crumped napkins, and a nickel-plated twenty-two automatic the size of a bar coaster. It looks like a toy, but it's loaded. Six rounds.

"My cousin," apologizes Miguel. "Sometimes there is trouble."

I turn to Jake. "We drop you off inside the gate. They'll be in the only open hangar. Come in the back door and keep anyone from getting out that way."

He nods in agreement. "Any ideas on how I do that?"

He still looks old, worried, but his eyes burn with a growing fire. Something stirs, adventurous and long missed.

"You weren't always a janitor," I say.

He smiles a tight, mischievous smile. "True. What about you?"

I set my jaw. "Miguel and I ram the plane."

"*Que*?" Miguel pulls up to the gate.

"Stop here," I command.

The van grinds to a stop.

"I'll see to it Cousin Pedro gets a new van."

Miguel purses his lips, fingers drumming on the wheel. "It is okay. No one in the family really likes Cousin Pedro."

Jake throws open the side door.

"You sure about this?" he asks, jumping to the pavement.

I reach out my open window and grasp his hand in a firm shake. "No. But I'm doing it anyway." We share a mutual, unspoken thank you and he slips away, keeping to the shadows.

Miguel speeds us onto the flight line. Four hangar buildings are shoulder to shoulder on our right. The open bay of the last one shines light across the tarmac. The blue Buick sedan is just visible beyond. A golfcart-sized tractor emerges from the bay pulling a plane on its long tow bar. It's a twin-prop corporate job big enough for eight or ten passengers with one door in front of the wings and a smaller back by the tail. Tricycle landing gear.

"Aim for the nose," I command, pointing Miguel at the front of the plane, the furthest possible point from Julia and any fuel tanks likely to go boom. "Duck right before we hit."

"*Ay dios mio*," gulps Miguel. He crosses himself and floors the accelerator.

The engine roars. The chassis creaks. This thing was built to deliver packages, not win at Le Mans. The speedometer has us at twenty rumbling up to twenty-five.

Blood pounds in my ears. My breath's gone shallow. Fear fuels my focus.

Julia.

The tractor driver faces our onrushing headlights. He's not Bart, Simpson, or Jimmy, likely some late shift schmo just doing his job.

Welcome to the most interesting night of your career, bud.

His eyes go wide. His jaw drops. He makes one desperate effort to wave us off before leaping clear, arms flailing.

I grit my teeth and shield my face with my arms.

Impact is a blast of grinding, screeching, snapping, and crunching. Ringing metal. Splintering glass. Yells of pain. My yells. My ribs scream against the seatbelt. My injured shoulder blazes. My forearms feel like tenderized beef. We rock to a stop, rear of the van dropping with a bang back onto its strained axle. The engine chugs and sputters. I smell diesel, taste blood.

The plane's nosecone is sheared clean away. It rests precariously atop our smashed hood, then tumbles off to *thunk* on the concrete. The front landing gear has collapsed, tipping the plane forward onto the cockpit.

I shove the shattered, spidered windshield off me. A few shards stick from my arms. They're not deep, but I'm bleeding. So much for Earl's bandage. I pluck them out with a hiss, click free the seatbelt, and check Miguel.

"I'm okay," he says. He did as I said, ducking aside when we hit. A few scratches and a stunned look, but he'll be okay once he catches his breath.

BLAM!

A deafening shot echoes about our heads. Sparks fly as it glances off the driver-side pillar.

It's Simpson, face bloody and right eye swollen shut under an askew headset. He scowls past the shattered cockpit windscreen, a smoking three fifty-seven gripped in his raw fingers. Jimmy's gotta be out of options to put him at the controls. The guy was unconscious twice in the last hour.

"Shit." I pull Miguel down as Simpson shoots again.

A round rips through the driver's seat.

"Stay low," I command, scrambling to the back of the van. Miguel is right behind, cursing in Spanish while shot after shot blasts through his cousin's party ride.

We throw open the back doors and tumble to the concrete. Plastic sprays as Simpson's fire shatters a taillight.

Miguel covers his head with his hands, shouting incoherently.

The hangar is big and high, a dozen halide fixtures suspended from the rafters. Loaded pallets rest on the floor. The walls are lined with metal shelves and safety placards. The back is a workshop area with tables, rows of more loaded shelves, and a couple offices. We've blocked the bay door. They're not getting out of here by plane. And the tractor driver vamoosed.

"Get behind the engine block and stay there," I command, checking the little pistol cousin Pedro left us. Six rounds. Better than nothing.

Miguel swallows and nods. "*Si*, I will draw his fire." He's off before I can protest.

Simpson fires for the front of the van as Miguel curses him in Spanish.

I sprint for the cockpit. It's five strides away. Three.

Simpson catches my movement. He twists in his seat so we're face-to-face, eye-to-eye.

He yells, tries bringing his pistol around, but the cockpit is cramped and I've forced him to fire across his body.

I skid to the open windscreen, thrust Pedro's pistol through, and pull the trigger point-blank.

A soft, firecracker *pap* and his yelling stops.

Simpson's good eye goes crossed, straining to focus on the pea-sized red dot on his forehead. His lips flap. His arms go slack, and he slumps in his chair, a heavy *thunk* as his revolver hits the floor.

My heart's thumping. Breath is racecar exhaust. Glass clinks and tinkles off hangar concrete as I pull my arm from the cockpit like a robot going through the motions. It's been twelve years since I first killed a man. It was predawn, ground fog thinning, earthy sweetness of the jungle so pungent I can still smell it. We were pulling security in Phuoc Long when the shots rang out. I reacted, did what I'd been trained to do, what I'd seen the veterans in my platoon do. That VC shooter just fell sideways into the underbrush, thirty yards beyond the sight post of my M16. I never saw his face or his eyes. Too dark.

It's bright in here. Simpson had brown eyes.

"Is he dead?" Miguel snaps me back to the task at hand. He peers over the van's crumpled hood.

I swallow and nod, then gesture for Miguel to stay put. He gives a thumbs up and slips out of sight.

Chapter Fifty-Three

THE rest of the fuselage looks okay. Though a big crease warps the door in front of the wings. That's not my way in.

I go for the rear hatch, staying tight to the plane's belly and away from the windows.

The airframe creaks. Jimmy's bark from inside. Bart's grumble.

The tail is up in the air, but I can reach the handle. I lift the lever slowly, ready to pop whoever's inside, save Julia. The handle's ripped from my grip as the hatch bursts open, swings wide, and knocks me to my ass. A small arm and small pistol jerk out of the opening taking blind, *kak-kak* shots.

I scramble under the plane, ignoring pain in bruised ribs and everywhere else as Jimmy's bullets ping around me.

"I'm coming Julia!" I shout. No sense in being sneaky anymore.

"You are a real thorn in my side, Lawson," Jimmy yells.

Above me the plane shudders and jerks. Bart jumps down with a grizzly bear grunt, slam of his boots echoing off the concrete. The side of his face is scraped red, blood trickles from his broken nose and soaks through a makeshift bandage over my bullet wound on his arm.

"Goody-goody," he growls, grinning a vicious pink teeth grin. "Another crack at snapping your spine." He's weaponless, save for his huge, bunched, ragged-knuckled fists. Guess he didn't have any spare rounds for that hand-cannon of his.

Luckily, my pop-gun's loaded. I level the twenty-two at him.

Pap-pap.

He drops to the floor and scrambles behind a pallet loaded with big steel drums. I fire four shots in all. One pings uselessly from a drum—I pray that's not aviation fuel— a couple hit home. I think. Don't know if they did any more than tear his flannel shirt.

"I'm gonna make you eat that gun," he shouts.

A bang and click above me. Jimmy's muffled shouts. Prick's closed the hatch. I would if I were him. He's got Julia. He can wait while Bart deals with me.

I know there's only one round left in my little pistol, but I check the chamber anyway. Best save it for the prick with a sidearm. I pocket the gun and slip back into the brass knuckles. I'd rather have a knife or a sword or a board with a nail through it, but I'll take any advantage I can get.

I bolt for Bart.

He stands at the sound of my charge. His eager snarl twists into a grimace of pain as I launch myself feet first over the pallet and catch him square in the chest.

Bart crashes back against a set of metal shelves laden with airplane parts.

I don't stick the landing, but I'm not flat on my back. I twist to my feet, fists raised only to duck as Bart swipes at me with a set of jumper cables snatched from the shelf. The heavy red copper clamp misses me by inches. That be the positive or the negative?

Before he can backswing, I shoot in and crack him with a stiff jab. It was meant to be a stiff jab, but my left arm isn't quite ready for prime time. The punch mushes against his face with all the impact of a half-filled water balloon. Surprise slows my cross. He ducks.

Bart slings those cables across my calves and heaves, dumping me backwards.

I manage to tuck my chin so my back slams against the concrete and not my noggin. My left shoulder screams. I hiss out an angry breath and suck another in with no time to lose.

Bart tosses away the cables and stomps his size thirteen boot at my balls. I roll aside, thrust a quick kick right above his knee, then spin away upright.

The big guy's leg buckles. He growls and gets right back up.

I can't take him toe-to-toe. Can't wrestle with him either. What's that leave?

He's bandaged on both bicep and wrist. His nose is broke. His face is a mess. I've already softened one knee.

Hit him where he's weak. Use his strength against him. Swear somebody wearing a black-belt told me that once before mopping the floor with me.

"Come on Barty-boy, we gonna do this or what?"

Bart spits then rolls his shoulders and comes right for me.

His rush is headlong, a lineman going for the sack.

I ignore his rage, his yell, the sheer mass of him, to focus on that weak wrist. He's a step away and I move, slipping sideways and snatching that meaty right hand of his in both of mine. I pivot with his momentum, then just as quickly pivot against it. I force his arm in the opposite direction his body is headed. Shoulder, elbow, and wrist all seize. His legs fly up as if he slipped on a banana peel. I dump him hard on his back.

He crashes to the concrete and lets out a bark of pain.

I stand at his right shoulder, controlling his right arm. I crank on that wrist, forcing it back over his shoulder the way he might strain to get a bad itch. Only I'm doing this to stretch out the muscles along his exposed ribcage. I crouch, trapping his bent arm with my left knee. Then I let fly with my brass-enhanced right fist.

I nail him once. Twice. Solid shots that thud against meat and bone. I'm Rocky in the freezer punching a slab of beef.

Bart grunts each time.

My third shot lands. Then Bart shoots up his free hand to snatch my collar and toss me off him.

My turn to slam against the metal shelves. The breath blasts from me.

Goddamn he's strong.

I shake my head to clear stars popping around my vision. Bart's back on his feet grimacing, right arm tight against his side. He points a sausage finger at me.

"You're dead, Lawson."

No Bart. Julia's right there. I will save her. You're just a big stack of trouble standing in my way.

And I can't afford to play any longer.

I crack my neck first left then right and flex my fingers around the brass knuckles. "Remember what I told you atop the grain elevator?"

Bart's eyes narrow.

I attack before he can recall. Rushing him, I feint right then slip left, ducking a dodgy punch and snapping a hard kick to that softened knee. It connects with a satisfying smack.

He gasps but doesn't fall.

I keep moving, dancing away from his swinging backhand to land a crunching shot to his battered ribs.

Bart growls and reaches for me.

I twist aside, switch-kicking the inside of first one leg, then the other, blade of my shin nailing that tender sweet spot no amount of muscle can protect.

Bart drops like a fat man on a broken chair. He howls in pain and rage, legs doubled up beneath him. He pants there, on his knees.

I'm in front of him, right fist flexing, throbbing, itching.

The big bastard smiles, blinking against the hangar lights as he looks up at me. He's a mess. People come through car wrecks looking better.

He snarls and lunges for me with the one good hand he's got left.

I swat it down and let loose. Julia's dead family. Niles Fergusson shot through the heart. Marcus Beane dumped in a motel bathtub. Chad's burned body. Holly. All of it adds jet fuel to my blow. I hit Bart's throat so hard the brass knuckles bounce off his spine.

His eyes bug. A mewling wheeze whines from his gaping mouth. His hands paw helplessly, clawing for air his lungs can't draw in.

I step around him, immune to his thrashings. It's too late Bart. You're done. The message just hasn't reached your thick head, yet.

The brass knuckles slip off into my pocket and I grip Cousin Pedro's pistol once more. Time for Jimmy.

Chapter Fifty-Four

"Come on you asshole," I whisper into air fouled by diesel, avgas, and mechanical solvents. The van still idles at the hangar entrance. My head rings with echoes of crashing into those metal shelves. There's a chill as night deepens. Cool sweat trickles down my forehead, down my back to tickle my scar. The thing hasn't itched once all night.

I walk toward the plane, leaving Bart splayed out behind me, face blue, hands at his crushed throat, right foot feebly twitching.

A yell inside the plane.

"Julia," I mutter to the night. "I'm coming."

I slip around the pallet of fifty-gallon drums, pistol ready to take the shot.

The hatch swings open.

I take a shooter's crouch, looking straight down the snub barrel to make sure my last shot counts.

Julia hops into the doorway. She's bound wrists and ankles with duct tape.

"H-hi, Larry," she says with a forced smile.

A short arm raises a short gun at her head. Jimmy calls out, "Back away hero. This one is coming with me. I don't want to kill Miss Rourke, but there is a lot of pain I can induce while keeping her viable. And I'm pretty sure that is something you don't want to see."

"Where you gonna go, Jimmy?" I say, mouthing 'You alright?' to Julia. She nods. "From the look of things you've lost everybody on your side that can reach the gas pedal. Can't see you getting away on foot."

"Oh, you would be surprised at my ability to improvise."

Julia shifts her gaze repeatedly from me to the hangar floor beneath her, then raises her eyebrows in an appeal for my approval.

I get what she's thinking. It might work. If I do my part right. If I—

She jumps. Dropping from the hatch she lands hard. For the first time ever I see her fall, tumbling sideways to the concrete.

"No!" shouts Jimmy.

I spring, legs pumping fast as my heart.

Jimmy's in the doorway, framed like a pistol target.

I'll never get a cleaner shot. But his gun's trained on Julia. I don't think. I dive.

I land atop her as his first shot rings out. White hot pain lances into my back. Once. Twice.

"Gah!" Jimmy cries like *he's* hurt.

A clang.

Something heavy and metal hits the ground beside us. A piston head?

"Go!" It's Jake, fastballing engine parts at Jimmy from behind the steel drum pallets. He throws again and again, forcing Jimmy to duck for cover.

"Come, *señor*. Let's get you out of here." Miguel dashes from under the plane to grab my arm.

A pair of guardian angels here to save the day.

"Help me." Together he and I drag Julia beneath the fuselage to the other side of the plane, well out of Jimmy's line of fire.

Bangs and clangs behind us. Jake's still throwing.

We prop Julia behind a stack of heavy boxes. She twists against her bonds.

"Can you?" I ask Miguel, pointing at the tape.

He nods and clicks open an Exacta-knife. Janitors come prepared.

"You came back for me," whispers Julia as Miguel frees her wrists and ankles. Her spiky hair is mushed flat on one side. Her field jacket hangs off her shoulder. Other than that, she looks alright. No tears. My spunky, amazing girl.

"I told you I would c-c—" My words choke off in a wet gurgle.

She touches the edge of my mouth. Her fingers come away red.

I touch where she touched and see blood. Bart never hit me in the mouth. Then I collapse sideways and cough, a red spray splattering across the concrete.

"Oh God, Larry," Julia takes me in her arms, cradling me like I've done her so many times. Each a heartfelt memory that adds another layer of ache.

The night's pains are gone. Weakness takes over. Jelly arms. Wobbly legs. Quivering lips. A blob of pinkish spit drops to the floor with a conclusive *pat*.

Jimmy hit a lung.

Another bang from behind us. Jake's doing his best.

"What can I do?" Julia pleads.

"Get him up," says Miguel. In a heartbeat Julia and I switch places—me against the boxes, her and Miguel crouching protectively over.

"Get away," I whisper. "Both of you. J-just get away. Get safe."

KAK!

We all look. Jimmy's firing back.

Jake has ducked out of sight.

"Go now," I order.

"No." Julia's tone is matter of fact. She pulls my right arm across her shoulder. "I'm not leaving you."

God I love her spunk.

I cough again, bloody spray missing them. The first shivers of shock start tingling. I clench my muscles, force them to cooperate, remind them who's boss. Keep focused on the task at hand.

Save Julia.

Miguel dips beneath my left shoulder and they get me up. Something hard digs into my side.

I gasp.

"Oh, sorry." Miguel pulls a pistol from his belt.

"Wh-whcrc did you—?"

"It was the pilot's," he says, hefting the revolver. "I figured he did not need it anymore."

"Come on," insists Julia, leading us away.

Kak-kak.

A shout from Jake.

I jerk my head to see him slump against the barrels, then drop behind them.

Miguel's eyes go wide.

My panicked heart kicks into second level overdrive. I pull away from Julia and reach for Miguel's gun.

He doesn't respond, standing statue stiff staring at the spot where his boss got shot.

A thump.

Jimmy has joined our little hangar party. He crouches twenty feet away where he dropped from the rear hatch. His back is to us.

I rip the pistol from Miguel's limp hand and twist to get my shot.

The little prick's faster. He spins and shoots. He misses.

Julia ducks away calling my name. Miguel tumbles sideways.

I'm left wobbling in between, body threatening to give out. I clench my jaw and keep in control. My turn, Jimmy.

BLAM!

The round knocks him back a step. He staggers. Groans. Then drops to his ass ending up on his side.

I cough bloody phlegm and collapse. Simpson's gun hits the pavement and skitters from my grasp. My back's wet. Sticky.

Miguel's to my right, on the floor, clutching his shoulder. Blood leaks past his fingers.

Jimmy didn't miss. He evened the odds.

Too many. One is too many. Tonight, my efforts got four people shot or burned or otherwise in need of an emergency room. Four. That's not counting Jimmy's asshole crew. Four hurt because I couldn't do my job.

My scar itches.

"Ow." It's Jimmy.

I lift my head to see him struggle back to his feet, pistol still in hand.

"That...really does sting." He probes the hole I made in his shirt with his free hand. "Good shot. I'll give you that. You should have gone for the head, though."

Chapter Fifty-Five

JIMMY taps his chest. "Kevlar. Something you obviously don't have." He draws a bead on me.

"No, stop!"

Julia throws herself across my chest, shielding me, obscuring Jimmy from me and me from Jimmy.

"Just stop," she says, one hand in the air. She's trembling. I can feel her heartbeat in a race against mine. I want to throw her off, draw his fire so she can run, yell for her to leave me and save herself. I don't have the breath.

"Move, Miss Rourke."

I hear Jimmy sidle closer. Go girl. Get out of here.

"Please, don't kill him." She shifts, scooting her supporting hand behind her, closer to me. "I'm begging you."

"Touching," says Jimmy. "Truly. But we are in a hurry. Move."

Julia shifts again. Her hand stops next to mine. There's something smooth and hard beneath it brushing my upturned palm. It feels like wood and steel. Familiar. As if I just held it.

"Let him live. Please."

Her pleading hurts as much as the gunshot wounds. What she is plotting, though.... Gotta love her spunk.

Jimmy sighs. "I get the loyalty, Miss Rourke, I do. Lawson rescues you from our first effort, keeps you under the radar for over half a decade, pulls you out of that Milwaukee dyke bar. Still, this smacks of more than professional between you two."

She presses the pistol grip into my hand.

Do I have the strength? Can I make the shot? Do I have a choice?

"I'll come with you if you let Larry live," says Julia.

She's playing for time, getting Jimmy off his guard. Still, those are words I never wanted to hear from her.

"Oh, you're coming with me no matter what," says Jimmy.

Miguel grunts. He's out of the line of fire, but he's leaking. God knows how Jake's doing.

One chance. I grip the gun tight.

"Jimmy," I gurgle. "K-kill you..."

"What's that? Still fighting, Lawson?" He chuckles.

I tap Julia's wrist with the barrel.

"Count t-to three..." I steady my breath.

"Out of curiosity, Miss Rourke," says Jimmy. "Did he ever tell you the full story of that first rescue? That time when you came home to find mommy and daddy and little brother on the floor?"

Julia goes stiff.

Focus, kid. Don't let him distract you.

"One," I say.

"Now, what you saw were the bodies of your family, and when men came at you from the shadows your shining knight here rode in to cut them down and sweep you away."

"I s-said, I'll come with you..." Julia trails off.

Task at hand. We can talk this later. If I live.

"Two." I tense, ready to make the last effort.

Glee flavors Jimmy's voice. He loves twisting the knife. "You never wondered what FBI Agent Lawrence Lawson was doing there? How he just happened to be in the right place, at the right time? You never thought about it?"

Her shoulders tremble. She grits out, "Fuck off, Jimmy."

My spunky girl.

"He was on the team," Jimmy cackles. "He was one of mine. Was it her father you killed, Lawson? I forget."

There it is. The truth that has eaten me from the inside out every day since *the* day. The darkness I've shoved down deep, prayed would go away. The evil that's been biding its time, waiting for the opportune moment to destroy me.

The op was set as a raid on a human trafficking safehouse. I was the last to breach. Dad stood in the living room with a shotgun. Not an assault weapon, more for duck hunting. I remember thinking what an odd choice, that bird gun. I ordered him to drop it. He didn't. He raised the barrel toward one of my team already in the room.

I fired.

It was only after he collapsed to the floor did I see the ten-year-old boy at his feet. Dead, two rounds through his small chest.

I haven't shot a man since. Until today.

Julia turns, a thin, frail, resigned smile on her face; the one she gave when I left her in the circus. The same one she gave me at that Milwaukee bus stop. She reads my face. I don't like what she's seeing, but I can't hide it any longer.

I'm sorry. I've been sorry for six years. I'm still sorry.

She knows. A single tear trickles from her right eye, something else that hasn't happened since that day. I thought nothing would make her cry again, nothing could hurt her the way losing her family had. I was wrong.

I have no words for her other than, "Three."

She drops to the ground.

Jimmy stands ten feet away, pistol held at his hip, grinning. His shoulders shake with triumphant laughter. He's won. He knows it. He exudes it.

I obey his last bit of advice.

BLAM!

Jimmy's head snaps back. His mocking chuckle cuts off in a gasp. He wobbles, teetering like a nudged bowling pin.

Julia holds her breath.

Me, too.

FBI Special Agent in Charge and my one-time supervisor James Morgenstern Hopwyth the Third, Jimmy the Fist, Opposition team lead, murderer, kidnapper, and hunter of Julia for the past six years, tips over on his heels. His head hits the floor with a satisfying smack. His pistol skitters from his lifeless hand. His wingtip-shoed feet splay open. The little prick is no more.

I drop Simpson's gun.

My head thumps back onto the concrete. The halide lights of the hangar shine down, welcoming me, beckoning me to a place where everything will be alright. I feel buoyant, as if a great burden has been lifted from my chest.

An angelic face haloed in shimmering gold appears from the heavens.

"I told him to fuck off."

Julia. Spiky hair and all. Smiling.

"He didn't listen."

Goddamn I love her spunk.

She crouches over me. She sniffs, breath shuddering, tears flowing freely, and touches my cheek.

I hate seeing her hurt. I want to hold her and guard her and let her know everything will be all right. I can't snap my fingers let alone pull her to me.

So, I lie here and wheeze.

"Thank you for rescuing me," she says, words gruff with melancholy. "Again."

Any. Time.

"I wish you'd told me," she says, swallowing hard. "I wish..."

Me, too. I suck in a haggard breath. "N-not...t-t..."

She closes her eyes and nods. "It doesn't really matter now, does it."

"Julia..." I whisper.

"I can't do this anymore."

I feel her hand on my chest. She kisses my forehead then whispers, "Goodbye, Larry."

What?

Shuffling steps. Movement. Someone's coming.

She stands.

"How is he?" Jake's voice.

Miguel appears as Julia takes a step back. He blinks, fighting gunshot pain. He's more concerned with me, though.

"*Mierda*..."

Julia steps back again as Jake arrives. He's pale and bare-chested, his shirt a bandage around his hip.

She wipes her eyes on her sleeve then glances around the room.

Julia? What do you mean goodbye? I don't have breath to say it, to plead, to beg. The world's going fuzzy.

"Where's he shot?" Jake.

"In the back." Miguel.

Hands slip beneath me, but I can't tell whose they are.

She's at the edge of my vision. Her tears shimmer. For a moment I think she's changed her mind. Then she touches her lips, shakes her head, and bolts off into the darkness.

Julia?

"Where is she going?" Miguel.

"Help me." Jake.

Julia!

Chapter Fifty-Six

BEEP.

I didn't know. I swear. It wasn't supposed to happen that way.

"Mr. Lawson?"

Beep.

It all happened so fast...your mother's screams...your dad with the shotgun...your little brother crumpled on the floor. He wasn't moving.

I'm sorry, Julia.

Beep.

"Mr. Lawson?"

That's not screaming. It's a woman's voice, a kind voice. Vietnamese accent. Nam region by the lilt on the s.

Christ, am I back in the shit? No. I'm not drenched in sweat. I'm not in the hangar, either—no Avgas stink. Mouth doesn't taste of blood. This place smells clean, antiseptic. And my scar doesn't itch. But my nose does.

Pop always said, "Situational awareness, boy. If you don't know what to do, at least know where you are."

I'm on my back, chest bound bandage tight. A sheet lays soft and loose on my bare shoulders and bare feet. The woman's breathing is close by.

Beep.

And what the hell is beeping?

"Mr. Lawson?"

Fine.

EXCEPTIONALS

My eyelids are gummy. They creak open like an old man working broken blinds. I blink against needles of glaring white light. Ouch. Still, a bit of focus. Wherever I am is pale, sterile, and chill.

Letting in that little bit of the outside world has a cost, sending a sonar wave pinging off ache after ache till it pops past my toes. Every limb, every digit feels bowstring tight. Each muscle is waiting for me to move so they can take turns complaining.

Yeah, I'm not in the best shape. Wish that damn beeping would stop.

"Take it slow," says the woman.

Not much choice. I clear my throat. My immediate reward are lancing burns from gut, back, and chest. I spasm and gasp, then whimper as a tender hand eases me back down. At least I'm not bound, not a prisoner. Not that it matters. I'm helpless as a newborn.

I squint through the jabbing light to see my caretaker. She's small boned with the wide eyes of southeast Asia. Her black hair hangs in a ponytail down to the elbows of a white lab coat.

A tangled interchange of colored wires lead from me past her to the small room's backdrop of electronics, the source of that incessant beeping.

No Julia.

"Here, sip this." She places the smooth shaft of a straw against my lips.

I sip. Water, cool and clean. The swallow is blessed pleasure moving down my throat.

My caretaker pulls the straw away.

"Not too much. Better now?"

I nod.

She sets the water aside. Her lapel badge reads: Rapid City Regional Hospital, Doctor Sherry Nguyen, Surgeon.

"Welcome back, Mr. Lawson," says the doc, voice gentle but cool, detached, professional. I know where I stand—or lie helpless—with her.

"It is about time," says another voice.

That voice I know. I love that voice! I turn my head, vertebrae grating like rusty gears.

Holly's here, seated beside my bed, so beautiful all that's missing is a heavenly host singing above her.

"Hey you," she whispers.

Seeing her, hearing her, sends tears welling. God, at least she's alive. At least I saved one.

"Didn't...know," I say, voice like sandpaper.

She lays her hand on mine. Warm and cool at the same time. Smooth and calloused in all the right places. So familiar. So welcome. "Didn't know what?"

I squeeze in reply. "Julia. By the time I reached her family..."

"Hey," she says, now holding on with both hands. "No. Shh. That's...that's all in the past."

I blink at the ceiling. "I should have told her."

Holly says nothing, just holds on, and stays beside me. I love her for it.

Doctor Nguyen's pencil clicks and scratches on her clipboard.

When I look back at Holly, she shows a wan smile. A plastic medical bracelet is on her wrist. Then I notice the hospital gown she wears, and the wheelchair handles behind her shoulders. I'm already flat on my back, but I've just been leveled by a Rockentanski right.

"Oh God...Holly. You. Y-you're..."

"What?" She catches my line of sight, shaking her head at the fear and shame written plain across my face. She lifts my hand to her cheek. "Oh, no. It's okay. I'm okay. Really. I'm fine."

Doctor Nguyen touches my shoulder. "Professor Chisholm's wheels are not permanent. She, like you, should not move around too much, though."

"The doctor's right," Holly soothes. "This is only until the sutures come out. A couple of weeks at the most. It's..." She cuts short her words and swallows hard. "I'll be fine. So will Chad. He's awake, recovering. The burn unit here is the best this side of St. Paul."

Our karate kid, our Exceptional karate kid. Holly's Julia. Can't believe I'd nearly dismissed his fate out of sheer will to focus on my acrobat, and Holly. Task at hand? Sometimes, Pop, it's more humane to cover the spread and make sure no man gets left behind. At least all this wasn't in vain.

Holly's face is drawn and weary, her hair frazzled. She must be exhausted. Lord knows what she went through. What I put her through. She's in that wheelchair because of me. Her suffering is because of me. Could I have found a way to stop her from coming? Maybe. But the past is the past and if I could change it I'd be running the world right now, not clinging to it. I needed her beside me in that elevator like I need her beside me now, and because of my needs, she got shot.

"My fault," I whisper.

"Oh, shh," Holly says, reaching up to stroke my cheek. My wet cheek.

"It's just...I am so, sor—"

"Uh-uh. No." Her hand is firm against my face. Her eyes take hold of mine. "I told you to stop saying you're sorry. I meant it. I still mean it. Chad's alive, because of you. He's not a lab rat because of you."

I sniff. "It's just...oh, hell. I'm blubbering like a kid, here."

Holly leans forward and kisses me with aching tenderness I don't deserve. I shake my head as she pulls away.

"Kiss number two," I say. "We still need to talk about that first one."

Little laugh lines crinkle around Holly's eyes.

"That conversation will have to wait," Dr. Nguyen says, lowering her clipboard and folding her hands in front of her. "First things first."

Holly pats my cheek.

"Okay," I say.

The good doctor checks my eyes with a pen light and lets me have it point blank. "Mr. Lawson, when you were brought in, you were comatose. Your heart had stopped in transport. You'd lost nearly three pints of blood. You suffered two bullet wounds, five broken bones, numerous lacerations, and contusions deep enough to threaten liver and kidney function. Not to mention damage to your rotator cuff that looks like it had been treated by a field medic."

"Not my best day." I try a smile.

Neither the doc nor Holly find it funny.

Doctor Nguyen continues, "You were fourteen hours in surgery and then recovered under sedation. It was touch and go for a while, but once you did stabilize—"

"For a while?" I ask. Holly's squeeze tightens on my fingers. "How long have I been out?"

The doc presses her lips into a thin line. "It has been a long—"

"How long?" My voice takes on a desperate rise in pitch. "Please."

The doc nods. "Ninety-eight hours."

I'm too addled for math.

Holly rescues me. "Four days, Larry. You've been unconscious for more than four days."

Four days. Holy Christ. I scramble through those last moments before I slipped into the black—gunshots, Jimmy tipping, Miguel cursing. Jake with his bandaged side. Julia's goodbye.

"Julia," I murmur, then plead with Holly wordlessly.

Her response is a slow, uncertain shake of the head. She lets go my hand and tries to speak, but a knock on the door interrupts. A buzzcut in a sheriff's department uniform pops his head in. Sergeant stripes are on his sleeve and a nervous crease is on his brow.

"A visitor," he says in a gruff voice.

"No more visitors," Doctor Nguyen tells him in a tone that brooks no debate.

"Um," says the officer. "This is *official*. And she says that—"

"I don't care if it is President Reagan. Close the door," barks the doc.

"The President couldn't make it," comes the response from outside.

Another voice I know. This one I'm not in love with. It is good to hear, though.

A woman and two men brush the officer aside and sidle in.

"Excuse me," snaps Doc Nguyen stepping up to confront the intruders. "This is a secure wing. You have no authority to—"

"I have every authority, Doctor."

Hello Geraldine Tabor.

She's distinctly out of character in jeans and a leather jacket. One of her companions I know all too well—JC Penney suit, iron gray landing pad hair, square jaw that a sledgehammer couldn't crack, narrowed eyes that don't miss a thing, including my new look.

"Laying down on the job, Lawson?" Typical Jack Underwood.

"Hi, Jack," I say.

The lean suit with them I know, too, but not so well. Gone is the flannel shirt. Gone are the aviator glasses and unkempt hair. He stands there clean-shaven, every neatly groomed inch of him screams Fed as much as Jack, more so.

"Kevin?"

My regular local cabbie lifts a hand in greeting.

Were Holly not here, I'd slip back into that coma, now.

Kevin and Jack flash badges at the good doctor. Geraldine Tabor doesn't bother. She's above badges.

"My authority," she says to the doc, "moved your patient to this secure wing. My authority placed this room under round-the-clock protection. My authority is why you've been removed from rounds. Until Mr. Lawson here is discharged, you have no other priorities."

Doctor Nguyen's flexed jaw and flaring nostrils reveal the truth of Tabor's words.

I nod my ascent and feel a second wind at potential answers.

"The others that were with me, how are they?" I ask before badges are even tucked away. "And where's Julia?"

"We'll get to that," Tabor says. "Doctor, if you'll excuse us."

"She stays," I grumble with as much force as my weak voice can muster.

"No," countermands Tabor, "she doesn't. Close the door on your way out."

Doctor Nguyen looks about to retort, but swallows whatever daggers she had to throw. She musters her dignity, hooks the clipboard on the foot of my bed, and strides from the room. The door closes behind her with a defiant chuff.

Jack leans toward me and whispers, "Told you she was in charge."

Chapter Fifty-Seven

TABOR crosses her arms. "You look like hell, Lawson."

"Nice to see you, too," I reply, then glance at Holly and grip her hand. "She knows about what we do."

Tabor gives an indifferent wrinkle of her nose. "I figured you've filled in Professor Chisholm on the broad strokes of our mission or else she wouldn't have been party to your very public stunt Saturday night. I had planned on sleeping in and letting the hubby serve me coffee, instead I get a predawn phone call telling me of gun fights, explosions, and smashed aircraft."

"Some of my jobs are more exciting than others," I mutter. "The rest? Julia?"

Tabor sniffs. "If by 'the rest' you are referring to your odd little band of custodial misfits, then they are fine. Both mister Jake Two Feathers and mister Miguel Peña have been treated and are under supervisory care. All of that crew have been debriefed. From what I could tell, they're neither conniving enough nor clever enough to spread any credible rumors."

Oh, you'd be surprised.

"I have to say, Lawson, you do pick some winners."

Tabor in a room with Pornstache. I'd be surprised if she didn't have to be restrained from slapping the crap out of him. Sven likely gave her the long version of his family tree. And paranoid Earl? Bet he twitched like a wet chihuahua and spouted conspiracies about the government controlling his brain.

The thought is enough to make a guy smile. I do need to thank them.

"There was a kid. College kid. Trevor—"

"We brought him in, too. Don't worry about that part."

I shake my head. "He was...important. To Julia."

Tabor paces. "We gathered that. Now, curious at all about how I found you?"

A chance to brag, Geraldine?

I look at Kevin. "I'm guessing *he* told you. I didn't know agent redundancy was in the budget."

Tabor clicks her teeth. "It isn't. Well, not yet. Long story. Anyway, he's not one of ours."

"He's one of mine," says Jack. "Sort of. I called in a favor."

"Nice," I say, then look at my ex-chauffer. "Your name isn't really Kevin, is it?"

He straightens his jacket. "No. It isn't."

The gears of my battered, medicated mind slowly start grinding. "You left that care package at my hotel."

Tabor and Jack raise eyebrows at Kevin.

"What?" he says. "The guy needed a toolkit. I wasn't about to let a fellow officer go at it unarmed."

Jack turns aside. Tabor rolls her eyes.

I knew it.

"And you found me at the hangar," I say.

He nods. "I intercepted the 911 dispatch call from a hyperventilating flight line employee. What with the commotion at the grain silo so close, I figured your activities might have moved to the airport."

"Some backup would have been nice," I chide.

319

"Those weren't his orders," Jack interjects. "You know better than anyone that we have to play every card close to the vest."

"Observe and report?" I ask, though it's not really a question.

He nods.

"Sounds like 'Nam," I say and look again at the ceiling, frustrated at the complications of it all. There must be a better way. "Thanks for the tools and thanks for getting there when you did."

"No problem," he says.

The room's quiet for a moment. That monitor beeps. Holly's thumb rubs gently at the back of my hand. Jack clears his throat.

"Julia's gone, isn't she," I say.

Kevin answers, "About Miss Rourke, or Reardon or Richards or whatever she's using, bottom line up front is that I don't know where she is. No one has seen her since Saturday. Her car was still in campus parking. Keys were in her room. When I spoke with the roommate, she did mention some of Julia's things were gone. No recollection of seeing her come pack up, just that there was a lot more space in the closet."

If the cops don't have her and The Opposition doesn't have her and *we* don't have her, then...

"She's free," I mutter.

Free. And alone. And vulnerable. Out there in the world. I'm floating and crushed all at once.

"Her bank accounts," continues Kevin, "were emptied and closed three days ago."

What was that?

"How did you get access to bank records? Who are you, Kevin?"

Tabor keeps pacing. Jack cocks a sideways smirk.

"U.S. Marshals Service," says Kevin. He steps up and places a firm hand over my own in a rough semblance of a handshake. "Deputy Marshall Blaine LeFleur, nice to meet you."

I size him up. He's no bumbler. No rookie. The guy knows his job and I owe him for what he's done while I laid here on my ass, not to mention the chatty cab rides, and saving my life. Thanks can wait. I'm sure we'll be talking again. "And that's how you got Julia's records."

"Yes, it is." He steps back beside Tabor. "I've been briefed on the who, what, and why of your little organization. It's an interesting secret you've all been keeping, and one I'll to hold on to. But we don't have a lot of options here. Your Exceptional has luggage, cash, and a motive to stay well below our radar. While I've tracked fugitives with less, I'd like your help to find her."

"I'll help," I say. "But we won't find her."

Deputy Blaine tilts his head in question. "And why is that?"

"Julia's had three identities in six years. She knows how to survive off the grid. The only time her cover was blown was because the guys in D.C. let a mouse in the cookie jar. I hope that problem is well and truly fixed."

Tabor purses her lips and nods. "It is."

"And she had a great teacher showing her how to disappear." Holly gives my hand another squeeze. She's not reprimanding or judging me. She's proud. "You trained her. You prepared her. She watched you set her up with a new life time and again. Julia will be all right. She just needs time alone."

I slowly shake my head and smile, recalling the fake ID in Julia's school bag. Looking for Sandra Guttridge would have to wait.

"For now," Holly adds.

"She's gone," I say, wistful. My gut flutters, partly because I'm happy that she's not in Opposition hands, partly out of fear for her without me as a guardian, and partly because I've been fed through an I.V. for over half a week. Mostly because I failed her. I failed her six years ago and I've failed to make up for it ever since.

Six years. Seems like a lifetime. Julia felt that three times over, only her lifetimes were incomplete, fragmented. Now, maybe she can have some semblance of the normalcy I tried so hard to make for her.

I rub a hand across the smooth ripple of my chest bandages and breathe deep the room's sterile, ammonia-tinged air, "I know my girl. She'll do okay. If things get hot, she'll send up a flag."

"Let's hope so," says Tabor, stepping up to me, heels clicking on the tile. "Our friends on the other side aren't going to give up. We have five of their operatives in custody. You killed three more."

"Two. Simpson was a merc."

"Simpson?" she asks.

"All in black. The pilot. He was a contract player."

Tabor taps a tight rhythm on my bedrail. "That's new."

"Yeah. Landscape's changing."

"So are we," says Tabor. "Anyway, you dealt them a blow they won't soon forget."

"Good. The bastards deserve it." I ache all over. My throat's gone dry, again. I want to fall asleep with Holly beside me, nothing more. But Tabor's words have my scar itching. "Who's talking to the prisoners?"

Tabor pats my arm, "We can discuss that later. You get some rest, now. I need you back and I need you healthy."

"No more unfortunate suicides," I say. "We need what they know."

"Let me worry about that." She gestures for Blaine to get the door. "I'll check back in a few days."

"A few days?" I ask, raising an eyebrow. I'm still itchy. It doesn't look like Tabor or Jack are going to scratch it, though.

"Yeah," she says, tucking her hands in her pockets. "I've never been here. Figure I'll take in Rushmore, Deadwood, maybe a cave. I read a brochure on that Crazy Horse monument they're building—supposed to be something else."

"Well, you've got yourself a decent tour guide." I turn to Blaine. "He will bore you to death with stories of this place."

Blaine smiles and pulls open the door.

"Thanks," I say to him.

He gives me a loose but genuine salute.

"Get better, Lawson," says Jack. "I'll be close if you need me."

He steps out the door.

"Geraldine," I say before she can leave, "Thanks for coming."

My boss cracks a rueful grin, "Well, if I thought a bouquet of carnations could send the right message, I would have gone that route." She steps forward to whisper in my ear. "I can't afford to lose you. You understand me?"

We lock eyes as Doctor Nguyen storms back into the room.

Tabor and I come to an understanding with that look. It's a shared respect for our roles in this fight and a shared need to keep fighting. Something powerful is hidden beneath the changing exterior of this woman and it demands she treat what we do as more than a job and to treat me as more than an agent. This is personal to both of us. Someday I'll ask her why that is.

I give a small nod in response.

"Will you please go, now?" Doctor Nguyen barks at her.

"Rest Larry," says Tabor following Blaine outside. "You've earned it."

The doc lets out a resolved sigh as the door shuts.

Holly shifts her grip on my hand. "I don't like that woman," she says.

"I'm not surprised," I tell her with a wink. "Just how many people *do* you like, Professor Chisholm?" My voice is getting slow and sleepy.

"The list is short," she retorts with a wink of her own. "I should be going, too."

I hold her hand a moment longer. It's firm yet gentle, smooth but tough, just like the rest of her. "Not too far." My effort to be charming loses out to a deep yawn.

"No. Not too far." Her words are as warm as her smile. The doc holds the door for her and I drift off to sweet dreams of loving angels, and dark nightmares of a girl on a highwire falling into the abyss.

Chapter Fifty-Eight

IT'S a bit of déjà vu. The same lone window, the same fluorescent lights. This room is identical to mine, right down to the hospital bed's pale blue blanket, framed print of a Badlands sunset, and the deputy posted outside the door. Only this morning, I'm not the one hooked up to wires and drips and beeping machines.

"How do you feel?" I ask the young man in the bed.

Holly's ditched the wheelchair. She stands beside me fidgeting. I lean forward on the walker I've been shuffling around with the past few days.

"Better," he says, though his clenched jaw and pinched face betray a body still plagued by agony. "The view's improved."

Chad regained consciousness before I did. While I've been building up strength to shuffle from bed, he's been living each day face down and peeing into a pan so the skin on his back could mend. Thanks to Tabor, his grandma has been allowed in to sit with him a few hours every day. But the young man she visits isn't Chad Ellis. Officially, a motorcycle accident victim named Dustin Frie occupies that bed. There are still a lot of arrangements and paperwork and counselling to be done. Those will wait for another day. Today Chad got to turn over and give his grandma a smile. She left happy as a new bride.

Holly clears her throat. "The doctors tell us you're healing faster than expected."

Chad gives a shy smile.

"You always were exceptional," she says, wincing at her own pun.

The kid fingers the edge of his blanket. "Yeah. I've been wanting to talk to you about that..."

I've already filled him in on the why of what happened; on Exceptionals and The Opposition and their scheme to purify humanity while exploiting people like him for pharmaceutical profit. Since then, he hasn't touched the topic.

"Hey, we don't have to." Holly waves a dismissive hand. "You shouldn't worry about that. Just focus on healing up."

He looks at me, not his *sensei*. Today the kid is ready to talk.

"How do we stop them?" he asks, tightening his grip on the blanket.

"The Opposition?" I ask, standing upright and giving his question my full attention.

"Yeah. How do we keep them from taking others? Keep this," he sweeps a glance across his bedridden form, "from happening to anyone else."

I can feel Holly stiffen. It's the same question she asked me once I had the strength to chat longer than ten minutes. My answer hasn't improved since then.

"Kid, sometimes we win, sometimes they do. This country is a big place with a whole lot of people, a few of which are Exceptionals. Even if they're only one in a million, that still means over two hundred people to protect and there's just a handful of us to keep them safe. Save everyone?" I shake my head. "We save the ones we can."

Chad doesn't respond right away. He looks at the ceiling, breathing easy.

Holly clasps her hands behind her back and keeps a game face.

I know seeing him suffer hurts more than Jimmy's bullet ever did.

"I want in," Chad says.

Holly answers, "Now, wait Chad—"

"It's not Chad. Not anymore." His nostrils flare with effort and anger. "I want to do what you do, Larry."

Holly is sputtering. I can feel her anxiety about to erupt and I raise a hand for peace.

"I want to protect others like me and shut down The Opposition." He thumps his fist into the bed. Pain flickers across his face, but he masters himself with a breath. I'll give it to the kid, he has heart.

Holly's voice is soft, quavering. "This is not the time for big decisions. You have a long road ahead."

"Six to eight weeks, *sensei*. The doctor told me with the skin grafts done, my recovery is six to eight weeks. Then I'm out of here." He turns back to me. "And I'll be eighteen. So how do I join up? How do I become a protection agent?"

Holly looks to me, searches me, eyes worried and proud at the same time, begging me to deny him. What can I say? The kid wants it. After what he's been through, he deserves the chance to lead the life of his choice. Hell, that's what I'm fighting for after all. That's my job.

But she's scared. Scared as any mother to put her child in harm's way. Scared he'll end up back in another bed like this, or worse. If the roles were switched and it was Julia asking...I don't know what I'd do. I wouldn't want it sugar coated. Pop always said the truth is medicine best used early and often.

"Well," I say, eyes on Holly, "you don't. There is no recruiting office or application to fill out. We don't work that way."

Chad's asks, "Then how?"

Holly swallows, releasing me with a shaky nod. I want to hold her, comfort her, let her know the kid will be all right.

"We find you," I say. "Agents like me observe and report potential candidates to our superiors and, if given the green light, take them into our confidence. If they accept, we gain a new agent, if they don't..."

"Then what?" he asks. "You eliminate them?"

"No. We don't work that way, either." I ease him down. "Should a recruit turn us down, they are sworn to secrecy. Since most come from places requiring background checks and a security clearance, they tend to understand the damage my higher-ups could do to their livelihood should they start spreading stories of government agencies hiding *exceptional* Americans."

Chad takes this in. I can see the gears working as his gaze drifts across his bed. "So, to get in..."

I shuffle closer and Holly is right behind, hand on my shoulder, her very presence bolstering me. I hope I'm doing the same for her. "Kid, I know a million things are zipping through your mind right now. I know that getting back at them is priority number one for you. If you want to do what I do, then start by doing what's right, where you find yourself."

Confusion narrows his eyes.

I place my hand on his arm, on a place I know was unburnt by the explosion. "You get better. You heal. You stay strong for your *sensei* here. She's gonna be lost without you." I give him a wink. "When the docs say you're ready to go, you go. You'll be assigned to a protection agent—"

His eyes widen. "You?"

Sorry, kid. Julia was a lesson I should have learned six years ago. "No. Not me. Someone you don't...share history with."

He lets go a long breath. "Fine. Then what?"

"Then study and work and train and follow a path of helping people. Become a cop or a soldier or an EMT or something. Do the job, well. Do it honest. Then, maybe."

Small tears well in Chad's eyes. He squeezes them shut and takes my hand with his own. "But, what if I can't...do those jobs? What if...my burns...?"

Damn exceptional, kid. Reminds me of someone else I know. "Then you Bruce Lee up," I say.

"What?"

"Bruce Lee survived his first Opposition attack. Media said it was a training accident." I shake my head. "They damaged his spine, left him in chronic pain the rest of his life. Doctors said he wouldn't walk again, much less fight."

"But he did," Chad mutters, two thin wet lines running down his cheeks.

"He did," says Holly, coming up to lay a hand on his head. "He fought through it. And you will, too."

Her nerves are hidden, only pride shows.

The Black Hills Bruce Lee. The kid has drive aplenty, he keeps cool under pressure, and he can fight, boy can he fight.

But for how long? Can he keep pushing forward no matter what? He's been baptized by fire. Now, he needs time. Least I can do is give him that.

Damn, I sound like Pop.

Chapter Fifty-Nine

AFTERNOON sunlight glints off the silver badge sitting heavy in my hand, heavier than something so small should be. Perhaps its heft signals the responsibility that comes with it. The badge is a simple thing—just a ring encircling a five-point star centered on a stars and bars shield. Not much to look at really. And yet this piece of metal changes everything—resources, influence, legitimacy. It opens doors I need open and closes ones I want shut. Stamped blue letters around the circle's edge are rough under my thumb. They read, "Special Agent National Protective Service."

"What does that mean, exactly?" Holly asks. She sits beside me on a wooden bench in the recovery ward atrium.

A gentle July breeze stirs the birch leaves above us and the loose hairs about her face. Her auburn waves are back, long and curly, the way she wore it when I first met her on a summer's day much like this, in a hospital not too different, with my mind just as mucked up as it is now. Back then she wore the whites of hospital staff. Today she wears the slick green skirted suit she was in when we locked eyes at Sally's restaurant. The happy night I shared a burger with Julia—and laughed.

"Tabor's made us part of the U.S. Marshals," I say, still not used to the feel of the badge, still not sure this thing is real. "It means I now operate with the full force of the United States government. And I get to carry a sidearm."

"But, how do you know if..." She tilts her head inquisitively. "If *they* aren't there, too. In the Marshals."

EXCEPTIONALS

I cup the badge, flip it, and catch it. "I don't." I keep my voice soft, so it won't carry to the sheriff's deputy perusing the latest *Field & Stream* ten yards away. "But Tabor's thorough and Jack knows his stuff. Plus, we got Deputy Blaine on our side. Besides, the FBI is The Opposition's beat. They know the bureaucracy, the scope of power. The Marshals haven't been involved in our Exceptional issues, until now. And let's face it, keeping people secret and safe is kind of what they do."

"So, that's a good thing, right?"

"I guess so." I pick up the padded envelope Blaine dropped off and slip the badge back inside, accompanied by Tabor's letter and my new ID. Their arrival feels premature, what with my having at least a couple of weeks left of physical therapy before I can walk out of this place. Guess they're intended to boost my morale or some such. Like giving a shot-up soldier the Purple Heart. Thanks for suffering on our behalf. Here's a shiny medal.

"Mr. Lawson?" The officer walks over, magazine under his arm. A stiff square of paper in his hand. "An orderly brought this for you."

I take the card and thank him. He goes back to his reading.

"What's that?" asks Holly.

"Postcard," I say. It shows an image of the Hollywood sign and bears a week-old postmark. The back side has no message, just my name, the hospital's address, and a Crayola drawing of purple pants.

I sniff, cheeks tightening in a smile I don't stop, couldn't stop, even if I wanted to, which I don't. I encourage it until my heart's swelling and my face hurts. Of course she picked Los Angeles. God, I love her spunk.

"Julia's okay," I say.

Holly presses against me.

I kiss the top of her head. Now's the time. "I left not just to protect Julia, but to protect you, too."

She doesn't respond, doesn't move. The warmth of her melts away the old barriers, letting the story out in a flood.

"My last job with the FBI was a cover for an Opposition raid. I didn't know about them or Exceptionals, we were supposed to be breaking up a human trafficking ring. Young girls shipped off into prostitution, that sort of thing. Once we breached, well, everything happened really fast. I got Julia out of there, but not before her family was dead. Her dad... I...."

Holly squeezes my arm. "You did the right thing as soon as you knew what the right thing was."

Wasn't soon enough.

"I'd never met Jack Underwood until that night in the hospital, Julia getting checked out in the ER. Oh, I'd heard of him, he was sort of an oddball legend, fanatical about cold cases, antisocial, the kind most avoid making eye contact with in the hallway."

He hasn't changed much.

"Jack comes to me out of the blue and explains things. It made sense, weird as it sounded, all the quasi-comic book stuff, it made sense."

The wind shifts. Strands of her hair tickle my face.

"Saving Julia changed me. I knew I would do everything to protect her. Everything and anything for as long as I could. Only, to do that, meant giving up who I was, what I had."

Holly lifts her head, quiet tears in her eyes.

"I had to leave our life behind." My own tears come. "Or you would be in danger. They could use you to get at me. To get at Julia and the others. You see?"

She nods and lays her hand back against my arm.

I pull her close, feeling lighter than ever for getting that out, for finally letting her in. I also feel like a piece of shit for these past six years. Comes with the territory, I guess.

We sit like that, holding each other, until the quiet gets uncomfortable, until it's obvious she has something of her own to say that'll be hard for me to hear. I tuck the postcard in Blaine's envelope.

Holly sits up and wipes her eyes. She crosses her legs with a slight wince. She may never be one hundred percent again.

"I also have something I've been needing to get off my chest."

My throat's dry.

"Please," I say. "Tell me."

I squeeze her hands the way she did for me back when our relationship was purely therapist and soldier. It always gave me strength. Now, I get to return the favor.

"I brought my life back from the brink after you left. I fought to leave that pain behind and move on. And I had moved on, I really had. I even convinced myself that seeing you again changed nothing." She takes a shuddering breath. "When you came into my office that day, I said that I no longer worried over why you left me. That was a lie. I believed it at the time, but it was still a lie."

She looks me full in the face, a thin smile dimpling her cheeks. "I understand the choice you made. I understand it and it still rips me apart."

I'm beat up all over, all over again. "The last thing I ever wanted was to hurt you."

"Shh. I know." Now she grabs *my* hands. "There's more. When we kissed that night, when I said those words..." She rubs her thumbs over my palms. "I meant them. I meant it all."

The breeze lifts her hair across her face. I reach out and push it back, brushing her cheek gently as I do. She tips her head into the caress and my fingers tremble.

"Holly..." No other words will come. My throat is clenched against them.

"We were good together, weren't we?" she asks with a teary smile.

"We were."

She takes my hand from her face and holds it in her lap. "I want you to know, in the years to come. That I forgive you. That I'm all right. And that I wish you well."

My dry throat is joined by a sour stomach. I'm not sure I follow.

"Wh-what are you saying?" I ask.

"I'm saying I love you, Larry Lawson," she smiles and grips my leg. "I never stopped. Even when I hated you, I still loved you. But you have a job to do, one the world needs, and I...I have one, too."

Another unwelcome pause comes between us. I look at her, soft and serious, and then take in the blue sky, the drifting clouds, the subtle healing beauty of this garden space, and my life drops away. The badge, The Opposition and Exceptionals, all slip away to show *me*, alone in the end, scared and desperate.

"What if I didn't?" I say, still eyeing the sky.

"Didn't what?" she asks.

"Have a job to do." My gut sinks as I say it. My mind protests. But my heart is running the show right now.

Her firm hand pulls my jaw around to face her. "Don't say that. Don't think that. With what I know? With people out there being hunted by some evil league straight out of Ian Fleming? Do you think I could be happy with you, knowing you stopped protecting people so we could be together?" She shakes her head. "With Julia out there?"

I dip my head and she lets go.

"I'm tired, Holly. The Opposition is so big, and Julia's gone...badge or no badge. It's hard to see the point. Maybe with you I'd have a chance at peace. At a life."

"Julia's not gone. She's out there and she's going to need you, again. Sooner than you think. Give her time. She'll find you when she's ready. Meanwhile there are others who need you to keep going. Need you to keep being there for them."

I'm trembling, gut roiling, head swimming.

"What about you?" I whisper. "What do you need?"

She kisses me. Her lips are flower petals. The kiss firm, unyielding, and long enough to make me ache from top to toes.

"I need," she says, voice hoarse, "to know that you are there, fighting the good fight, keeping Exceptionals safe. Otherwise, I might just have to track down Tabor and join up myself."

We share a weak smile.

"You're too stubborn," I say. "She wouldn't have you."

We chuckle and sit, foreheads together as the July breeze blows. Our fingers interlace and we enjoy a happy moment six years overdue.

"Can I call you once in a while?" I ask.

She wipes at her eyes.

"You'd better," she says with a smile, and thumps me on the shoulder.

A clown and an angel sit beneath a tree. I can't think of a good punchline.

• • • •

THE END

• • • •

Don't miss out!

Visit the website below and you can sign up to receive emails whenever Bowen Gillings publishes a new book. There's no charge and no obligation.

https://books2read.com/r/B-A-DABU-LSIFC

BOOKS 2 READ

Connecting independent readers to independent writers.

Did you love *Exceptionals*? Then you should read *A Night to Remember*[1] by Bowen Gillings!

AWARD-WINNING author. A lively cocktail of intrigue and mayhem shaken (not stirred) together with a dash of laughs on a sunset cruise for the ages, from the author of *Dawn Trouble* and *First Family*. "***A Night to Remember* was an all-nighter for me. After reading it, this author is on my auto-buy.**" – Donnell Ann Bell, award-winning author of *Black Pearl* After losing his lunch across Monterey's Coast Guard pier, nervous newly successful writer Walter Straub wobbles aboard the Diego Wind for a sunset cruise with a who's-who of celebrity authors. It takes a few fruity cocktails, a disputacious dinner, and some playful orca before he's comfortable in his rented tux and finds the nerve to speak with lovely, bestselling author Avni. All goes swimmingly until a guest becomes fish food. Then more writers turn belly up. When those left look to pin the deaths on him, Walter must either sink or swim.

Read more at https://storiesbybowen.com.

Also by Bowen Gillings

Dawn Trouble
A Night to Remember
The Wedding Guest
First Family
Exceptionals

Watch for more at https://storiesbybowen.com.

About the Author

Bowen Gillings is an award-winning author writing to bring fun back to fiction. His work has been published in anthologies and periodicals while he's been featured on TV, radio, podcasts, and YouTube channels. His quirky, offbeat tales are "perfect," "charming," "fun," and stories that "boggles the genre mind." He facilitates a variety of writing workshops and is an active member of Pikes Peak Writers, Rocky Mountain Fiction Writers, and the League of Utah Writers. He holds a Master of Education, five martial arts black belt certifications, and is an Army veteran. Travel enthusiast, outdoors lover, and RPG nerd, he also enjoys cooking big meals for family and friends. Born in Wisconsin, he grew up in the Black Hills of South Dakota, matriculated in

Minnesota and Alaska, and bounced around Europe with the Army.

Read more at https://storiesbybowen.com.

Made in the USA
Middletown, DE
23 August 2024